That Twisted Thing Called Truth

JOE STEIN

Ward Wood Publishing
www.wardwoodpublishing.co.uk

Published by Ward Wood Publishing
6 The Drive
Golders Green
London NW11 9SR
www.wardwoodpublishing.co.uk

ISBN 978-0-9568969-2-6

British Library Cataloguing in Publication Data. A CIP record for this book can be obtained from the British Library

Designed and typeset in Garamond and Times New Roman by Ward Wood Publishing.

Cover Design and Image: Catherine French
© Catherine French 2011
Cover Photography: Tim French © Tim French 2011

Printed and bound in Great Britain by
Imprint Digital, Seychelles Farm,
Upton Pyne, Exeter EX5 5HY, UK.

And one, at least, should be for my parents.
My first heroes and the most constant.

That Twisted Thing
Called Truth

The meeting had not gone well. Al had heard the raised voices from the inner office and could hear the tone even if he hadn't been able to understand what had been said. Now his client was coming out, followed by the Russians' top man, Lysenkov, and the body language wasn't encouraging. Lysenkov turned to Al, looked him up and down and, in heavily accented but good English, said:

"Mr Shapiro. You have a reputation. I hope for his sake it is justified."

Al didn't respond. Didn't even acknowledge the comment. Just made a point of keeping his eyes on Lysenkov, peripheral vision covering the other two men in the room, as he made for the door, checked briefly the corridor outside, and took his client out. In truth, it wasn't this point that worried him. He didn't expect any problems either in, or directly outside, the Russians' office suite, but once into the rest of the building and outside, where anything could be denied, there was room for a killing.

They were on the ninth floor, too far to expect an elderly and egotistical businessman to walk, and as there were two possible lifts to choose from, Al felt easier in calling them and not taking the stairs. He still reasoned it would be too close to the meeting to be chosen as the place for a hit, but automatically stood to the side as the right hand lift arrived first, adjusting his thinking to the fact that these were Russians and had operated in the bad old days following Perestroika, when it wasn't unusual to blow away a government worker on the steps of the Justice Building itself.

But this was London, not Moscow, and although these men were quite capable of extreme violence and would have no trouble in removing the CCTV from the office security to cover themselves, they wouldn't want the connection too close to home territory.

In the lift Al hit the buttons for the second, first and ground floors and they got out at the second. Getting into a lift was one thing. Getting out of it at ground level as a sitting target he wanted to avoid.

Before taking the fire escape from the second floor to street level, Al called through to the driver who had dropped them off at the front of the building earlier and had then parked up around the back. There was no response and there should have been. Waited fifteen seconds and tried once more. Still nothing. The driver might not be dead, but he wasn't in the game anymore. Which meant that since whoever had dealt with the driver would have his radio and would have heard the call, everyone now knew where they stood. There would be an attempt on his client and it would be here. The various possibilities flashed through Al's mind and, as ever, a part of him was fascinated at the almost automatic way that his brain analysed the options and made decisions. He knew he was good at his job and so did others, but that part of him still wondered exactly how he got to be so good at it. Hard work, training and experience he knew were the answers, but also that extra undefined something which grew with that experience and made him better than others. He knew it was there, just as he knew that at some point it would not be enough. Maybe it would be his error, everyone made mistakes at some time, or maybe just a judgement call that in some circumstances would be correct and in others, for reasons beyond his control, would be fatal.

Could be this time, he thought, and would have grinned to himself if he hadn't believed it would unnerve the man with him.

It was still light outside and the fire escape, whilst overlooked, had no windows opposite. There was no-one on the roof of the next building currently showing themselves and he thought that for a couple of minutes longer the Russians would still be expecting them to emerge from the front, or possibly even the back of the building, but at ground level. Transport would be the problem, but the alternative to moving would be to lose the slight edge that they had and to wait it out. Eventually the Russians would simply come for them and a gunfight in a corridor against superior numbers wasn't good practice.

Al stepped on to the fire escape landing, waited for a moment and then drew the man after him, shielding him behind his own body. Then, as the weight of the fire door swung it closed, he bent down quickly and wedged a matchbox in the doorframe, making sure the door didn't close all the way.

"We're going to go quickly but steadily down the steps," he said to his client. "You keep behind me. You move when I tell you to move. You stop when I tell you to stop."

Al's voice was calm and measured, the effect one of confidence and authority. The man nodded to him, knowing the situation. You don't survive the 80s and 90s in business in Russia without understanding the way some of that business is conducted.

They were at the first floor landing when he saw someone start to walk down the small road at the side of the building from the front. At a guess, the front was where the car would be waiting for them, but with a different driver. An old trick, but one that had worked before. If he had simply come out, not called first...

Stopping where they were, Al glanced to the rear, but that showed no-one. It was now a case of how long until the man below saw and recognised them. The image they were presenting was of two men, but he didn't want to split from his client, in case the man walking towards them was a shooter and good at it. Al eased his gun from his shoulder holster. He didn't like shoulder holsters, he preferred having the gun clipped to his belt, but this was London, not New York. Guns here were illegal and guns in shoulder holsters were hidden more effectively than on the hip.

The man approaching may or may not have been a gunman, but he wasn't too bright. He was supposed to be on the lookout for them, but hadn't looked up yet. Or maybe he was an innocent man. Another grin threatened. There was no such thing in Al's world. Everyone was a threat until proven otherwise. Or until they were dead.

Al rested his gun arm on the fire escape railing in front of him and covered the gun with his other hand. Showing a friendly, relaxed image. Told his client to stand close behind him, covering him with his own, bigger frame. Then he whistled quietly at the man, who was almost below them now.

The man looked up, couldn't disguise the recognition in his face and grabbed at his gun. Al slipped easily into firing stance and shot him three times, twice to the body making sure of the hit and then once to the head as the man fell. Again he noted, even as he manoeuvred his client, not down the remaining steps to the street, but back up the escape, through the wedged open second floor fire door and along to the internal stairs, that he'd automatically chosen the three shots to make sure of the kill, knowing that once the first had been fired, their position would be blown. And that was what he was going to use. Not everyone would move to the side and rear of the building, but that would be where they focussed. So when, ninety seconds later, they walked quickly from the staircase into the manned reception of the offices, there were no obvious Russian hit men present and the building's reception staff were looking out of the front doors to see what had happened.

Odd, he thought. You'd think if there were three gunshots, people would keep out of the way, but curiosity has killed more than just cats over the years.

If the car hadn't been there, the contingency was to either grab a black cab, which would have depended on blind luck, or simply to fade, possibly having had to deal with another Russian hood on the way, but in the event, he could see their car outside the front of the offices with someone who was not their driver and evidently didn't have enough *discipline to sit still in the car as he was supposed to. Instead he was standing by the open driver's door looking at where his colleagues had run to, following the shots. Al led his client quickly through the office's front doors, again keeping the man covered with his own body. The driver never even looked round. Al stepped up to him and discreetly placed the gun low into his groin while pleasantly asking him where the keys were and manoeuvring him away from the car. The keys, as he'd expected, were in the ignition and the engine was running. Gesturing his client to get in, and checking for any interested onlookers, he hit the driver a short blow to the windpipe, not enough to kill, but debilitating enough and, as the man choked and gasped for breath, he dropped into the car and drove away. His client was looking back and swearing in Russian, but Al wasn't. These situations weren't everyday occurrences, but they were what he was trained for and paid to deal with.*

'Good guys one, bad guys nil,' Al thought, as his subconscious worked on the next move.

*

I dropped the Mondeo back at Tony's car lot and stuck the keys through into the office, together with something for the use of it for the day. The job had gone well and I'd apparently impressed the Japanese businessman I'd been shepherding around enough for him to insist that he would ask for me again when he was next in London. Repeat business. Mick would be pleased, although there'd been enough work recently for me to be happy without building up a wider clientele. In fact the whole of the last year had been pretty good. I was earning enough to get by, Jenny and me were getting on well and no-one had seriously tried to kill me for most of that time. If everything kept on like this, I might even get rid of the feeling that it couldn't last. Jenny said that was just me being a depressed git and worse, a fatalist, one of the newer words in her vocabulary since she'd started college classes. Social Policy Studies. 'Comprising elements of politics, sociology, social history, psychology and cultural studies'. Part time. I'd told her it would be more practical in today's London to do something like basic plumbing skills, but I'd missed that this wasn't a joking matter. Trying to better herself, she said. I told her she didn't need to be better, which earned me some brownie points back, but otherwise wasn't taken seriously. Funny thing was, I meant it. But I couldn't say that, it would look like I didn't want her to go to the classes, didn't want her to widen her world.

I'd parked my old Saxo round the corner and it was raining hard enough that I got soaked getting to it. There was a note left on the seat addressed to me from Tony. 'Garron, the car needs an MOT in next couple of weeks, Tony.'

Tony is the only person I know who has to address and sign a note to someone when he's putting it in a locked car that only two people have the keys for. But I wasn't going to pull him up on that. Truth was, it was another one of his cars from the business, but this one well down the rust-bucket scale and there was an unspoken agreement that it was mine to use unless someone came to him wanting an old wrecked runner, in which case I'd nip it straight round and hand it back. Although I'd probably have to give it a quick hoover first.

I was never quite sure what Tony got out of this arrangement, although I did pay him something when I used one of his better cars for jobs, but maybe it was just his way of helping me out, or maybe of salving his conscience, in that he felt he was doing okay and he didn't think I was. I certainly wasn't going to question it.

The advantage the Saxo had over the old Cavalier of his that I'd been using previously, was that this one had a CD player instead of a tape deck. 'Course I had to buy some CDs, but the sound quality went up. I switched on the engine and up came Leonard Cohen 'Everybody Knows'. It was raining, I was working early the next morning and I couldn't shake that depressing feeling that the good times were an illusion, so I took out Leonard's disc and stuck in Deep Purple In Rock. Track one - Speed King. Checked no-one was looking and cheered myself up by screaming it out all the way through Tufnell Park.

*

I'd just parked up back in Camden, when the mobile rang. I'd switched the phone back from silent when I finished the job, but I wasn't prepared for it to ring with 'The Birdie Song'. For some reason

Jenny had taken to switching my ringtone to embarrassing themes every now and again. The worst had been when she'd recorded herself saying: "You wanna pick me up?" as the tone. Having that go off on the bus was enough to make even me cringe.

It was her on the phone and I got the same kick as I always seemed to when she called.

"Garron, you still alive?"

"Very funny," I replied. "One day I'm going to get someone else to answer the phone and say 'no, he's not.'"

"Now that isn't funny," she said. "Look, I've finished classes and there are a few of the guys going for a drink. Do you want to come down and meet us?"

- *No. I don't.*

- Shut up, I said to the little voice.

- *But I want her to come back here and not be somewhere else.*

- She can go have a drink with her friends if she wants to.

"Hey, you still there?"

"Yeah, I'm still here. I've just got back, haven't even got into the flat yet and I don't much feel like going straight out. Give me a bell when you're leaving and I'll come and pick you up."

"You don't need to pick me up, I'll get the tube."

"I don't mind, I'll - "

"Don't be silly, sit yourself down, eat something, have a drink, chill out, play with the cat, but don't get yourself out again."

"I'll lose a finger if I try to play with the damn cat."

She laughed. Jenny had been trying to domesticate my feline flatmate since she'd moved in, but the cat was ten-tenths street cat and had been squatting in the place before I arrived. We'd worked out a reasonable living arrangement and when Jenny had come on the scene he'd accepted it, but she'd never tame him. And if she did, he wouldn't be the same cat anymore.

"You don't mind me going, do you?"

- *Yes!*

She'd picked up on it, God knows how, but Jenny was intuitive like that, picked up vibes in person, over the phone, all the time. It was the sort of skill that I could do with, but just didn't have.

"No," I said, "that's fine, just give me a bell later on."

"Love you," she said and rang off before I could respond.

Yes, I thought, I guess you do. Which is good.

I trudged up the steps to the back of the flat, which was above the shops on the High Street. The fire escape always reminded me of the back of one of those New York tenements, but this place was okay. There was a front door, but we could go for days at a time without using it, depending on whether we'd taken the car, or where we'd parked.

As I unlocked the door and went in, the cat hissed slightly. He was in his corner, where we kept his food plates and next to the window with the missing pane of glass which I'd replaced with a cat flap. He, for some reason or another, had never got used to the fact that people could enter through the back door as well as the front. Tough. This was my flat now, not his.

I said hallo to him and he bolted out through the cat flap and into the night. Usual friendly attitude. I buy him food, tolerate his nasty side, even painfully de-flea him once every six months, which is an incredibly difficult and irritable experience for the both of us and one for which I've worn gardening gloves ever since the first clawing. What do I get in return? A totally non-tactile relationship, hisses and yowls of annoyance and regular dead creatures dragged in and left on the carpet. Jenny once asked me why I didn't close up the window and keep him out. I didn't tell her the truth, that when I'd first moved in, I'd needed the cat's company more than anyone else's, which was an indication of how far gone I'd been. I just answered that everyone needed a place to be and he'd been here first. I'm not sure she agreed with my reasoning, but the cat stayed and at least we never had mice or rats. Not live ones, anyway.

I debated for a minute getting a takeaway, but we had food here and I was trying to make an effort not to eat unhealthily all of the time. That didn't extend to drinking, so I cracked open a can of Strongbow and stuck on the small TV. Terrestrial only and nothing good, so I put on a Big Joe Turner CD and tried to find where I'd left my harmonicas to play along with it. Since there was very little furniture in the flat, which was only one big room with a kitchen and bathroom tacked on the side, it didn't take long to find them. It also helped that almost everything in the one wardrobe and the chest of

13

drawers belonged to Jenny. I only had about two places where anything of mine could be.

It was a small place for two people, more of a bedsit than a flat and the walls separating the main room from the kitchen and bathroom were really just partitions, but it suited us. We'd been good together here for the last year now and I couldn't see any reason why that would change. And I genuinely didn't mind her being out with her friends, I just didn't want to be with them. Unsociable? Yes. But I always had been the sort of person who stuck with small groups. Even when I'd been fighting and started to get known, I'd been uncomfortable going out in groups with the hangers-on and people I didn't really know. Jenny would probably call that insecurity now that she was on this course, but I didn't think of it like that. I didn't think of it at all most of the time. Except recently.

I picked up the D harmonica and started playing along with the CD. 'How Long Blues'. I tell you, I should have been a musician, even if no-one else thought so. For the moment, this was all I needed. And Jenny, of course, for the rest of the time.

*

The client couldn't go back to his hotel, that was clear, so Al registered them into rooms in a small b&b near Euston. It was difficult enough to get in anywhere these days without using a credit card as security, but cash is cash. He'd not actually stayed in this place before, but it was one of the range of possibilities from small guesthouses to larger hotels that he checked on regularly and kept a note of. This one had a rear fire escape from each floor, which, whilst not being perfect, meant that at least there was the possibility of another way out.

The next thing was to get the man out. Certainly out of London, preferably out of the UK. Like any good or worried businessman, the Russian had kept his passport with him, so it was going to be possible to get him on a plane. Friends in Romania, he'd said, and that was the aim. Al left him at the guesthouse with a charged up mobile to call Romania and arrange that he'd be there as soon as possible. Meantime, the man needed luggage and clothes so that he wouldn't stand out at the airport. Calling in at a local travel agent to check the times of flights to Bucharest wasn't a problem and there was a six pm flight from Heathrow, or a cheaper budget flight from Gatwick. Heathrow would be easier if no-one knew he was going to try to leave for Romania and it was unlikely, although it had happened before, that someone would try to take a man out at the departures gate inside a major airport. As long as Al didn't let anyone get too close to the man, he should be all right, although Al himself would have to be unarmed inside the airport. He would have to get rid of the gun now in any case. The police wouldn't be on to it yet, but the Russian he'd shot at the offices was dead, he was sure of that and the gun was now hot.

Money should be manageable. He'd stop with his client in a bank on the way to the airport and have him draw cash to pay him back for the outlays he'd made. Even if Lysenkov's people were monitoring the client's bank accounts, it would be too late for them to track where they were and get to him. In theory, it would be better for the man to pay cash for his plane ticket, rather than use his credit card, but then again, he would be travelling in his real name. It all depended on how well connected Lysenkov was. Russian Mafia could be tapped into Russian government sources, or individuals within government departments and their reach if they really pushed would be extensive.

With the stops for flight information, luggage, some basic clothes and a couple of sandwiches, it was well over an hour before Al returned to the b&b. As he walked down the road towards the guesthouse, he knew something was wrong. It wasn't something he could quantify, but it was a feeling he'd learnt not to ignore over the years. Automatically he glanced up to check where there might be CCTV cameras, most of central London was covered with cameras, but this particular stretch didn't have one immediately visible.

The black Range Rover close to the front of the guesthouse was wrong. Blacked out windows and the engine running, but the door to the b&b was closed and, given that it was terraced, the only other way in would be from the rear.

Al crossed the street to the other pavement and walked to the next intersection. Turned right, walked down to the next right and turned again. Eighty yards down the road he was outside the property that backed on to the guesthouse. He stopped for a moment and put down the luggage he was carrying.

How had the Russians got on to this place? It had to be through the client, the b&b was clean. The client had called his friend in Romania, not realising he wasn't his friend anymore, or his wife in Russia whose phone was probably compromised. All he'd needed to do was mention the name of the place, or the street. It didn't matter. It was done now.

Al could just walk away. The Russian was nothing to him personally and no-one would ever know that he simply hadn't got back here in time. Then he smiled to himself. This thought process was just part of the game. He couldn't walk away. He'd contracted to bodyguard this man and, if he didn't, he'd be reneging on every principle he'd worked to throughout his life. He glanced up and down the road and stowed the luggage with the new clothes packed inside behind the low front wall of the property in front of him. The thought that he could get some help flashed in and out of his mind. There wouldn't be time. The professionals he knew wouldn't thank him for dragging them into a last minute unplanned operation against Russian Mafia and it was unlikely that any armed police would arrive in time, even on a 999 call. Whatever was going to happen, was going to happen now. The Russians weren't going to wait for them to come out of the building. They were going to go in after them. If they weren't already in there. Besides which, the police option could leave him open to all sorts of trouble about the dead Russian.

Briefly, Al thought of calling the kid. He still thought of Garron like that, although he wasn't much of a kid anymore. He might be nearby, but although he was a hard lad he wasn't trained for this, it was far too dangerous. He'd start worrying about Garron, rather than his client, and they'd all end up dead.

He was just using up time now. Another quick look both ways up and down the road and then he approached the building, which had a side door to an alleyway running back behind the property. This was the exit for the fire escape from the b&b. There was broken glass fixed to the top edge of the door frame, so he went back to the luggage, took out some of the new clothes and used them to cover the glass. Better than ruining his own jacket. He then wrapped a couple of other items of clothing around his hands and reached up for the top of the door frame. For a split second he thought about the fact that he'd done this kind of thing so many times before. In London, in New York, in Europe, in the Middle East and that sooner or later...

He didn't bother to finish the thought. This was what he did. So he might as well get on with it.

*

16

It was late on a Sunday evening and I'd been round the weekly rent collection. It had become fairly routine recently, as the group of tenants were relatively stable. No knowing when one might clear out, but on a weekly payment, the risk was small. I was tired and I'd already planned to go round to Mick the next day, so I reckoned passing the money on to him to forward to the landlord, or landlords, whoever they might be, could wait until then. I had to park up a couple of streets away from the flat, which is one of the problems of living in non-suburban London, but at least I was legitimate in Camden with my genuine residents' parking permit that Jenny had got for me. I used to have a pretty good fake, but when she moved in we started putting stuff in her name, which was useful and meant I stayed anonymous.

We live above the shops and as I walked to the service road that runs behind the flats, I could see a group of six or seven lads, ten yards into the back street. Working on the principle that even if you don't hide from trouble, you don't have to go looking for it, I thought I'd walk past and take the front door in. Yeah, I know all the arguments about misunderstood youth, but I grew up on a closed estate and a group of half a dozen hooded teenagers hanging around on a street corner when it's nearly dark and they've had a while to get themselves tanked up on booze, glue, boredom, or whatever else they can get their hands on, spells trouble in most inner cities. If you can avoid it, then do yourself that favour. Problem with this little group, I saw as I walked by, was that they weren't just hanging around. Instead they were concentrating on something else and chucking stones at it. A rat, I thought as I looked past them at what they had cornered against a wall. But it wasn't a rat. It was a cat. My cat.

I was quite surprised at how angry I suddenly was and at the fact that I'd immediately thought of the cat as mine. He was right up against the wall, back arched, tail up, ears flat and hissing his anger at these humans throwing lumps of rock at him. If he could have got at one of them, he would have ripped the guy's face to pieces, but they were throwing the stones fast, landing them either side of him, the noise and impact stopping him from running in either direction. One of the 'kids', although they looked to be at least sixteen or seventeen, had picked up half a brick and he wasn't going to waste that on just a positional shot.

I was unarmed. I don't usually think I need to carry in order to collect the rents, but the moment I stepped in here, I would become the focus of seven violent teenagers carrying stones, bricks and possibly other weapons. The kid directly in front of me with the half brick looked like he was maybe the leader, all these groups have a leader of sorts and he was facing away from me, so as he drew his arm back I grabbed it with my left hand, twisted the brick out of his grip with my right and shoved him away from me. It would have been nice if he'd fallen over, but he didn't, just stumbled and recovered his balance. I stood there with half a brick in my hand and seven hostile people in front of me.

The cat did a runner.

There's gratitude for you.

I waited to see whether they were going to be obvious and start the pre-amble, or just rush me, which would be worse, but at least would be quick. Maybe they were only half-feral though, because the one I'd pushed started talking.

"What you doin' then? What's it to you?"

Predictable, but I wanted to walk away, not fight, so I answered and tried to keep the tone easy and the conversation going forwards, giving them a chance to calm down.

"I thought it was a little unfair, that's all," I said.

"Who the fuck asked you?"

Very predictable, but the problem is that they're dangerous as well.

"I'm from the RSPCA," I told them, half-joke, half just to keep it non-confrontational.

"The what?" another one said.

"The Royal Society for Pissing on Complete Arseholes," I said.

Not brilliant, but the best I could do on the spur of the moment and I was getting fed up. I thought how easy it might have been if I'd had the gun. Just a quick threat and they might have backed off. Or maybe pulled their own.

They were quiet for a moment and then the penny dropped and one of them said:

"You calling us arseholes?"

It should've been funny, but I had no illusions. These teenagers

18

were street kids and would be quite happy to stamp my head into the ground. I'm not six foot six and seventeen stone, so I wasn't going to physically intimidate them and there were more of them than me. I hadn't had a serious confrontation with anyone for a while, but this had the possibility of being just as bad as some of the previous trouble I'd had. I didn't want this to degenerate into a fight. I didn't want them to know that I lived in the area and now I had directly challenged them. It also suddenly occurred to me that I had four properties worth of rent in my jacket pocket.

Where was a bloody policeman when for once you needed one?

I could either climb down, which they might not want to let me do, force a standoff, which would depend on whether they were able to understand and be worried by the fact that I could hurt them, or I could take the initiative, thump the leader and hope they'd all back off. So from about six feet away, I chucked the half brick at him and caught him full in the face. The body would have been a bigger target, but I thought a bit of blood might help shake up the others. Besides which, I was still angry about the cat.

It's not usually a good idea to throw away your only weapon, if you hang on to it, you might get to use it more than just the once, but there was a two foot length of copper tubing off to the side, so as I saw the brick hit the guy and he started to fall, I took the three steps to the right fast, picked up the pipe and faced them head on again. Two of the gang were helping the kid on the ground, who was shouting and swearing. The others were looking at me with expressions that clearly showed that they thought I was mad, which in their eyes, I probably was. One against seven. Not the best numbers to start a war with.

I was half crouched in front of them, two foot of metal pipe in one hand and they weren't quite sure enough to go for me. Especially without their leader to push them on. He was getting to his feet now, face covered with blood, maybe, I hoped, with some bone damage as well and with one hand pointing towards me. He was shaky though and his mates were helping him stand.

"You're fucking dead, man! Dead! I'm gonna fucking kill you!"

I smiled at him.

"Maybe, son, but I don't think you're quite up to doing it today, are you? And your lads are looking a little worried as well. So you keep looking for me and I'll remember that when I'm miles away."

With that, I backed well away from them, keeping hold of the pipe and when there was enough distance, turned back the way I'd come and jogged away. I'd go the long way around to the High Street at the front of the flat. Unless, of course, I saw them on the High Street, in which case I'd cross over and fade till later. This was a pain, having this happen on my doorstep, but I hadn't seen any of them before and with a bit of luck, they weren't local. Camden's always full of visitors out for the night. Two streets away I saw a phone box and with a false tourist name, called in a fight between two gangs at the place I'd left the group. It might do nothing, but it couldn't hurt. Then, given that you can never know an object's history, or what might happen later, I wiped my prints off the copper tubing before I dumped it and went home.

The tired feeling had gone, driven away by the adrenaline rush, but I was looking forwards to a quiet night in.

*

When I got to the flat, Jenny was in the kitchen, washing up. She had the CD player on loud and hadn't noticed I was there yet, so I stood for a few moments and watched her. It was only a little over a year that we'd been together and she hadn't changed at all in that time. The dark eyes, the black-brown hair, the high cheekbones. And yet she had. She'd relaxed more. She was still cynical, probably had to be, living with me, but she'd opened up, learnt how to enjoy herself a little, learnt that the past may have been bad, but it was still possible to get something out of the present. It was good to see and I felt good that some of that may have been down to me. The defences were still there, but they weren't up all of the time now and for the most part, they weren't there at all with me, which made me feel very responsible for her and a little scared. Which for someone who'd just faced down seven yobs with only half a brick and a piece of copper, was an odd position to be in.

She turned, saw me and nearly jumped.

"Jeez, Garron," she said, "you scared the hell out of me. You're

20

not working now, you're allowed to make some noise, say hallo or something."

"If you didn't have Squeeze on at 110 decibels, you'd have heard me come in. And," I said, moving into the kitchen and picking up a dishcloth, "I didn't say anything 'cos I was watching you and thinking."

"That's creepy."

"No, it's a compliment. Make the most of it, they don't happen too often."

She smiled at me and put the large frying pan on the drainer.

"You take this," she said, "and I'll take the compliment. Second one today, actually. One of the customers at the restaurant said I looked like a film star, but he couldn't remember which one." I opened my mouth to interrupt, but she carried straight on. "Before you say a thing, he didn't mean Lassie, or Shrek, or Skippy, or whoever. I know it was a corny line, but it was still a compliment."

She was still smiling at me and as I looked at her, looking at me, I was struck again as I had been many times over the past year, not every day and not all the time, but regularly, consistently, that this was it. This was real. This was what people wanted and ached for and searched for and prized. And I had it. We had it.

So I put down the dishcloth and stepped forwards and took her face in my hands and said:

"Guy's an idiot. You don't look like a film star. You look like you. And that should be good enough for anyone."

For a moment, as neither of us moved, I debated telling her about the gang outside and what had happened, but by then she'd packed in the washing up and was reaching to kiss me, so I let it go. Given where I was now, it wasn't important anyway.

*

"Julot?"

I'd said it too loud and at the change in my tone, the dog looked up from its position in the doorway between the hall and the lounge. Mick lives in a small, ground floor council flat and there's not much room there, certainly not enough to dodge a trained attack dog. Or guard dog. I was never sure which it actually was, but it was trained and big and that was enough for me. It did occur to me that although the dog knew me, I still shouldn't be shouting at its owner if I wanted to be sure it didn't get the wrong message. And with this dog, any message other than 'friend' would be the wrong one.

I'd gone round to Mick to drop in the rent money and check on the jobs he had coming up for me and I hadn't expected to be confronted by a name from the past. Certainly not that name.

"You know him?" Mick asked.

I started to answer and then stopped myself. Mick was a real friend, but he'd often told me that he didn't want to know things that he didn't need to know and I wasn't one of those people who felt some huge need to talk about things to anyone. Thinking about it, I was pretty sure that what happened in that factory building all that time ago wasn't something that Mick would want the details on. He'd got me the gun and he'd known something had happened, but that was enough for him. So I bit it back and said, yes, I knew who he was, a heavyweight face from Europe, but that was all.

"How did he get hold of me, then?" said Mick.

"Not through me, mate, you should know that."

He looked at me for a moment and then blew out a breath.

"Yeah, I'm sorry, I do know that. I just don't like it when someone can get to me and I don't have an idea how, or who they are. But I suppose it doesn't take much to put you and me together if you ask the right people, or in the right place. It's not good, but it's going to happen after a time."

I sat on the chair opposite the sofa which as ever, he was occupying, although this time he was at least sitting up and not sprawled across it. Not that he's lazy, Mick, he's just relaxed, which if you're a fence and know half the dodgy types in North London, is probably a good way to be.

Julot. Out of nowhere. Asking for me. And getting to me through Mick.

"It doesn't have to mean he knows anything about you," I said to him. "It could just be that he's asked in the local and they've said you could get in touch with me. Might not concern you at all."

He looked up at me from his roll up.

"You're not thinking straight," he said. "No-one would give out anything about you or me, unless they had a good reason to."

"Money or muscle."

"Or grudge, or favour, but yes, that's about it. Any idea which one it is?"

"You suggesting I've annoyed someone?"

He laughed at that, which was a rare event in itself and at least released some of the tension in the room.

"For someone who says he tries to avoid trouble, you piss off a lot of people."

"It's not deliberate."

"No, it's definitely a gift," he said and laughed again.

But he didn't take it further, just as he hadn't wanted to know about the gun way back then and last year when he hadn't asked me about Hillier although he'd known, he must have known, it had been in all the papers, on the news, everywhere and he had left it, even though I knew that he had his own contacts, his own sources of information, yet he'd never asked, never mentioned it and for the first time in my life, I wondered how much of that was to protect me, as I'd always thought and how much might be to protect himself.

Bad thought, Garron, let it go. Mick is more than a friend, he's been a refuge, a sounding board and if you're going to start getting paranoid just because Julot's name has come up, just because a piece of your past is sitting up and snapping at you, then you're going to be in a lot of trouble. Right now you might need the small number of friends you've got and maybe Mick more than most.

He was still talking, working on his cigarette and speaking to me as though I was still paying full attention. So I did.

" – the pub after eight tonight. You going to go?"

"Sorry, missed part of that."

He looked up again and shook his head.

"I said, if you could just stay with it for a moment, that this Julot wants to meet you tonight at the pub sometime after eight. Which I guess means he's asked locally how to get in touch with you and that's the connection you to me."

Or, I thought, he knows all about you already and just wants you to think he doesn't. Don't try to second guess him, Mick, 'cos he's too

23

good. Al might've been able to, he could think around how people worked. Not trained to do it, it was just natural. But you can't, Mick, you don't. But I didn't say it. Mick is a privacy nut and the thought that someone might be able to get close to him without him knowing would have freaked him out completely. And then I wondered why Al had jumped into my mind again just at the time that I was feeling threatened. Was I still that dependant on him? On his presence in my mind as a reassurance?

I stood up. Too much thinking. I used to suffer from that, though I'd got over it a bit since I'd been with Jenny. But having Julot and Al in my head at the same time that I was questioning Mick, was a bad combination.

"I'll go," I said. "With someone like Julot, it's better to do what they want when you can. Makes it easier to say no when you have to."

I glanced at the huge dog still lying just outside the room, filling the gap in the doorway and then back at Mick's small frame hunched on the sofa.

"I don't suppose you'd lend him to me for a couple of hours?"

I was joking, but Mick answered anyway.

"He wouldn't go with you, mate," he said. "And Garron - "

"Yes," I said, stopping him. He didn't have to complete the sentence and I was a little narked with him for even starting it. Whatever happened, he would be kept out of it. But then, as I was pushing past the dog to leave, I realised the other thing that was nagging at me. It wasn't only Mick who couldn't second guess someone like Julot. I wouldn't be able to either.

*

A year ago, I'd sat here in this same pub with Hillier, when he'd told me, in effect, that I couldn't touch him. That he was too powerful. Julot wouldn't be doing that. He wouldn't overplay his hand. He had class. He also scared the hell out of me.

He was already sitting at a small table when I walked in. It had been nearly a year and a half since I'd last seen him, standing over me on the waste-ground outside that bloody factory, but he hadn't changed. A large, heavyset man, with an air of authority that meant he was comfortable anywhere. I looked around the pub, got a nod from the barman and went over to get a half. Only a half. I was already tired and I wanted a completely clear head talking to Julot. It was still early evening and the pub was quiet. I couldn't see any obvious support for Julot, no heavies hanging around, although there were a couple of new faces, a middle aged man in a leather jacket at a table and a non-descript, smallish, younger man in a trench-coat standing at the bar. 'Middle aged man', I caught myself thinking. He couldn't have been that much older than I was.

I took my drink over to Julot's table and said hallo. His faced creased into a smile and he stood up for me. Class, like I told you.

"Garron, my friend, thank you for coming here to talk with me." Still sounded French to me, even though he was Belgian and quite pleased about not being French. "You have a drink already?" he carried on, "good, then sit and we can talk."

Compare and contrast to Hillier. Just like in one of Jenny's essays. Hillier was tough, knew it and wanted you to recognise it. Julot was tough, knew it and didn't care about letting you know it unless there was a point to it. He was so confident in himself that nothing had to be on show. Not unless there was a reason for it. Yet he had manoeuvred me around almost at will eighteen months ago and would have killed me in cold blood if it had suited him. Maybe that was the difference between them. Julot would only kill for a reason, not because he was worried about the act itself, although I'd like to think that he was, but because if it wasn't necessary, then why do it. It only caused complications. Hillier would kill to make a point. That made Hillier sound like he was harder. He wasn't.

Julot was watching me, relaxed in his chair, tonic water in a glass by his hand and dressed in an expensive, but not a flash suit, dark shirt and a quiet tie that blended in. No waves, don't stand out, keep in the shadows, be professional.

He didn't spend long on the small talk.

"You know, Garron, that I keep out of England in the main. I do not need to be here. I run my small enterprises in some European countries and I keep myself to myself. I have only been in London once since we last met. Although I have tried to keep, as you would say, an eye, on what you have been doing. I know that you had a fight

25

a while ago which caused quite a stir. That surprised me. I thought you would have kept away from such things."

"Wasn't by choice, Monsieur Julot, I would rather have passed on it."

That was all he was getting. If he was fishing, I wasn't going to bite.

He shrugged. "That is good, it is never clever to draw attention to yourself."

There was a silence and I waited for him. He had brought me here for a reason, it was up to him to make the running.

He drank some of the tonic water and sat forwards a little.

"I have business interests in many places, Garron. Some of these rely on activities that are...not looked kindly upon by the authorities. Some of them are entirely legitimate. I have recently come under increasing pressure to hand over control of these enterprises to a third party. This I am not prepared to do. This third party's name is Vsevolod Lysenkov. He is Russian Mafia and controls a large 'business' empire in Russia and extended to some of the Baltic States. When he is not in Moscow, he lives much of the time in London, where he runs some clubs and gambling, but nothing in his name that is expressly illegal. There is almost certainly some prostitution run from the clubs, probably some drugs and it will be his, but it will not be easy to connect him to that. He is, as far as the London Police are concerned, more legitimate than not. I would think that they would know he is involved in activities elsewhere, but he keeps himself clean in this country. It allows him to live here easily. When he travels elsewhere he is well protected. In Russia, he is all but untouchable, not least because of his connections. But he has threatened me and my business."

Julot put his glass down on the table, looked directly at me and in the same tone of voice said:

"And so I must kill him."

I gave him no reaction, this wasn't anything to do with me and I wasn't going to comment on it.

"I do not take this lightly," he went on, "I always think that such things should be at the end of the line, a, er...last resort, but having failed to push his way in on my business in Marseilles, he will come for me. Without me, my businesses will be open for him to walk in. I will have to get to him before this. There will then be confusion in his organisation, there will be power struggles, internal divisions and I will continue in my own small way undisturbed for a while longer."

I said nothing, but I'd started worrying. Russian Mafia? And somehow Julot wanted me involved.

"What I need you for, Garron, is nothing too taxing, although I cannot pretend that it does not hold a certain risk. I would not ask you to make the kill for me. You are not an assassin, but you are a bodyguard. Which is what I need for the man who will carry out the killing."

I didn't like this, but I didn't want to say no straight off. In one way it was quite flattering. Top European mobster wants me to look after his pet killer. Something to put on the CV. But I still didn't like it.

"And who is this killer?" I said, more to be polite before I said no, than because I was interested.

Julot indicated with a turn of his head. "At the bar, in the coat."

The smallish man with the trench-coat. Slim build, clean shaven, short brown hair, nothing remarkable about him at all. He certainly didn't look like someone who was going to take on the Russians. But this was Julot we were talking about here and if he said the man was capable, then either he was more than capable, or there was some deeper game being played.

"His name is Michel and don't be taken in by the fact that he is not so big, or threatening. In a fist fight, you might destroy him, but with a weapon, almost any kind of weapon, he is an expert. I have put time and effort and reputation into Michel and he has not disappointed. I have put, I am now putting, my life into his hands again. He will deliver this time as well."

I looked over at the man again. He held himself well, was very contained, but against the Russian Mafia...

"He's one man, Monsieur Julot, I don't see how he can do this."

Julot smiled at me. "You will take the job, Garron," it was still a question "and then I will tell you why it is a job for just one man. Plus," his smiled broadened, "his keeper, of course."

I sat back. I didn't want this job, didn't want to put myself back out there, when I was working steadily along. And I had Jenny to consider. She'd blow her stack if she thought I'd taken something this

27

dangerous on when we didn't need it. But then Julot must have thought about that. He'd know I wouldn't just do this.

"Why me," I asked him, "why come to me?"

He held my gaze and answered directly.

"Garron, you are a survivor, you are not stupid, you will not take risks and rush in. I need someone like that who will get Michel to where he needs to be. I will pay you well and," he shrugged again, "I know where the bodies are buried. Oh, that is not a threat," he added quickly, as I started to reply, "but just a fact. I could cause you some discomfort with that, but I think I would not after all this time. It would not be worthwhile. But we do share an experience there."

I thought for a moment. That was a neatly stated non-threatening threat. Designed to make me realise that he could drop me in trouble, even though he wasn't going to, so I really owed him a favour. With just the possibility that he would do it anyway.

I looked around the pub. It was beginning to fill up now. A few solitary drinkers and some small groups having their little conversations at the bar, or at the tables. I'd been here before talking about violence and now I was talking about murder. I wondered how many other conversations like this had gone on in this pub. Maybe it happened all the time.

"One more thing," Julot was saying. "A little piece of information. This man Lysenkov, is the man who caused the death of your friend, Al Shapiro. His bodyguards killed him while he was protecting a rival Russian 'businessman'."

I would remember this place, the set up of the tables, the placement of the glasses, where people were standing. I would remember the details and I would remember the sudden chill at the mention of Al's name. After all this time, with Mick not even fully knowing what had happened, could Julot really know?

He'd stood up, looking down on me. Dropped a piece of paper on the table in front of me.

"My number until this time tomorrow. Call and we will set up the next meeting for the details."

I picked up the number without looking at it and opened my mouth to ask a question.

"Yes, it is the truth," he said, before I'd begun. "This Shapiro was well known in his profession. In our profession. I know his connection to your friend Mick, and I know his connection to you. I do not think you will want this job because you look kindly on me, nor for the money, although that will be good. But paying a debt is always a better reason."

He turned to leave the pub. I looked to the bar, but Michel had moved before his employer and was already in front of him at the door.

Al's killers. I'd wanted to know about this for a long time. The question now, was what I was going to do about it.

*

There was nobody in the alleyway, so Al dropped down as quietly as he could, bending his knees into the landing, and then removed the clothing from the top of the door frame. He suspected they were already here, but if not, there was no point in advertising, or in making things easier for them.

He drew his gun as he moved down the alleyway towards the back of the b&b. He didn't want to use it and alert anyone that he was here, but he couldn't ignore the fact that the Russians would be armed and would expect there to be shooting. Again, that part of him registered that he ought to be more worried, but as ever, he was just getting on with it. Maybe, he thought, without any feeling of arrogance, he was the ultimate professional. Which meant, he thought again, not letting himself get carried away, that within the next two minutes he could easily become the ultimate dead professional.

The end of the alleyway led almost directly to the bottom of the guesthouse fire escape. There were two men standing there, one of them facing the back wall of the building talking into a radio, the other looking upwards at the steps.

'Amazing,' Al thought, 'another one who doesn't know how to work around fire escapes.'

Taking them out silently was no longer an option, since there were two of them, so he waited until the man on the radio had finished whispering and signed off and then stepped out from the shadow of the alley and shot the radio man in the centre of the chest twice. Without moving forwards, he shifted to the second man who had drawn his gun very quickly and

29

shot him once in the chest and a second time in the head.

It was now a race if anyone had heard the shots, so he moved quickly to the metal steps, firing once more to the head of the radio man, who was still moving, as he passed him. Up the stairs to the second floor and along the fire escape to the furthest left hand room. The half-length window was shut and he took a half a second scanning the room inside before deciding he didn't have the time and simply kicked the wooden frame open where the two sides met in the middle, breaking the frame and some of the glass with it. His client, having heard the window breaking, was running into the bathroom on the other side of the room when Al called to him. The man took no notice, didn't look round and slammed the bathroom door behind him.

'Dumb,' Al thought, 'but understandable.'

Time was the thing now and he strode over to the bathroom door calling the man's name, but as he passed the front door of the room, he heard the slam of it breaking inwards. The thought that he should have had more time flashed even as he turned towards the splintering door and a huge man, bigger even than Al himself, staggered slightly as he battered through the thin wooden panels and almost fell through the door onto him. The two of them fell to the ground, the big Russian landing heavily on top of Al, but almost before they had landed Al had smashed the butt of his gun into the side of the man's head and as the Russian fell sideways, he brought his elbow up inside the man's arms and slammed it backwards into his face. Half a second's respite as the big Russian fell off him to the left and he saw the second man entering through the broken doorway. Two targets, ahead of him and to the left and the instincts took over, automatically evaluating, instinctively raising his gun hand to the man ahead of him, the unhurt man, the man who wouldn't need time to recover, but as he fired and the second Russian fell backwards he felt a huge slamming force into his face that actually knocked him sideways. Correct professional instinct it might have been to take out the man in the doorway, but somehow the big Russian to his side had recovered fast, faster than he should have been able to from the strikes he'd taken and had got to his gun.

Al felt no pain yet, but he knew that he'd taken a shot to the head. He tried to turn to face the Russian next to him and found that he was lying on his front. He pushed himself up on his left hand at the same time that he realised he couldn't see. Tried to say something and had no control over his mouth. He felt a rising tide of panic and killed it stone dead.

30

He'd been shot before and survived, he told himself, even as he knew this time was different. Then he felt his right hand moving beneath him and actually smiled to himself as best he could with his shattered jaw, as he realised that again his instincts were taking over, his body was still trying to survive. Shoot the man and maybe, maybe... But even as Al fired once more he knew that was it. 'Luxury,' he thought, 'time to think at the end'. How many seconds, split seconds had passed... Had that shot hit... He felt himself struggling to hold on to the thought, felt everything slipping, tried to remember something, someone, anyone and then briefly felt what seemed to be a huge kick in the side of his head as the second bullet hit him.

The big Russian got up off his knees. His right hand still held his Serdyukov SPS, but he was using his right arm to cradle his broken and bleeding left hand. He couldn't believe the dead man had been able to shoot him after he'd blown half his face away. And that bullet could have gone anywhere, could in fact have killed him, instead of just shattering his left hand. His legs were shaking, something he couldn't remember experiencing before, the side of his head and face were hurting and pulsing and the pain in his hand was excruciating. But containable. It had to be containable. He took a deep breath, steadied himself (when was the last time he'd had to steady himself) stepped forwards and kicked in the bathroom door. His target was in the furthest corner, next to the toilet. He aimed the gun casually, one-handed and fired three bullets into the man, the first two to the body, the last to the man's head. Left him slumped over the toilet seat.

The Russian pulled a hand towel from the rail and wrapped it loosely around his left hand to stop the blood from trailing after him. The pain was increasing, but it would have to wait for a while yet. He didn't even look further at his hand to see the extent of the damage although he estimated it was significant. Turning quickly, he walked past Al's body, noted his dead colleague in the doorway, saw the broken window and realised what he would find below. He glanced out over the fire escape and then put his gun away. Took out his radio and called the car from the front to pick him up from the street at the back. How much time did he have to cover traces? Enough maybe to clear the man in the doorway, but not the two men he expected to find dead at the foot of the fire escape. If they could have picked the time and place, if they could have taken the man out at their offices, then they could have sent in a cleaner to cover things. Now though, they would have to leave. Daytime, in London, the police would be here soon enough. None of the three dead Russians would be carrying any identification, but it wasn't how it should have been. He'd left his own blood there as well, but there was nothing he could do about that and there was no DNA match that he knew of to tie it to him.

He looked back at where Al was lying. Lysenkov had told him about this man, told him how good he was supposed to be, but he hadn't believed it. Hadn't really thought that someone could be better than he was. It simply wasn't in his way of thinking. He couldn't conceive that anyone could take him out.

And he hadn't, he thought. He hadn't. It had been close, but he was the one walking away from this. Bloodied maybe, but the only one standing.

He tucked his broken hand wrapped in the towel inside his jacket and stepped carefully through the broken window on to the fire escape. Quietly down the steps, past his two dead colleagues, down the alleyway and through the latched door. A check on the environment in the street behind, then into the black Range Rover with the darkened windows and away.

*

"He says this Lysenkov killed Al. Or his people did. That's his hook for getting me involved."

We were in Mick's living room, that bloody dog sitting as ever in the doorway in case his food provider decided that he didn't want me to leave. Even though he knew me as a 'friend', it wouldn't stop him tearing me to pieces on Mick's word. I'd once asked Mick what would happen if he collapsed while I was here and I had to try to resuscitate him. What would the dog do, seeing me grabbing his master who was laid out on the floor. His answer was that he didn't know, he hadn't thought about that one, but with a bit of luck it wouldn't happen, otherwise we'd probably both be dog food. Which was a real comforting thought.

"You think he's lying? Just to get you to go along with it?"

"It's possible, but I don't think so. He doesn't know that we're all a bit in the dark about what happened to Al and at some point I might get to ask someone some questions. Stupid though it may seem, I don't think he'd lie to me. I think he'd have me killed if he thought it was necessary, but I don't think he'd lie like that."

Mick looked at me like I was an alien species.

"Right. Of course. Major European criminals don't lie to get what they want. They always play it straight."

Of course he was right. But Julot was a little different. The way he dealt with people, with situations, always the minimum effort, always in control, was different. Reminded me in fact of Al. But I didn't think of Al as a criminal. Although as Mick would point out, he was when he felt like it.

Mick stood up from the sofa, pushed the dog out of his way with his foot, something I'd never quite had the nerve to do and went into the kitchen. I could hear the noise of tea making.

"Look, it sounds about right," he said. "I know Al was looking after some Russian when he was killed and that it was all covered nicely over which ties in with a powerful bloke who can move bodies and block questions. I just don't know whether it's this Lysenkov or not."

I got up to go into the kitchen, but stopped at the door. That was one of the little tricks Mick had taught the dog. If you were in a room on your own and Mick didn't say the word or give the signal, you wouldn't get out of that room until Mick came back. Just some basic security he called it. Bloody paranoia as far as I was concerned. I stayed in the living room, but leaned my head round the doorway. The dog grinned up at me.

"But you could find more out," I said.

He came back into the room, sat down again.

"I don't know," he replied. "Part of the reason I didn't push too hard at the time was because I was worried you'd go off on one, trying to get at whoever killed him. Now you're asking me to get you the same info."

"But I'm older now, more mature, less likely to do something dumb."

He looked at me.

"Older yes, I don't know about the other two. But you're also more dangerous now. You've grown up a bit, but you've also become aware of what you can do. Remember, I'm the one that got you the gun when you asked for it." He shook his head. "Al didn't want you to get

33

too involved in this way of life. He thought when you had to stop fighting, that you'd move away from it."

I felt myself getting annoyed with Mick, which was unusual.

"But I am in it," I said. "And you know that I'm even more in it than I tell you, because you don't want to know everything that goes on. Yes, I'm grateful for the jobs you get me, but it works both ways and I'm a long way past being sheltered by you."

I noted that the dog had looked up, catching the change in my tone, but I carried on with it, because Mick was getting to me now.

"Look, I'm not about to run off and shoot someone, just because we find out a little more about what happened to Al, I'm – "

"I think that is maybe exactly what you're likely to do," he cut in "and given that this could be Russian Mafia we're talking about, you'd end up dead." I started to say something, but he carried on. "You remember what we used to say years ago about not messing with the groups at the time, the Yardies, or the Triads? Well the Russians are worse. They're organised, they're completely ruthless and unlike the others, they don't always stick to their own. London's a good place for them. The police for the most part play by the rules and they can be almost legitimate here while running things elsewhere. You start upsetting that and there won't be any warning, they'll just be fishing you out of the river."

It was quite a long speech for Mick and I thought about it. I didn't like to admit it, but I felt guilty about Al. Not that I would have been able to help him at all, but because towards the end, we'd not been in regular contact. I'd been trying to hold down a steady job and I think he'd felt that I'd have a better chance of doing that if some of the people I'd been running with, including him, weren't getting in the way. He'd been a friend, a teacher really for years, but I guess I knew what he was doing and I didn't keep in touch. I tried to make a different kind of life. And now look where I was.

The other thing that I didn't want to admit was that Mick was right. There was a part of me that wanted, if not revenge, which sounded a little dramatic, then at least to find out what had happened.

Mick was still talking.

" – really think that Al would want you to go and get yourself involved with these people just to get back at them for his sake?"

34

"I don't know, Mick, Al always said – "

"Al was a professional bodyguard. He knew the risks when he worked and he knew that eventually something could happen to him. And it did. That's it. End of story. We go home and carry on with the rest of our lives and don't go looking for trouble."

I looked at him for a moment. Someone I'd known for years. The person who, with Al, had given me most guidance, most help and with my background, almost brought me up. Allowed me to make my mistakes, not judged me, but helped me to pick up the pieces and carry on. He was telling me to let it go. I trusted him. He was Al's mate as well and he was telling me to walk away and yet...

"Mick, Al always said the most important thing was family. You and him. You were my family. Don't you think he might want someone to finish this for him."

Mick sighed and turned himself sideways to lie back on the sofa, his usual position.

"It *is* finished for him, Garron. It's done. There's no mystical Al calling on you to 'avenge his walking spirit'. Anything like that is coming from your head, nowhere else."

He was right of course. I was still looking for some kind of approval from Al, something which I never looked for from anyone else. But it was just me, no-one else. I would be the one to decide whether I wanted to push this or not.

And then Mick sat up again and said:

"Ok, here's the deal. I'll very gently have someone ask some questions about this Lysenkov, so quietly he won't know it's happened and we'll see what we can dig out. But your side is that you don't take on this thing for Julot and you don't go anywhere near anyone to do with Lysenkov, or any Russians at all. Then we'll talk again. But this is just to get some detail. For information. I still don't want you to do anything and certainly not in someone else's show."

I knew that Mick sometimes traded in information as well as being a fence and setting up the minding jobs for me, but it was so out of character for him to go looking for something that he didn't actually need, that I wondered whether he himself had come to terms with the lack of detail about Al's death. But it wouldn't be a problem for me to turn down Julot. I'd be quite happy keeping out of trouble for a few more days. Jenny would say that I was even getting good at it.

"Deal," I said to Mick.

He gave the hand signal to the dog and I left. When I closed the front door of the flat behind me, the dog was standing right there in the hallway. Big, alert, vicious and with what looked like a huge grin all over his face.

*

"Haven't we had conversations like this before?"

Jenny asked the question after ten minutes of me trying to explain why the fact that Al was dead didn't lessen my obligation to him. The flat was warm, the dinner was cooked and smelt great and I didn't want to have this conversation, but I wasn't going to have a choice about that.

"No," I said, "we've had conversations about friends and what you do or don't do for them."

"But this one is dead," she said, which I guess seemed like a reasonable argument to her.

"Yeah, but that doesn't make a difference. In fact it makes the tie stronger, because he can't release me from it. Not," I added quickly before she could cut in, "that I'm trying to look for a way out of it."

"I don't get it - " she started.

"I know," I cut in and then stupidly added, "you wouldn't get it."

She looked at me, with the one that says be very careful what you say or do next, mister.

"Just why wouldn't I?" she asked with a tone that backed up the look.

I sighed, too loud, which didn't help and pushed myself off the wall I'd been leaning on by the window. I wasn't sure where this was going, but I had that feeling that it wasn't going to end well unless I backed down and on this point I didn't think I could. Hell, I didn't want to. I looked out of the window briefly at the night. Clear sky, no rain for once and my mind straining about what I could say to her to try to make her see it.

"Jenny, how many of your friends, if they said to you that they needed you to drop everything straight away, there and then and drive

36

to, I don't know, Scotland or somewhere, to bring them back, how many of them would you do that for?"

"I don't know, I don't have many friends like that, but - "

"No buts. How many people would you do that for, not with a discussion of whether there was a better way to do it, which meant you didn't have to go and put yourself out for them, or lose holiday from your work, or pay for the petrol, or anything. So no questions, just yes, I'm on the way."

She was quiet for a moment.

"Now, how many would you put yourself out for physically, possibly into a dangerous situation, or financially, or to an amount of hassle that really hurt, or could have repercussions."

"But people – "

"That's it, you see. There are 'buts'. And I know that there are soldiers who save each other and although that's brave and beyond the call of duty, that's what they do. They rely on each other all the time as their job. And there are kids in gangs who fight for each other, but that's also different. They haven't got anything else and they've got the peer pressure to make them do it. There are strangers who suddenly dive off a pier to save someone who's fallen in the sea, but again, that's spur of the moment. I'm talking about in general living, people who have that understanding that they'll put themselves out for each other. Some will do it for family, some won't, but there's not that many will put themselves in that position. But that's what I've got. Not with everyone, just with a couple of people. And with Al, even though he's dead."

She sat down, always a good sign in an argument. "But you and Mick and Tony and this Al, you're a bit like the soldiers example. That's almost how you view the world. You're fighting along with each other to survive it. In your own ways."

I was wrong, she could understand it. She'd almost got there.

"But where do you draw the line?" she asked. "What can you ask of each other?"

"Jenny, the trick is to know where that line is." I stopped for a moment, thinking about the lines I'd crossed in my life and whether I was looking to cross another one now. "The real thing is knowing what you can reasonably ask of someone else and where to stop." I

37

tried to think of a good example. "Like last year, when Pete tried to get me to take that unlicensed fight, I wouldn't do it, even though he expected me to and he'd told everyone I would take it."

"But if Al or Mick had asked you that, you'd have done it. Right?"

I shook my head. "That's the point, Jenny. They wouldn't have asked me to do that. They'd know that would be wrong, a step too far across the line."

"Okay," she said, "I get what you're saying, but Al isn't asking you to do anything here. He can't because he's not here. So where does that leave you?"

"That leaves me trying to work out what it is he would expect me to do and that's not easy. It's too simple to say that he'd want me to leave it and keep clear." Even though that's what Mick said he would do, I thought to myself. "I'm not sure that he wouldn't want someone to go and take on the bastards that killed him. And then again, it's too easy to say that *is* what he would want. He wasn't one-dimensional. He might just shrug it off as the price to pay for the job he did and expect everyone to forget about it."

And I don't know, I added to myself, how much of what I'm thinking is me projecting my thoughts onto Al. Then throw in my stupid pride in wanting to do something to the people that killed him.

- *What's worse, you're keeping that thought from Jenny.*

I sat on that little voice very quickly and concentrated on what Jenny was saying. She'd paused after my last comment and had gone a bit quieter.

"What about where I come in?" she said

I moved towards her, but I didn't touch her.

"You," I said, "are at the top of the list. In fact," I tried to make a joke of it, "you're on a different list altogether."

"But that time, when I asked you not to go to – no, don't answer that. That was me, though, changing what I'd said before."

But she was quiet and I knew why. She was talking about the time I went to see Hillier and might not have come back and she was right, she had, before that happened, said she wouldn't ask me to change, but I'd known then and she'd known, that there would come a point where she would have the right to ask me to be different for her. And when that point came, I didn't know what would happen. I didn't know if I would be ready to change how I lived. I didn't know if she would be ready to ask me to, or to accept me if I couldn't. And I didn't think Jenny knew either.

So we left it there, like an illness that you know is there, but no-one wants to talk about. But it had been noted now and it wouldn't easily be cured.

*

I didn't sleep much that night, just kept thinking over what I should do. Mick said step away and he'd known Al well and for longer than I had done. But he didn't know him to work with, he hadn't been there when Al had been on a job, totally in control, totally professional. I'd learned so much from him, not just about working the bodyguard jobs, but about how to survive, the right way to live, ignoring your own ego, when to fit in and when to stand out, how to be what you needed to be and I felt there was a debt I hadn't paid. With maybe some guilt for the fact that towards the end I'd not been around that much, I'd moved away from Al and the people I had known when I'd been fighting.

It was just a natural progression, a move towards what was supposed to have been a better job, a better life, but I guess I had tried to cut some of the people out. Not Al, but he'd recognised that I had to make a break with what had been my life for years and he hadn't pushed me to keep going back to the same pubs and the same people. People who had cheered me in the ring, but somehow couldn't face the fact that I hadn't got to the top. No matter why, it hadn't happened and some of them didn't seem to like the idea of me getting a decent job and working a nine to five.

I wouldn't have drifted long term from Al and Mick and I'd always stayed in touch with Tony, but I just needed to get some time to concentrate on living in a different way. It was such a massive change from the training regimes and the odd jobs that I'd done for Al and with him. But that change hadn't worked out and then Al had been killed while I was still finding out that I was flogging a dead horse. That had brought me back a bit towards Mick and my old haunts, but it wasn't the same anymore. I felt like an outsider and I was already beginning to live like one.

Was Mick right then? Just to leave it. Or did I know better? That Al would want me to go after his killers?

I got up off the mattress we slept on and went quietly out of the back door onto the fire escape landing. It was a warm night and although you could hear cars on the main road from out the front of the flats, they were isolated sounds, in the main it was quiet.

No moon, it was cloudy, and though it was nice to think that I could stare into the sky and get some kind of answer, that wasn't going to happen. I pulled myself back to reality. I was probably guilty of projecting what I was thinking onto a dead man. If I was him, I'd want someone to go after these guys. Or would I? Would it matter to me? A couple of years ago, I'd had trouble not thinking what Al would've said, it was almost like he was talking to me, but now I couldn't get a word out of him.

And Jenny, what did I owe to her? Staying alive would be a good start, but then I would always have something like this that could come up unless I changed what I did to earn money. Changed the whole way I lived. Back to that again. But not Russian Mafia, I thought to myself, that is pushing it a bit.

So what then? Do I stop and pick and choose what jobs I should take? Or does Mick already do that for me? I had a sudden thought. Did Mick protect me from jobs that were too difficult for me? Did he give those to someone else? Or were there no other types of job anyway?

That hurt my pride a bit, but it started me thinking. How much of wanting to take on the job from Julot was just my own pride talking. Or if not pride, because I hoped I was beyond that, how much of it could be the desire to find out if I could take them on. If I was good enough. That was a thought. I could die from a thought like that. And what would I be leaving?

- *Jenny of course.*

- And again, you're butting in.

- *I never go away.*

I squashed the little voice, but not before I had noted what it had said. And it was true. I had to consider her as well. This wasn't a controlled environment like when I was in training, or even an uncontrolled but known situation like in the ring. This would be stepping outside of anything I had known and dealt with before. It should scare the hell out of me and I worked out after a minute that the only reason it didn't was that I was too stupid to have thought it through properly yet.

Russian Mafia!

But if I did think it through, I would have to admit to myself if I was too scared to take them on. Or kid myself that there was another reason to leave it alone.

- *Which there is.*

- Ah, shut it!

At which point Jenny arrived at the back door of the flat, eyes full of sleep and voice throaty and tired and asked me why I was out here in the middle of the night.

"I couldn't sleep," I said.

"I thought you were better with that now," she said.

I'd had trouble sleeping for a long time and it was only after Jenny had moved in that I began to put a couple of nights sleep together at a time.

"I am better," I replied, "just thinking things through. Go back to bed and get some rest."

She held out her hand.

"Come back with me," she said. "I don't like lying down without you."

So I took her hand and went back inside, realising that whatever debt I owed to the dead, there were some I owed to the living as well.

And the dead, I felt, would understand.

*

The next morning I walked to a phone box and called the number Julot had given me. A thin, quiet voice answered in English, but with the French or Belgian accent and told me that Julot was not available.

"Give him a message then," I said, "from Garron. Tell him, no, I'm not taking his job. Tell him I appreciate the compliment of him offering it to me, but the answer is no."

There was silence at the other end of the line and I wondered if the man had gone to get Julot, but then he said:

"It is nothing to me, but Julot will not be happy."

"Maybe not, but I owe something to the living, as much as to the dead."

But then, because I realised that I had made a mistake there and that if Julot had been on the call, he would have picked up on it, I added:

"I'm living and I owe it to myself to stay clear of trouble, as much as I owe anything to dead men."

They didn't know who Jenny was, or even that she existed, but just in case, just in case, I had to keep it that way. I had to protect her. The living had to refer to me. Not to anyone else.

There was silence again and I wondered if this was Michel, Julot's hardened killer, but even if it was, he couldn't kill me from the other end of the phone line, so I hung up and walked away.

Above me, the clouds thickened and darkened and although it was a warm day and the constant exhausts and engines of the cars on Camden High Street made it even warmer, I shivered. I'd fought in the ring and I worked as a bodyguard and God knew I'd met some tough and scary people and maybe been lucky to stay in one piece. And yet I was more worried about Julot than anyone else I had ever confronted, even though he had never been a direct threat to me at all.

If asked, I would have denied the shiver, but the truth was that it was a reaction. I'd turned him down and my psyche didn't like it. I told myself that I would have liked dealing with Russian Mafia even less, but that didn't help. What helped was the thought that I was now going to keep my head down.

*

It was three days later and I was standing in an old and dark pub in south London about ten feet away from a booth where a very nervous jeweller was reluctantly allowing a possible buyer to handle some stones. I had no idea where the stones were from, or what they were worth, but the jeweller had promised me they were genuine and perfectly legally acquired and all that he was doing was removing some tax from the government and conducting a little cash currency conversion.

Like I cared.

All I was worrying about was the fact that he was an idiot who had allowed this meeting, or exchange, or sale, or whatever you wanted to call it, to go ahead in a place of the buyer's choosing in a part of London that he himself didn't know, without anyone to check the money properly. This was amateur hour and if I was lucky it would all be legitimate. If I wasn't, then any or all of the other people in this public house could be heavies for the buyer and there wouldn't be a thing I could do about it. There was another option of course. The jeweller could be the crook and some or all of the stones could be fake. As ever, I hadn't got a bloody clue of what Mick had landed me in. Occasionally, I got a decent job where I got to plan what I was doing and where I would be doing it, but all too often it was like this. Collect person X, take him to Y. Meet Z. Get him back in one piece. And if I was lucky, someone else's assessment of how dangerous it might be, or if I was very lucky, some background information that would let me make up my own mind.

Concentrate, I told myself. Keep your eye on the people around here, as well as on where the two men are sitting. The buyer knows the jeweller brought you with him. He knows you'll react if he tries anything. If he's planning something, he has to consider you in the equation.

The jeweller had nothing with him except a small carry bag. The buyer had one of those small soft top cases that look a little like laptop carriers, but cost about a fiver from the local street market. He'd come in on his own, but that meant nothing. There could be a dozen of his men in here and I wouldn't know, but no-one else seemed to be paying them much attention. It was mid-afternoon and the usual suspects of unemployed, unemployable, pensioned off and those knowingly termed 'self-employed', were dotted around the place, propping up the bar, clocking the racing on the TV and reading the evening paper. One day I'd move upmarket, I promised myself. Go to meetings in decent offices and hotels, instead of cheap clubs and grubby pubs. But then I'd done a few of those as well and the truth was, they were no better or worse than this. Trouble could be anywhere or nowhere. In a moment it could all be off, or we could all amble back to the drop off point, business concluded and everyone happy.

Ringtone and movement and the buyer took out his mobile and started speaking into it. He paused in the telephone conversation and apologised to my jeweller, asked if it was okay for him to take the call, he wouldn't be a minute. The jeweller of course obliged and the buyer wandered a few steps away towards the door leading to the toilets. He was a slim man of around fifty maybe, with glasses and an earnest expression and I could hear him saying as he passed me:

"No, I can't talk here, it's not private, I'm in the middle of a pub."

Then a pause and:

"But I'm in the middle of a transaction here, I can't just stop and discuss this with you now."

He'd turned back towards the jeweller, raising his eyebrows in a 'what can you do' sort of way and that was really quite good, but he overplayed it a bit when he went back to the table, still on the phone and said to my client:

"I'm sorry, it's my partner, could you possibly just look after my bag for a minute. He's got himself in a difficult position with a client, I just need to calm him down."

Very assured, very well done and he wasn't of course going to leave the pub, he just wandered further away and when he got to the door leading downstairs to the toilets, put his finger in his other ear, said:

"Sorry, I can't hear you properly, I told you, it's a pub here. Hang on a moment" and slipped through the door.

Perfectly natural. Perfectly done. But wrong.

I gave it a count of five and followed him down the stairs which led to the toilets and also to a service stairway to the kitchens. Which led to another fire exit staircase, which led to the back yard where I caught up with him by the gate to the street.

I wasn't sure exactly what he had got away with, but it had been something.

He wasn't going to stop for me calling to him, so I jogged the last five yards and manhandled him face first against the yard wall. I was gentle about it. This looked like a con, rather than an attack and most con men want to talk, they don't want to fight.

"Okay, okay," he said, "I knew you were trouble the moment he walked in with you."

I was surprised. "You're admitting it," I said, "just like that."

"You win some, you lose some. There'll be no trouble over this. He's hardly going to call the police about it. I don't think he wants to do that."

He'd had a well educated voice upstairs in the pub. It was slipping a bit at the edges now, out here in the yard.

"How do you know I won't take it out on you, if he asks me to?" I said. "Extra payment for teaching you a lesson."

He was still facing the wall, but he smiled back at me over his shoulder.

"I don't think so. You've done your job. I don't think you'll work me over unless I give you a reason to do it and I'm not going to do that."

I checked him quickly for any kind of weapon and then turned him around. He could still be dangerous, but I didn't think he was.

"Neat touch," I said, "leaving the bag there."

"Four ninety-nine from the cheap shop."

"So what did you do to him? And yes, I am going to drag you back up there if you won't go under your own steam."

"Palmed a couple of the stones."

He opened his left hand to show me four small pieces that looked like diamonds, not that I knew a diamond from a piece of glass.

"Wouldn't he miss them?" I asked.

"He's got about thirty-odd small stones there. He'd miss them, but only when he counted them. This is enough for me to be keeping going on."

A small time con man. No thought of the fact the jeweller was carrying twenty thousand pounds worth of stones, he just wanted to skim a little off the top. A thought occurred to me and I started him moving back into the pub.

"What's the hurry?" he asked.

"I want to get going in case you're keeping me talking here waiting for some eighteen stone heavy to come in through the back gate."

"I'm not, but I did think that maybe if we got talking I could interest you in two of the diamonds. Just tell him you couldn't catch

45

me in time. I had a car waiting, there were four of us..."

I laughed and pushed him towards the kitchen door of the pub.

"Tempting," I said, "but the thing is, I've got what's left of a reputation to protect. I can't be taken by some con artist as easy as this. Besides which, I couldn't be sure you hadn't switched them again. These may be fake bits of quartz, I wouldn't know the difference and the real ones could be in the lining of your jacket by now." He started to protest, but I gripped his arm tighter and manoeuvred him inside. "So, Mr Small Time Con Man," I continued, "I think we'll take you and your stones back up to my client and he can take a look and see what these are and whether you're one trick cleverer than you look."

*

I was quite chuffed coming off that job and it had been a 'pay direct' deal, where the client paid me and then I dropped Mick's cut back to him. Most of my work came the other way and Mick simply gave me an amount. I usually didn't know what the overall price was for a job, but if I couldn't trust Mick on something like that, then I couldn't work for him anymore.

I parked up a little way from Mick's council flat as I always did. It was always possible that someone, somewhere on the spectrum between police and villain could be watching it and I didn't need to step into trouble that easily. As I walked the last couple of minutes to his place though, I could see something was wrong. There were police cars all over the car park area outside the flats and the entrance to the building was taped off with that yellow and black 'crime scene' tape. I started worrying straight away and had a choice between turning in mid-stride and heading back, which, if anyone was paying attention, might have looked suspicious, or of walking on down the pavement, past the front of the car park and casually looking at what was going on, as anyone would.

It didn't have to be Mick, I told myself, it didn't have to be anything to do with him. Walk past, see if there's anything obvious and then on to the pub and hear what the local gossip has to say, but as I moved on there was a neighbour of Mick's, another of the ground floor flats, standing by a police car talking to a plain clothes, so a detective of some sort and she was too close. I turned my face away, but too late, she'd spotted me and the call came from the plain clothes man.

Keep going or stop, but it was no go. He was too near for me not to have heard and if I kept going he'd just call one of the uniforms in to pull me up. I should have been holding the mobile, on a call, with a reason to ignore him, but it was too late for that, so I walked over to them and nodded to the woman who I'd seen many times over the years, but whose name I didn't know. The man didn't even bother to show identity, just said:

"I'm DI Dayton. Lady here says that you're a friend of Mr Lennox. Do you know him well?"

I'd had a few seconds to choose a line and I went for the easiest.

"Yeah, reasonably well I suppose, we've had a few drinks in the pub together and I come round here occasionally, play a bit of music. I play the harmonica a bit and Mick plays the guitar." I smiled at him then, nice and friendly. "Doesn't play very well, but then I'm not so good either. What's up? Has something happened here?"

The detective was in his early forties I guessed, looked fairly fit, wearing the usual low key suit with a standard shortish haircut. But sharp eyes. Hard, sharp eyes.

"Were you on your way here, Sir, to see Mr Lennox?" Usual police tactic. Ignore your question and ask their own.

"No, not this time. I was on my way to the pub. You know, top of the road, turn right."

He was looking at me critically and I knew what was coming next. No chance of pulling the moody name bit here, so I thought I'd get in first.

"Don't tell me," I said, "you think you know me from somewhere."

"No," he said, "I know exactly where I know you from. Name's Garron. Nearly fought for the British middleweight title about three, maybe four years ago. Hand injury and you had to give it up."

"Wrist injury," I said "and it's nearer five years than four, but that's pretty damn good." I was all friendly and smiles now and I wondered if being recognised would actually work in my favour for once.

"And you're a friend of Mick Lennox."

Loaded meaning and I backed away from it.

"Well, friend might be too strong for it, but we get on okay." I was getting really worried now as the conversation stayed on Mick. I could feel my heart rate increase and I got that slight tightening in my gut that I hadn't felt for so long. I didn't want to show out, but I had to know what had happened. I had to ask.

"So what is going on here? Has there been an accident? Is Mick okay?"

Too many questions, but I hoped it came across as a concerned acquaintance, not anything more.

The neighbour started to say something, but Dayton cut her short and then probably figuring that I'd find out from her anyway, started in.

"Truth is, Mr Garron, we're not sure exactly what has happened. We have a slightly strange situation in that there is a lot of blood - "

"Loads of it, all over the place!" the neighbour broke in and I felt the grip in my stomach tighten more and the sweat begin to break out and the panic rise in me and fought to keep it all under control. Was Mick dead?

" – yes, thank you, Miss Flannery." Looking back at me, he carried on. "As the lady says, 'loads' of blood in the foyer and in the hallway of the flat, but no-one in the flat itself."

So he could be alive. Or dead with the body removed. But why would anyone want to do that? Take a body. So he had to be alive. Maybe he wasn't even in the flat when this happened. But then why the blood? As far as I knew, Mick didn't have a weapon, although I could be wrong, but then how did anyone get past the dog? What about the dog?

I realised I'd been quiet too long and that the policeman was staring at me. I tried to recover, but I wasn't doing too well.

"I'm sorry, it's a...a bit of a shock. How could there be no-one there? What about the dog? Mick had a dog."

He was looking at me and I realised I'd used the past tense for Mick and suddenly he was much more interested in me and I cursed myself for being so stupid and also for assuming the worst.

"Come with me," he said and turning to the woman he thanked her for her help and asked her to ensure the uniformed officers had all of her possible contact details as she would be required to make a statement. I wanted to get out of there, but I couldn't. I'd made the slip and this man had picked up on it and had some idea that he wanted more from me. I could have tried to justify what I'd said, but it might only make it worse, so I left it and concentrated on trying to breathe like I wasn't going to have a heart attack.

I followed him to the entrance of the building, ducking under the tape and seeing on the way the blood stains on the ground in the car park and in the foyer of the flats. Someone had bled a lot. The door of Mick's flat was open and had obviously been opened by force. The door was broken and the doorframe splintered at the side. A few feet inside the hallway was the dog, looking as big as ever, but now lying still on its side, covered in blood with part of its head shot away. There was blood all over its mouth and what I guessed could have been bits of flesh as well.

"There's the dog," the DI said.

"Jesus Christ!" I was stunned. It had never occurred to me that anybody could have got past this dog, although that was a dumb way to think about him. He could be shot as easily as a person and obviously had been. I looked up from the dead animal to the policeman again and something in what he saw in my eyes, something of the shock, scored me a few points with him. I evidently looked in a bad way to him, because I was. If they got past the dog, they got to Mick. Whoever 'they' were. I had to say something and I tried to get some ground back with Dayton.

"I'm sorry," I said, "this is a little difficult to take in."

He was quiet. The old police trick of leaving a silence and waiting for you to fill it. Well, I would fill it, but hopefully with a good enough performance that would get me off the hook. If the police had been in, they might have been through the flat and found anything. What I said now had to leave me clear, leave Mick clear, in the hope he was all right somewhere and yet not be so totally innocent that it made me out to be a liar and know more than I was saying. All this flashed through my mind while I was still recovering from the sight of that monster dog lying there dead and the carnage around him. Then I realised that although there was blood on the floor and the walls, it didn't go right the way into the flat. There were bloody footprints further on down the hall, but not pools or sprays of it. I needed to see inside the main room.

"Look, can I sit down for a second?"

"Not here," he said, "you can't stay here, or go in any further. This is a crime scene. We can go outside again. If you're a friend of Mr Lennox, then you may be able to fill in a few gaps for us."

No chance to get inside then, but as I turned I caught sight of the corner of the small table that Mick kept just inside the doorway to the lounge and it was clear. Which meant either his stack of scribbled on post it notes and scraps of paper had already been removed by the police, which seemed unlikely at this stage, or they weren't there because Mick had cleared them and with them, contact numbers, initials and everything else. Unless whoever had been in had taken them. Either way, I was going to play it without any reference to my jobs, or to Mick's work. A bit of second hand goods dealing maybe, but nothing else.

Outside the air was clear, which it hadn't seemed before we'd entered the flat and DI Dayton leaned himself against an unmarked police car.

"You've known Mick for a while, then?"

First name only now, I noticed. I could play it hard, but there was no point. I was in this now and the thing to do was to give him enough of the truth to keep him satisfied without drawing myself in any more than anyone else might be. The lady neighbour for example. That level of police interest would do me fine.

But if Mick was dead, then everything had changed. Even if he hadn't been in the flat, even if he was alive somewhere unaware of what was going on, then he wouldn't be coming back here. Mick was paranoid at the best of times. This was possibly the worst of times. The sun shone, there was a light breeze, elsewhere the world turned on and I started to pick my way through the conversation that could keep both Mick and me out of trouble, or land us both in it.

"I've known him a few years, I guess," I answered, "not too well, but well enough to come round to his flat often enough, play a bit of music, have a chat, that sort of thing. It was sort of a pub friendly type of thing. I don't know too much about him or his family, or anything."

"Who would do, Mr Garron, who would know about his background? Did he ever mention any family, any close friends?"

I shrugged and shook my head. "He pretty much kept himself to himself. You could ask at the pub, but he was usually at the pool table, not with anyone particular. Actually," I said, feigning a bit of surprise, "I don't remember him really ever talking about family at all. He just didn't talk about himself much."

"And you didn't think that was strange at all?"

"I didn't think about it much. You know, you meet someone at the pub, get talking, find out you like the same kind of music, saw the same films, or the match at the weekend, or something like that and it kind of stays at that level. I know he did odd bits of gardening and stuff for cash, but I don't know if that was his job. He always had a load of cigarettes handy and I thought he probably got them cash in hand off someone, but he obviously didn't make any money out of that, so I guess he was on benefits, but he never talked about it."

He was quiet for a moment and I wondered if I'd overplayed my hand with the cigarettes bit, because this Dayton was no fool, but then he said:

"What's his mobile number?" and it almost caught me out, him not asking if Mick had a mobile, but just asking for the number straight out.

"I don't think he has one, at least I've never seen him with one."

"What about you, do you have one?"

I smiled: "No," I replied, praying that Jenny wouldn't pick this moment to call me. Why hadn't I switched the damn thing off, or put it on silent. "I'm not doing too well at the moment," I went on "and I've cut out anything that costs money. If I need one now, then I try to borrow one for a couple of hours."

He looked surprised.

"Not married, then? No girlfriend?"

"No. I know it's a bit of a stereotype, the ex-boxer on hard times, but the reason it is a stereotype is because it happens. Not quite sure what to do with yourself, can't knuckle down to anything for long and you end up drifting a bit."

"Yes, I can see that," he said, "but a lot of them end up drifting

51

into trouble, don't they?"

I didn't like where this was going.

"Not me, I keep my nose clean." I made a joke of it. "It may be broken, but it's clean."

Stupidly, it seemed to work as a deflection, or maybe he was just allowing me to move past that because he let it go. But not too far.

"I hope you're right, Garron," he'd dropped the 'mister' now and his voice was a touch harder. "Because something here is very wrong. If your friend has been abducted, then it must have been for a very specific reason and if you were to know anything about it, then you could perhaps help us to find him before he maybe vanishes for good."

I tried for the aggrieved innocent tone, which in this case wasn't too difficult.

"I don't know any reason for anything like this to have happened. It doesn't make any sense." Which it didn't. Mick was ultra careful, completely paranoid and didn't stick his head up anywhere where anybody could take a pop at him. I pushed it a bit further though. "Mick's just a bloke from the pub who I have a drink with, play a bit of pool with and sometimes he plays a bit of guitar. That's it."

He looked hard at me, but then eased off.

"All right, leave your address and number with the uniform over there." He turned away and then back to me quickly.

"Never mentioned any foreign people he knew, did he?"

"Not unless you count foreign footballers taking over the Premier League."

"No Eastern Europeans, or Russians, then?" he said and I went cold.

"No," I managed to say and I knew I had to get myself out of there and right away. But I also had to know why he'd said Russians. And the sweat had started out again on me and I didn't want this detective, this on-the-ball detective, to pick that up from me.

"Nothing," I continued, "why should there be?" Which was a weak way to ask, but I thought he wanted to give me the lead, to let me think about it.

"Two of the neighbours called in when they heard gunshots. We reckon that's when the dog was shot, although it could have been more than just the dog. But before that, your friend Ms. Flannery, who is right there in the next flat, heard the door going in and then men shouting and then she says screaming, in what wasn't English. We think that might have been the dog going for them when they burst in. Then there were the shots and then more shouting until they quietened down a bit. She was looking out of the peephole in her front door and didn't see too much because it's the wrong angle and it's filthy as well, but she saw figures dragging other people away. Could have been your mate Lennox, or just the men removing one of their friends after the dog went for them. She's not even sure how many people were there, but again she heard a language that wasn't English. When we pushed her on it, she thought the accents may have been Russian." He paused for a moment. Then he said: "Although that is based on her saying it sounded like the baddies in old James Bond films."

I almost felt sorry for him for that.

"Did they drive away? Anybody get the plates or the make?"

"Oh yes, we've got witnesses for two cars here for definite, but five or six possible makes and models, four variations on plates, which I would guess won't be real anyway and even three colours for the two cars." He held out a card. "So if you can think of anything, any comment he might have made recently, any throw-away remark, that would help. We'll get something from the forensics, but maybe not in time for your friend if he's with them. If you think of anything, the number here will put you through to me or let me know you've called. Don't forget to give your details to the uniform."

He turned and walked back towards the flats and I turned away. Straight into one of the uniforms who was anxious not to let me leave too quickly. But I wasn't even a witness and once he accepted that and I'd shown him the card that his DI had given me, he began to lose interest and I managed to convince him that I was dossing on a friend's floor since I'd been thrown out of where I'd been lodging. I gave him the address straight out, without hesitating, of a house next to one of the places I collected rent from, which meant that I knew the post code which helped impress the uniform and from my point of view, meant that I knew it was also a place with three or four people renting, probably for cash. It wasn't great, but it would muddy the waters a little.

On another day, or with a different uniform taking the details, they might have given me a harder time, but there and then I walked away, with the police as unable to contact me directly as they had been before. Dayton knew who I was, but that couldn't be helped. What I needed to do was to get clear and I forced myself not to run as I left the area. Once out of sight I called Jenny straight away. It went to voice mail. Shit! She'd be working now and I called the restaurant and held while one of the other waitresses called her over.

"Hi," she said, "What's up?"

"What time do you finish your shift?"

"Five this evening. What's the panic?"

How the hell did she know I was panicking?

I kept my voice calm, but the words were not reassuring.

"I'm going to pick you up. Wait for me there."

"What's happened?" Now *she* was panicking. "What's gone wrong?"

"Maybe nothing," I lied, "but we're not going home to the flat tonight."

There was a silence.

"What have you done?"

Which was a new one on me. She'd never said that before.

"I haven't done anything, but Mick may be in trouble and until I know, I want to be sure he hasn't told anyone about where we are. Where I am."

Another silence, so I carried on.

"There's no reason why he should have done, but I want to be sure. It's just me being extra careful."

"Where are we going to go, then? How long does this last for?"

"I don't know, Jenny, I think just for tonight. We'll go to a hotel, or a Travelodge, or something."

"I've got no things, no - "

"We'll buy you a toothbrush, Jenny, that's not important."

More silence and then:

"All right, Garron, you be here at five, but I want the full explanation. I want to know what is going on and what you've got me involved in. No part stories and half-truths. The whole thing."

54

"I always tell you the truth."

"No," she said, "you never lie to me. That's not the same thing." Her voice hadn't changed, it was still the same quiet tone, but there was something there.

"If I ask you something," she went on, "you tell me the truth. But I don't always know the right questions to ask and you don't always volunteer everything. Maybe for the best of reasons. Maybe because you don't want to upset me, or worry me. But not this time. This time it's affecting me directly. This time I want to know everything you know and I want to know everything you think."

And she hung up.

But I didn't have any part of the story. It could have nothing to do with me at all. It could be a completely separate deal Mick was involved in that had gone badly wrong. But all I could think of was the Russian accents and Mick saying he was going to very gently have someone ask some questions about Lysenkov. 'So quietly,' he'd said, 'that he won't know it's happened'. And I wondered if Mick's questions had been too loud.

Mick and Tony were the only people who knew where I lived. If they had Mick, I thought, did they have the link to me as well?

*

We pitched up at a hotel on the dividing line between Willesden Green, Kilburn and Brondesbury at just after six. We could have stayed closer to home, but I wanted a little more distance and this was fairly straight down the Edgware Road from where Jenny worked.

There wasn't much said in the car and I didn't push it. I'd already called Tony at the car lot and I couldn't think that there was anyone else to contact. Tony had been really upset, which was strange, since although he knew Mick well, he wasn't that close to him. But maybe it was my problem that I couldn't understand that. I'd lost the ability to feel for anyone that I wasn't close to.

The hotel was basic, but clean and once we'd signed in and got to the room, after a couple of dodgy looks from the girl on the desk since we had no luggage, I asked Jenny what she wanted to eat.

She wasn't hungry.

What she was, was angry and she wanted to know what was going on.

So I told her, while she sat on the bed and listened in silence. I told her everything that I knew, which wasn't much. She already knew about Al and the Russian connection and Julot wanting me to help him, but I also told her about Mick having some questions asked about the Russians and how there could be a connection there. But that it could just as easily be to do with some other deal Mick was cooking up.

"I thought you said he kept his head down, stayed out of trouble." Her tone was accusatory.

"He does. Just this time not far enough down. Look, until we know, if we get to know, then there's no point in guessing. But if it is Lysenkov's Russians and if they want to know why he's asking questions about him, then maybe my name'll come out. And if they then want to find me, Mick knows where we are." I sat down next to her on the bed and took her hand. "I'm just trying to be extra careful, not walk into anything."

She took her hand away.

"Wouldn't Mick tell them a wrong address, or something?"

"Depends on how good they are," I said and hoped that she wouldn't ask any more about that. Which I realised, was exactly what she'd accused me of doing before, but what did she want me to say? That if they were good, they'd beat or torture the true address out of Mick?

She didn't ask further. But she still didn't want to eat yet, so we put the small telly on and watched the news on each channel in case any bodies had turned up.

At a quarter past seven my mobile rang. I didn't recognise the number and I took a deep breath before I answered, half expecting to hear a Russian accent at the other end. Instead a voice I knew said:

"All right, mate."

Mick.

The breath came out of me in a rush.

"You know who this is?" he asked.

"Oh, yeah. I know. The guy who's given me half a dozen heart attacks in the last four hours."

"Yeah, sorry about that, but I had to sort a couple of things, get a new phone, get clear of home and stuff."

"You were there?" I asked him and then before he could answer I said: "You on your own now?"

"Yeah, I'm very much on my own."

"In one piece?"

"Yep."

On the phone, Mick is Mr Communication, even worse than me.

I found I was standing up, but the relief running through me made me sit down again. Jenny was staring at me, so I told her.

"It's him. He's okay."

I didn't expect Jenny to have the same reaction as me to the news that Mick was alive and apparently well and most of her relief would be for herself and me, but she half smiled at me, patted my arm, stood up and walked to the window of the room, giving me space to talk to Mick. Or putting some distance between us. I'd think about that one later, but for now I wanted, I needed, to know what the situation was.

"Ok, mate, you'd better tell me all."

"There's not that much to tell. They tried, missed and I got out."

Pulling teeth, that's what it was like. I never understood how someone who could talk so easily face to face, just clammed up when he was using a telephone.

"Just tell me what happened."

"I was sitting down, having a cup of tea, middle of the afternoon and the dog starts growling, you know how he does when someone walks too close to the windows at the back there. He knows better than to bark, but his growl's still loud, so I shut him up and have a quick look from behind the nets and there's a guy there standing close. I don't know if he can see me or not, but he's not Old Bill, you can tell, so I shovel me papers into a Tesco bag and I disappear."

"What do you mean you disappear? How can you disappear? Was there no-one out the front?"

"Ah. Well. I've, er…got a little hidey hole there."

"What? Where? In a one bed ground floor council flat?"

"Yeah, in the kitchen, there are those panels in the ceiling. There's about two foot between them and the floor above and I took out the

57

electrics ages ago, which is why I've got the other light there on the plug and if I stand on the step-stool thing I can get myself up there and lie flat. Wouldn't stand up to a full search, but if someone's only got a minute then I can get away with it. Practice it about once a month, just to make sure I can still do it and how long it takes."

I couldn't believe it. "So you were there when they came in?"

"Yep."

"Don't just bloody say 'yep' like that," I shouted down the phone, "tell me what happened!"

"Not much to tell. They broke the door in, maybe used one of those police type 'forced entry' things and the dog went for them. Must've been hell for the guy who went in first. I could hear it. He was really going for them and I could hear the screams and the dog snarling and after a few seconds there was a shot and I could still hear the dog going at them, I swear I could almost hear the flesh being torn off them and then another two shots and I reckon that's when they killed him."

I was silent and so was Mick. I felt like saying something about the dog, but Mick sounded so matter of fact that I didn't.

"Then they ran in, saw no-one there, pulled open a couple of cupboards and scarpered. I think they had to. They'd made too much noise and this is a block. They may have thought that they'd get away with the door going, just a thump, but they must've realised someone would be calling the police after hearing the shots. So I waited a few seconds, nipped down, checked the back, pulled some cash and walked. Story over."

"That's it? Story over?"

"Well, mate, what do you want me to say? Do you panic after something happens on a job? No. It's over. You survived, so you get on with it. I can't say I'm happy about it, but something like this was always possible. Sort of an occupational hazard and the plan to survive it worked. What else do you want me to say?"

I couldn't think of any reply for a moment and although part of me recognised his logic and knew he was right, I was having trouble believing he could be so matter of fact about it, so I said:

"Hard on the bloody dog though, isn't it?"

He got a bit angry then.

"Don't start about the dog. He did exactly what he was supposed to do, stop them coming in, give me enough time to get myself away and if necessary get killed for me. That was his job. He wasn't a sodding lap dog, Garron, he was a guard dog and an attack dog and he's saved my life here. I'm not welling up over him because that's exactly what he was trained to do and why I had him there."

He was right of course and the truth was that dog had always scared everybody. It was why Tony hardly ever went round to see Mick, but I'd always liked the dog even though what he could do terrified me. I sometimes thought that he liked me as well, but that of course was rubbish. Given the word, he'd have ripped me to shreds like he'd been trained to do.

"How did you find out about it?" Mick was asking, so I told him about going round to the flat and thinking he was dead or taken. And about the neighbours reporting the Russian accents and the police interest in the whole thing.

"Russian!" he said. "I thought I could hear something that wasn't English. Can't be from the Lysenkov thing though. It just can't be."

I noticed he was using names, if not his own and remembered that he'd said he was on a new phone. It would be pay as you go and he'd either have had it with him in the flat as part of his contingency plans, or he'd bought it since leaving.

"It has to be, Mick, it's too coincidental otherwise. Whoever you spoke to has tripped a wire somewhere to cause this."

There was silence for a moment and I let him think. He knew how he'd made the approach, he'd work out what could have gone wrong.

"I don't see it, mate. I don't see how it could be unless they'd take out my source as well."

He obviously just realised what he'd said and went on:

"Yeah, I'll check it out."

There was another pause and then:

"I'm not surprised the police are interested, must've brightened up their whole day. Did you see who was leading the investigation?"

"There was a Detective Inspector Dayton there, he seemed to be in charge and he was right on the ball."

"Yeah, Dayton rings a bell. I'll see what I can find out about him." Mick had contacts everywhere, some of them I was sure were in the police itself and when he wasn't trading goods, he would sometimes be trading information.

"Listen," he said, "I'll give you a bell later, let you know what's happening."

I didn't ask him where he was or where he would be staying. He wouldn't want to tell me. Not because he didn't trust me, but because it wasn't, at least at this stage, necessary.

"You're not at home, right and you've got Jenny with you."

It was a statement not a question. He knew it would have been stupid for me to have gone home until I knew that he was okay and that my address hadn't been compromised.

"Yeah."

"You're okay, Garron, nothing's out of place. Your home's intact."

"For the moment."

It was a warning to him. Not a threat from me, but a reminder that these people had come for him for a reason, even if he didn't know what that reason was yet. If they found him, then we, as well as he, could be back in trouble again.

"Point taken," he said. "I'll call again tonight before midnight and then we'll fix when you need me to call in to let you know I'm still in one piece and running. Meantime, I've got to chase some stuff down."

I said okay, but there was one more thing.

"Another point," I added. "Your source for these questions on Lysenkov. He doesn't have to have been taken out by the Russians. He could just have been paid off by them."

There was a pause before he answered.

"You're a cynical bastard, but I'm not stupid enough to tell you you're wrong. I'll call later."

He hung up and I sat back on the bed. Jenny was still at the window.

"We can go home," I said. "Or we can stay here and pretend we're on the run from Russian gangsters."

She looked daggers at me.

"I don't know how you can joke about it," she threw back at me and thinking about it, it was a pretty dumb thing for me to have said.

"I'm sorry," I said, "it's just relief at the fact that Mick's okay and

60

that we're okay."

"Are we?" she said and let it hang there.

"Jenny, you are the most important thing to me. I wouldn't let anything happen to you."

"Except if you couldn't stop it happening. You don't control everything." Her voice was rising. "You're not that good. You're not God!" Then she caught herself and stopped. In a quiet voice she said: "I want to go home now."

"Yes. We'll go home."

I paid cash for the whole night and we checked out to another strange and questioning look from the girl at the desk. We drove home in silence and Jenny went straight to bed turning her back to me until she was asleep. If she was asleep. I was still thinking and worried about what had happened at Mick's place, but for the moment at least, it seemed it might not touch us at all. I would have a lot of bridges to build with Jenny, but we would deal with that. What she was feeling now was the aftermath of fear and shock and she was blaming me for it. There'd been no way for me to avoid this situation and once the shock had worn off she would see that and we would move on. I pulled out a half bottle of Haig from the kitchen cupboard and sat by the window in the main room. The cat was nowhere to be seen, but the sounds of Camden at night were keeping me company.

Stupidly, I felt really bad about the dog being shot, but less worried about Mick, now that I knew he was all right. Things could change though. Mick would either have to go to the police and be subject to all sorts of questions which he might be able to see himself through, maybe by just claiming he wasn't there and that they'd gone into the wrong flat. Although I couldn't see DI Dayton swallowing that. Or he'd have to vanish and either stay vanished, or emerge somewhere else. Which wasn't easy to do. I had enough money for the moment, but I still had to collect rents and get them to Mick and if he wasn't around, find work from somewhere.

All thoughts for tomorrow I told myself, thoughts for tomorrow. I closed up the whisky, reminding myself that not too long ago, before Jenny had been here, I'd have sat there and downed the rest of the bottle. I sat up for a while waiting for Mick to call as he'd promised and when he did and he'd assured me that where he was for the night was safe, we agreed that he'd call by eight in the morning and then at three hour intervals after that until he'd found out more of what was going on. I left a message on Tony's machine saying, without names, that everything was okay, but that our friend would be away from his home for a while.

Then I went to bed. Jenny had managed to sleep by then and had turned back towards me, so I didn't feel so much in her bad books as I lay down on the mattress.

And it was good to be able to be in my own home.

*

In the morning, Jenny had a college course, but I got up with her and after a few uncomfortable minutes of carefully not talking about the previous day, she said that she was sorry, but she'd been scared and she wasn't used to being stuck in some fleapit in Kilburn because she wasn't able to go home safely.

And I told her that she was being perfectly reasonable and I was really sorry, but I'd only wanted her to be safe and if I hadn't taken her somewhere else, until we'd found out it was safe, then it would have been irresponsible of me.

It was all very adult and polite, when what she really wanted to say was 'how could you do this to me, you bastard?' and what I wanted to say was, 'you know what I do and I've never pretended anything else and something like this happening was always a possibility and you knew that', but if we'd have said either of those things at that point in time, we could have been in big trouble, so there was a kind of tacit agreement to leave it at that.

When she left for the college, together with her essay on 'A study of how differing views and opinions regarding social issues and questions can be understood', she even kissed me goodbye, which in the circumstances I took to be a good sign. And I kissed her back, which hopefully she also thought was good.

Then I sat down and added up how much money we had left and how long it would last if I had no more jobs coming in from Mick.

I had the whole of the jeweler's money, although I'd have to take out Mick's part and somehow get that to him and I had money left over from the previous three jobs I'd done. But I'd have to know where I stood with Mick. He would need his cut and I'd have to know where to drop the rent money that I had collected. I still had the last week's on me.

We had Jenny's money from the restaurant, but that had decreased since she'd started with the course and anyway I felt bad if we used too much of that. I liked her to save it, although again it was necessary for her to show outgoings from her account to cover the basics and we kept money going in and out of it. I had no rent to pay on the flat, that was covered by my work collecting rents on the other properties and that was what made the big difference. Whatever happened, as long as I could still work that job, we had a place to live.

Feeling slightly better, I set up the matchsticks in the door frames and nipped out for a morning paper and some more milk. I never understood it, but it seemed like Jenny always finished the damn milk in the morning, even if she only had a cup of coffee before she went out. I checked front and back doors before I came back in, which was a pain to have to do, but I thought was necessary and then settled down with the paper and some cereal to wait for Mick's next call. The eight am call had been just a check in, but it had been useful as an alarm wake up, if nothing else. Somewhere around page seven of the paper, broadsheet not tabloid, as I actually wanted something to read with my breakfast, the cat came in and yowled at me. Other cats mew politely. This one yowled with a noise that suggested it was carrying some fatal injury, which unless you count terminal lack of manners as an illness, it definitely wasn't.

I opened a tin of tuna for him, drained it and dumped half of it in his bowl, before I realised that that was the last tin and Jenny had asked me to keep it back for supper. Now I'd have to replace it. Unless I could blame the cat and persuade Jenny that he'd opened it himself. Possible, I thought, but probably the evidence of having used a tin opener would give it away.

The cat had jumped back on the window sill next to its improvised catflap while I'd been sorting its food out and only came back to its bowl once I'd moved away. I wondered if I hadn't moved, whether he would just have stayed there out of range all day, or whether hunger would have forced him to come closer while I was still there, but I knew the answer. He'd have stayed there, or left and scavenged for food elsewhere.

"You could at least say thank you," I said to him, as I carried on with my breakfast and went back to the paper. "I could have left it until I'd finished my breakfast, instead of getting yours and letting my weetabix get soggy."

The cat ignored me and ate the tuna.

At a little after eleven, Mick called.

"You ok?" I asked.

"I'm fine."

Like nothing had happened. Like he was on a day trip somewhere. But if there'd been anyone with him, he'd have said something else, made me aware there was a problem. As yet there wasn't.

"How's Jenny doing?"

"Very upset and a little scared at having to leave her home for a while."

"Not surprising. What are you going to do about it?"

This was a new one on me, Mick being worried about my domestic arrangements.

"I'll work it out," I said. "We'll work it out."

"If you say so, mate. Meanwhile, this is getting difficult."

That wasn't what I wanted to hear.

"The guy I spoke to about the Russian, he says that he's heard nothing and has no idea that what he's dug around for could produce this reaction."

"Well, that's good isn't it?"

"Not really. Now he's panicking and he's vanishing for a while in case it is because of him. Well, because of us, but through him. He doesn't want to be seen as a link. Which you can understand. He wants me to chase down where this has come from and make sure it has nothing to do with him."

"Which you can do?" I asked.

"I don't see how. Unless I contact the man, play the innocent and find out why he targeted me."

"You don't want to do that?" It was a question again.

There was a sigh from the other end of the line.

"They screwed up a hit. They have one or two dead or very

64

seriously injured men who they almost certainly couldn't get to a hospital, although the guy probably has enough money to buy a couple of doctors if he wanted to, but the damage is done. They missed me. Whatever reason they were going for me, they missed me. These are not people you can reason with. This is the Russian Mafia."

There it was again, the phrase that stopped everything in its tracks. The Russian Mafia.

"So what are you going to do?" I asked him.

"Lie low and keep quiet."

"That's it? For how long?"

"I don't know, mate, I don't know. Maybe for a long time."

And for perhaps the first time since I'd known him in all those years, all those years of the troubles and worries that came with what he'd chosen to do and to be, for the first time I heard something like despair in his voice.

"If I knew what it was about," he said, "then maybe I could head it off. Talk to them somehow, but even then I probably can't get to him, to Lysenkov, without putting myself in his control."

"He wouldn't talk to you?"

"What am I going to do, call him up and say, 'hey, man, fancy a pint and a chat about what's been going on'?" There was frustration in his tone now, because I wasn't getting it. "I keep telling you, this is the Russian Mafia we're talking about and you don't seem to understand what that means. You can't threaten them and I haven't got anything to negotiate with."

"What would Al have done?"

I'd said it without thinking, almost as a reflex action. When in trouble, invoke Al.

There was a pause and then Mick said:

"I don't know. He may have told me to clear out. He may have tried to negotiate for me." After another pause he said: "He may have decided to blow Lysenkov's head off his shoulders."

I suddenly realised what I could do. Julot was planning to hit Lysenkov and I could help Mick by helping him. And a split second after that thought, I remembered that Mick knew that as well and that this whole conversation could be taken as a lead up to this. Mick couldn't ask me to do this, it had to come from me. But he could certainly remind me of what could be his only way out.

I stopped myself thinking like that. This was Mick and if he couldn't ask me for help, then who could?

- *Jenny.*

- Yes, of course, but –

- *And she'd want you not to do it.*

- Because she doesn't understand.

- *You don't think so?*

I took a deep breath and killed the little voice again.

"Mick, you sit tight. You call every three hours, like we agreed and if I don't answer, you leave a message, let me know you're still okay."

"What are you going to do?"

"I'm going to contact Julot, he's the way out here."

"I can't ask you to do that, mate, you don't know where it'll go."

"You can ask, Mick, just not straight out. But I know what you need and I can deal with it. I'll talk to you later."

"I'm not happy about - " he started.

"I'm not happy about it either," I cut in, "but I'll do it and I'll speak to you later" and I killed the connection before he could reply.

I looked at the cat.

"If I believed in karma, then this would be it. Turning down going after Al's killers, only to be forced back into it."

The cat ignored me.

"Lucky then, I don't believe in any of that stuff," I went on.

The cat continued to ignore me, so I went out and found a phone box and called the number Julot had given me. I wasn't sure anyone would pick up, but the same quiet, accented voice as before, told me a time and a place and I said I'd be there.

*

I met Julot in a pub near Baker Street tube station three hours later. He was evidently pleased to see me and we tucked ourselves round a small table in a corner, with Michel sitting at the next table apparently unconcerned at whether I was there or not.

I told Julot that I was a little surprised to see him still in London, but he said that even after I had turned him down, they still had to

66

continue and so there had been no point in returning to Belgium. Then he asked me why I had changed my mind about joining him.

"I thought a lot about Al," I told him "and I realised that I owed it to him to pay back the people who killed him. And, although I hate to say it, I could do with the money."

He laughed and seemed to buy it, even though it was pure lies. There was no way I was going to mention Mick. Then he pulled an envelope from his inside jacket pocket and put it on the table between us.

"I think, but I do not know, that I can trust you," he said in that rich, accented voice. He should have been a radio actor, or a voiceover man for macho Belgian cars. If there are any macho Belgian cars. "There is five thousand pounds here," he continued, "enough, if you choose, to run and hide for a while, but I do not think you will do that. And not just because I would look for you."

Nice little threat dropped casually in, but it made no odds to me.

"I won't be running anywhere."

"Good. Now this man, this Russian, I will tell you a little about him, just so that you know what you are dealing with. But I do not want you to worry. Michel will take care of the...the final act. You just need to take care of Michel, keep him out of trouble, watch his back as they say."

"That's fine, Monsieur Julot, that's what I do for a living."

"Good," he said again and sat back in his chair. He wasn't drinking and neither was Michel, just tonic water. I could've murdered a pint, but these guys were as professional as you got and I didn't want them to think any the less of me. But orange juice wasn't really hitting the spot.

"So this Lysenkov is only a very few years older then me, about sixty-one, sixty-two years of age. He was an intelligence officer in the KGB before *glasnost* and when communism crumbled, he was placed well to cash in on the new 'free' market. He worked for one of the top mafia groups and there were many mafia groups at the time, all carving up the industries and making Moscow as though it was the old American Wild West." The heavy face split into a smile again. In fact Julot smiled a lot, at times just a half smile, as though he found something amusing that no-one else could notice and I had the thought that if he stopped smiling I would see a completely different man. Not one I would want to know.

"Eventually the man at the top of this group was killed and there was an internal power struggle between Lysenkov and two other of the leading figures there. I call it a power struggle, but it was a war. The group split into the three factions and Lysenkov got to command his army. And he proved very good at it. He had a keen sense of when and where to strike and he was utterly ruthless. Totally committed to the destruction of his enemies." At this point Julot leaned in towards me. "I do not take him lightly, Garron, I do not take him lightly at all and I am aware that this will not be easy for you and for Michel. Five thousand pounds is nothing. That is just a gesture of goodwill. If you succeed," he paused, "*when* you succeed, I will pay you ten times that amount and you will not have to have been the one to make the kill."

I didn't respond. A professional hit on a man like Lysenkov could command higher than 50K, but it would do me, if I survived to take it. But of course, that wasn't my prime motivation. Not that Julot knew that.

"The war with his rivals for the control of this mafia group lasted four long and bloody months. Lysenkov personally hacked to death both of them after they had been brought to him by his, er..." he struggled briefly for the word, "...his lieutenant, a younger man, by the name of Kirilenko. This Kirilenko could have killed them himself easier, but the statement had to be made to the men's followers. So he took them from their bodyguards and brought them to Lysenkov, who killed them piece by piece in front of his own men as a demonstration. The groups were merged again under Lysenkov and they began to rebuild their businesses which had suffered during the four months of the war."

Julot paused and took a long swallow of his drink. During all the time he'd been talking, Michel had not looked over once to us. I guess he already knew the history, but the point was that they were on foreign turf here. Relatively safe in an unknown pub in central London, but only if they had not been tagged or seen by chance. Any threat would be coming in towards us and that was why Michel faced away from us. Standard procedure it may have been, but he had the discipline to hold to it and I noted that.

Julot was talking again. Jackanory, I thought, but with a dark tone and a lot more blood.

"Taking back control of the businesses was another task in itself. Some had been taken over by other groups which had moved in, one or two had decided to resist some of the 'protection' offered by Lysenkov, but here the man showed that he had a flair. He was ruthless enough to take back what he wanted and vicious enough to punish those who had walked away from him, even when he did not want their money anymore. But he also knew to expand. He became legitimate in many areas, which helped to hide those areas he was not legitimate in. Nobody had expected him to be such a good businessman. And still he knew when to bribe and when to coerce and when to threaten and when to destroy."

"You sound like you almost admire him," I said.

"No. I do not admire him." There was no smile this time. "He has over the years built a business, but it is one that is based on fear and hatred and, how shall I put it...*unnecessary* violence. He could not have operated in this way in Western Europe to the extent that he has in Eastern Europe. In Russia it was necessary, but I do not think he did this because it was necessary. I think he did this because he liked it. Now in England he behaves and is 'respectable' and in Europe he expands both legitimate businesses and illegitimate. And now he wants mine and there will be a war and many people will be hurt if we do not manage to cut off this man and leave his organisation headless."

He hadn't raised his voice, but the intensity was there and I thought that if Lysenkov had been in that pub now, Julot might have killed him there and then with his bare hands. Although Michel would probably have got there first.

"The way you're talking though, this Kirilenko could take over. Wouldn't you just have the same problem with him?"

"Kirilenko is muscle. Very big, very powerful, very skilful with a gun and a knife, but not a businessman. He would not be able to take over from Lysenkov." He leaned closer in towards me and lowered his voice. "But I will place a little bet with you if you like, Garron, I will bet with you that Kirilenko will not survive the death of his employer." The smile was there again. "You see, I have told Michel that Kirilenko considers himself the best at what he does. Michel is a professional, he will not allow himself to be deflected from what he is to do, but he will want to demonstrate to me that Kirilenko is wrong, you understand? The truth is, of course, that no-one is 'the best', but it will not hurt to have Kirilenko gone as well."

He sat back again.

"Michel does not especially want to work with you. He does not feel the need to have you around, but he is wrong. You know the geography, you know the set ups, you have more experience than him of how to get close to people. Michel is a blunt instrument. If I simply let him loose here, he would make too much disturbance and they would see him coming. And with his accent, the moment he started asking questions, someone in Lysenkov's organisation would put two and two together and come up with the fact that I am looking for him. You though, you could be anyone. You have the advantage of knowing the city and of being able to move around in it easily and without attracting any attention. And you are a bodyguard. Michel will need someone to watch out for him. I think it will work well."

I looked over at Michel, who was still sitting with his back to us. A small, slim figure, with apparently the capability to unleash seven kinds of hell onto a Russian mobster. He didn't look like he could, but unless Julot was playing some kind of long game, which he was certainly capable of, then Michel was a cold blooded, expert assassin. And I was going to be looking after him.

"All right, Monsieur Julot, we'll get moving on it. I'll need a photo of the man and also of this Kirilenko and addresses, businesses, places they might be and so on."

"All here," he said, pulling a folded sheet of A4 from his pocket. "All on one piece of paper except the photos which are these."

I looked at them briefly, noting that the obvious bodyguard looked slightly familiar, though there was no way I could have seen him before. But there'd be time enough to study them later on. Before I burned them.

"The photo of Kirilenko is not good, he takes care to avoid being pictured if he can, but you will know him. He is a huge man and always wears a glove on his left hand. He is very conscious of it, because it was shattered not many years ago and it has been operated on many times."

I thought of my own damaged wrist.

"Occupational hazard, I guess, but if it slows him down any, that's useful."

"It does not," Julot said. And then, "is there anything else you will need from me?"

I thought for a few seconds. I wanted as little as possible from Julot, but with Mick out of circulation for the moment, there would be some things he could help me with.

"I need some extra ammunition, .357 Magnum expanding bullets for a Smith and Wesson 686. I know Michel is the tool, but if I'm going to be there, I might need to back him up and I'm low on ammunition."

For a moment I wondered whether he would be able to get that in London, given this wasn't his home town, but he just said that he'd have it by tomorrow for me, so maybe he would have it brought in from France, or elsewhere in Europe. He must have his favoured suppliers.

"I'll need to hire a car as well." Might as well get Tony some cash out of this if I could. "Something very low key," I went on, "not flashy, probably a few years old, but something to get around in that can't be traced to me or to you."

"That is okay," Julot said, "take it out of the five thousand and I will make it up."

"Okay then," I said. "I'll spend tonight and tomorrow during the day looking at where we can easily get to and I'll meet Michel tomorrow evening."

"Here?"

"No," I said and gave him the name of another pub just up the road. Central enough and he would know how to get there easily.

"One thing, Garron," said Julot, "I have put on the list Lysenkov's flat in London and his address outside London in the county of Hertfordshire, but they are like fortresses. You will not be able to get to him there."

I nodded and stood up. So did Michel and I noticed that although

71

he was smaller than me, he moved very smoothly, very easily. Probably hadn't spent half his life being punched to pieces in boxing rings. His hat was on the table and he was wearing the same trench coat that I'd seen him in at the pub near to Mick's place. Mick's old place, I corrected myself.

"One more thing from me, Julot, get him some better clothes, something that'll blend in. In that coat and hat he stands out a mile, looks like something out of a forties Bogart movie."

I'm not sure whether I said that because it was true, or just to rile Michel for some reason, let him know who was in charge, but as a parting shot it was pretty weak and didn't seem to bother him at all.

I tucked my five thousand and my sheet of information and my two gangster photos into my jacket and left.

As I walked out of the pub, Mick called to say he was still all right.

I was glad somebody was.

*

It was early still and I called Jenny. She answered with:

"Is everything okay?"

I told her it was and that there were no problems. Not exactly true and again I was guilty of exactly what she had accused me of, of shielding her from what was actually happening, but I didn't want her worrying and I didn't want her getting angry with me again. She was going to a pub with some of her friends from the college and wanted me to meet her there. I had half a second to sound like I wasn't hesitating and in that time I realised that I had to go. She was getting more confident in herself and branching out and these were her friends, or if not friends, at least people she met with at the college lectures and tutorials. This was part of her life at the moment and I needed to show an interest in that because she wanted me to. And given the last twenty-four hours, it wouldn't hurt me to follow where she led.

So I went. To a redecorated pub with potted plants and neon strip lighting which was in Islington. There was nothing wrong with it. It just wasn't where I would usually go.

Jenny was sitting with a small group of five or six other students.

72

She qualified as a 'mature' student because she wasn't doing the course straight from school and in fact was ten years out of the little education she had finished. The rest of the students were younger, which immediately put my back up for no reason whatsoever, but it did. When she saw me, Jenny waved me over, stood up and kissed me, which served to stop me being quite so narked. Everyone was already drinking, but I don't tend to drink in public much, just the odd pint, so I was happy just to sit for a while next to Jenny. There was a list of names, Paul, Margaret, Sian, I lost the other two or three and then there were a couple of questions as I was introduced which I found difficult as I don't like talking about myself much, especially with people I don't know. So I fielded the ones about what I did for a living and whether Garron was my first or last name (they seemed to think it was some obscure Scottish nickname) until Margaret, or maybe it was Marian, said:

"Wait a minute, didn't you say, Jenny, that you met Garron when he was collecting your rent?"

And that started a whole new topic for them ending with the inevitable question:

"So what do you do if someone can't pay the rent? Do you beat them up, or something?"

Jenny tried to save me by saying:

"No, he ends up going out with them and then gets them to move in with him."

That brought a laugh, but Marian, or was it Sian, wasn't having any of it and pushed it further, so I said that no, I usually only broke a couple of fingers. I guess I should have made a joke of it, but they were annoying me by now with their extreme youth and their sureness about everything and I said it straight and the conversation died.

"That was a little bit like you meant it," said Paul, who seemed a nice enough bloke, just a bit studenty and I felt Jenny's leg against mine and saw where this was going, so I creased my face into what I hoped was a smile and said:

"No, of course not. If I did that, the poor sod wouldn't be able to work and then they wouldn't be able to pay next week either, so there'd be no point to it."

And everyone relaxed and sat back and I shut up and let the conversation flow around me.

But as it did, I wondered why I was so uncomfortable with these people. Was it just that they had no concept of my life, of how I was brought up, or rather not brought up? But that didn't make sense, because Jenny was no more in their social circle than I was and she was mixing with them without any problem. So it was me. Something in me resented their certainties and their education and their knowledge. Which was dumb. It was just the sort of prejudice that I hated when people looked at me and saw just the scar tissue and the broken nose. And then someone was asking me a question, what I thought about the fact that the government wasn't doing something about something that they should be and it was their fault that something else. And I hadn't got a clue what they were talking about.

"I'm sorry," I said, "I don't do politics much."

"But you must have an opinion." That was Sian. Or Marian. Or maybe Margaret, I think.

I was obviously expected to reply.

"No, really," I said, "I don't talk about politics too often, I'm not sure it's worth the effort nowdays."

Which wasn't true, I did talk about politics at times with Jenny, but somehow I wasn't comfortable talking about it with anyone else.

"That's just the problem," one of the girls said. I'd given up on which was which by now, they just seemed interchangeable. "Everyone's given up on politics. People just can't be bothered."

And I kind of resented that, because the implication was that I was one of those people who just couldn't be bothered, and that wasn't true. At least I thought it wasn't true. I could be bothered and I did think it was important, I just didn't want to talk about it with these people. But now I felt I had to.

"I just think," I said carefully, "that maybe governments day to day have far less control over anything than we give them credit for. They're always going to put taxes up and they can help or get in the way of the health service and stuff, but somewhere along the line, I think we've lost the point." I realised everyone was listening to me. Which stupidly, made me nervous.

Someone said: "What do you mean?"

74

Which was difficult to explain to people who hadn't come up from the same places as me. So I said:

"Well, it's not the government's life. It's your life. And it's up to you to live it. And if you can't because you can't get a job, or you're not well, then that's what the benefits are there for and that's quite right, but that's only a final help. Politicians get the blame for everything, but no government is going to make your life good. It might stop it being quite so shit, but it's up to you to change it if you choose to."

They were looking at me now and I felt like I was on trial.

"Look," I went on, "I don't mean that people don't sometimes need help and if they do, then we should help them. I just mean that we've got to the stage where everything and anything that goes wrong has to be someone's fault. And sometimes it isn't. Sometimes things just happen. Some stupid clerk forgets to lock up his files properly and one goes missing. Should we fire the government? No, we should fire the idiot that didn't lock it up. But we're always looking for someone else to blame. And sometimes it's us and we don't like that."

At which point my first political speech ended and I sat back. Why did I resent the way they were looking at me? But Jenny had taken my hand and I took a deep breath and reminded myself that these were only people and they were just bringing their own backgrounds and experiences to their own views. So I stood up and said the immortal words in a pub guaranteed to get everyone back on your side:

"My round, people, what'll it be?"

Jenny came to the bar with me to help carry the drinks and whispered in my ear:

"I'm proud of you."

"What," I said, "for saying all that rubbish?"

"No, for the fact that you don't want to be here, and that you don't like them much, but you're trying. For me."

And as we turned back to the group, I still didn't want to be there, I still had Russians and Julot in my head, but following Jenny back, I thought I might be able to stand it for a little while longer.

*

75

A little later, on the top deck of a half empty night bus on the way home, she asked me:

"Why do you dislike them so much?"

I said, flippantly:

"It's a class thing."

"No, I mean it," she insisted, "what is it about them?"

She was sitting by the window and I looked past her, out at the streets, London's dark streets. At the man sitting on his cardboard in the doorway there, at the couple arguing with each other, faces straining and arms flying, at the kids hanging out by the fast food place, when they should be somewhere else, anywhere else, but not on the street, not this street, not at night and I answered her.

"Because they're so sure of themselves. Because they're doing this college course to understand the world and everything in it and to make it better and that's just naïve, it just doesn't work like that. They don't have a clue and they don't know that they don't have a clue and for some reason, that really gets on my nerves."

She put her head on my shoulder and said:

"What about me? I'm doing the course as well."

"It's different," I answered, "you're starting from a different place. You know the world is lousy and unfair and that people make it that way. They still think there's a chance."

"Jeez, Garron, that's a terrible thing to say. The way you're talking, you think people should just curl up and die."

"And some of them do."

"But some of them don't. Some of them find something. Look at us. We found something."

And suddenly I wanted her to understand, to really understand and I moved her head off my shoulder and turned her to face me.

"That's my point, Jenny. We found something despite the world we live in, despite where we come from. Not because of it."

She was quiet for a moment, then:

"There needs to be a new word for you, Garron. Cynic doesn't cover it."

I shrugged.

"The world can be a beautiful place," she said, "it's all there."

"But not for everyone, Jenny, not for everyone."

76

"And what about the guys tonight? What's their crime? Being young and enthusiastic? Is that wrong?"

I shook my head.

"No, it's not wrong. It's how it should be. I just can't join in with it."

"Maybe that's your problem then, not theirs."

"Oh yes," I agreed, "it's my problem all right."

We fell silent again and looked out through the window at the dark and damaged city, as we were driven through its streets.

*

Jenny was at the restaurant for the lunch shift the next day, so we slept in late, only disturbed by the text message from Mick that simply said 'OK' which we'd agreed he would now send three times a day instead of the full phone call. After Jenny had left for work, I started checking through the detail that Julot had given me on Lysenkov. In theory, the job was straightforward. Get Michel close enough to Lysenkov that he could make his hit, without either of us getting taken out in the process. But if it was that easy, somebody else would probably have done it already.

Lysenkov owned, or had interests in, a number of businesses including a hotel, a nightclub, a couple of posh restaurants and strangely, a couple of low life drinking dens in East London that were marked as Russian hangouts. Maybe if he didn't import his muscle from his homeland, then these places were good recruiting grounds. Or maybe he just liked slumming it occasionally. But none of these schemes were in themselves illegal, although any one of them could easily be running drugs, or very likely prostitutes brought over from Russia and Eastern Europe, which is a major industry. And they were all good ways to launder money from his European enterprises.

There could be protection too, although that was more likely to bring his criminal profile higher which Julot seemed to think that he would avoid. This was where his family spent much of their time. He wanted to be clean here.

So where to start? I didn't want to just walk into one of the restaurants and ask for the man and I didn't think that hanging around outside one of his homes on the off chance that he would be at that house was a good idea. Even if we could be there without being spotted, his people would be too good to allow us to follow him and get close. I wasn't sure exactly what Michel would want. Julot had said to 'just get him close', but that could mean there would be a bloodbath with others getting caught in the way. Maybe Michel and Julot wouldn't care, but I would and not just for any moral reasons. I also had to carry on living here afterwards.

I tried to memorise the photos and then burnt them. Just in case this all went wrong, I didn't want anything in the flat tying me to these guys. I kept the list of Lysenkov's places for the moment on me and went round to Tony's car lot. For once I had a paying job where I could hire a car properly and it was only fair to give him his share.

*

He was in his little office when I arrived, even though there was a potential buyer outside looking at a couple of the cars.

"You doing so well you can afford to let them walk away, then?" I asked him.

He shook his head and carried on with the local paper crossword. "He's a pain in the butt, that one. Thinks he's God's gift and wants to tell me all about the flash cars he's driven in the past. If I stay out there, I won't sell him anything, I'll just end up decking him."

"Ah well, you can sit in here then and listen to me instead."

There was a grunt in response and nothing else. He wouldn't really have hit the guy outside. Not only is he not particularly physical, although in the past he's had a go when he's needed to and I've been there to see it, but Tony is one of the good guys in life and one of the very few I'd known. We grew up together on the same estate and he's the only one of us that I know of who managed to graft his way out. He's got the car lot, which does okay, a nice home, not flash, but nice, two kids and a wife who has the good judgement not to like me.

"Come on, mate," I carried on, "At least I'm not like him out there poking about at your cars. I know I'm not special. I mean, if I was God's gift, I'd be wrapped better, wouldn't I?"

Tony looked up and said:

"One day, Garron, you're going to realise that your jokes just aren't funny."

"One day, Tony, you're going to realise that you just don't have a sense of humour."

He sighed and went back to the crossword.

I smiled to myself and threw a thousand pounds in fifties onto the small desk in front of him.

He didn't look up, just said:

"What am I, your bank now?"

"Well if you were, you'd show a little more interest."

He put the paper down in resignation and said:

"You see, that is exactly what I'm talking about. Crap jokes that half the time only you get."

"It's the same reason I talk to myself, mate. Only way to guarantee a decent conversation."

He looked out of the window at his possible customer, probably working out whether it was more painful to suffer out there with him, or in here with me.

"How's Mick?" he asked. "You heard anything else?"

"Not really. Somebody he was asking questions about had a pop at him, but didn't get him. The dog held them up for a while before they shot him, but Mick got away. He's holed up and he's trying to sort it out."

Best I could do without showing my hand and I didn't want to do that. It wouldn't help Mick or me and it might stop Tony loaning me the car.

But Tony had turned from the window to face me.

"They shot the dog?" he repeated, with shock in his voice. "The dog's dead?"

"Yeah, the dog's dead."

He shook his head, I think in disbelief.

"Must be serious people, carrying guns into a man's home."

This was getting a little close for me, so I tried to close it off.

"You know what Mick's like, you can never know what he's into at any one time. And you never liked the dog anyway."

"Bloody terrified me, that dog did, but it still sounds out of character for Mick. He kept himself to himself mostly. He shouldn't

79

have got mixed into something where someone would come for him like that." He turned back to check on the man outside who was looking underneath an Audi for some reason. "Anyway, you can talk," he carried on, "like you ever tell anyone what's happening."

"Well, I'll tell you what's happening this time, okay," I said, seizing the chance to change the direction of the conversation. "I've got a good job for a few days. I need to hire a decent, but not flash car and there's a grand in it for you. Same rules. No-one knows I have it, no-one knows you hired it. No damage to the car."

He got up.

"One day that last bit will go wrong and then there'll be a world of hassle and pain over it."

But he'd do it. All the cars were insured on the lot and he'd never had so much as a scratch on any of the ones I'd 'borrowed' over the last couple of years. If anything did happen, the contingency was for me to call him straight away and for him to report the car stolen off the lot. For that reason I only used older cars that weren't fitted with immobilisers, or top grade alarms.

"Four door, or two?"

"Four," I said automatically, my brain then catching up to the fact that Michel wouldn't be riding in the back like a client, but all the same, we might possibly need to carry someone else at some point.

"Got the same Mondeo you used before. Five years old, 1.8 manual, little slow accelerating, but okay once it's going."

"Fine by me," I said, "it's only to ferry someone around in, I'm not going to be caning it anywhere."

He went to the locked strongbox that was bolted to the floor, keyed the code and took out a set of keys.

"One and a spare," he said. "How come you've got a real job? Someone legitimate drop out at the last minute?"

"European businessman," I replied truthfully. "At the top of his profession and spying a little on his competitors."

"I'm impressed," he said, "especially with Mick out of the picture for a bit."

"Personal recommendation. Asked for me only," I said, taking the keys. "I'm good at my job, you know."

He smiled at that, but as I left, I didn't mention anything about

Russian Mafia. I'm not sure Tony would've appreciated the challenge that represented.

*

Michel was in the pub we'd agreed on, tucked away at a table near the back fire exit and facing the rest of the pub. He'd changed his clothes and was now in black jeans, boots and a leather jacket.

But they all looked brand new.

It was an improvement though, on the trench-coat thing, so I let it pass. Where he was sitting was good positioning, but just where I wanted to be. I hate sitting with my back to a room.

He didn't acknowledge me as I walked towards him and only after I'd pulled the chair facing him round at an angle, so that I too was facing the room, did he say anything.

"You get here first, you get first choice of where to sit."

His voice was quiet, but not thin. The same accent as Julot that sounded French to my ears, but wasn't. None of the richness of Julot's voice, though. Just a steadiness that spoke of confidence, maybe arrogance even. I'd look out for that. It could be dangerous to both of us later on. He took a drink from his tonic water, or lemonade and I waited. This was going to be a tricky partnership and I wanted to see if he would try to set out ground rules. If he did, I'd tear them up.

But he said nothing, just sat there and finished his drink and then got up and walked to the bar. It wasn't until he was returning that I realised what he was doing. Giving me time to size him up. As well as putting his unspoken authority on the relationship. 'I will do what I do,' he was saying, 'I will not even allow for the social norms of introduction or interaction.'

Well, that suited me fine.

I watched him until he reached our table with his new drink (needless to say he hadn't bought me one) and noted again that he moved easily, with an economy of effort that was natural, not affected. As he sat down, he opened his mouth to start speaking and I got up and went to the bar. Boys' games, but I can be just as petty and childish as the next guy and I've got a good sense of timing with

81

it. When I got back with my drink he looked slightly put out, but I reckoned he'd get over it.

"Touché," he said and then leaned back in his chair. He reached into his jacket and came out with a Tesco's carrier bag wrapped tightly around a smallish box. Those would be my bullets. He placed the bag on the table between us, but didn't take his hand off the package for another minute while he spoke.

"I do not like you, Garron and I do not think that you are necessary to this operation, but Julot does and I accept that he knows better than I do about this." He leaned in again, took his hand off the bullets and prodded with his index finger at my forearm which I was resting on the table. "But I do not want you here. You may have been a good fighter, but you are an amateur killer. I do not like working with anyone else, but definitely not with amateurs."

I don't like anyone touching me and I really don't like being prodded with index fingers. For a moment I considered leaning in and punching him off his seat, but that wouldn't have been very discreet, so I contented myself with picking up the box of bullets, which for some reason he seemed to resent giving to me, looking him straight in the eye and saying:

"You put that finger on me again and I'll break it off. Then we'll see how easily you can pull a trigger."

He started to say something, but I carried on.

"You're right. I'm an 'occasional' killer as you put it and much the better for not being a proud, professional assassin, like you are. But I'll tell you, the people I've killed in my poor quality, amateurish way, are just as dead as those you've killed professionally. And I'm still here to tell the tale."

He looked at me hard for a moment, maybe not used to being challenged like this and then shrugged, almost as if to say, 'what's the point in arguing with someone like this who doesn't understand.'

"I will call an, er…agreement," he said.

"A truce, you mean."

"Ah, yes, a truce" and he even smiled, either at getting the word, or at the thought of having to enter into a truce with an amateur like me. "We will agree to get to the Russian and I will not kill you."

There was no smile and I think he meant it and for a second I wondered if maybe he had a breaking point, if maybe this cool, young killer had never really been pushed and needled and wound up, but then I dropped the thought. He was Julot's killer. He would be calm and relaxed. Unless taking on the Russians was a step up in class for him as well.

I smiled at him.

"Julot wouldn't like you to kill me. He thinks I'm good. He thinks you need me."

"And I respect his thoughts. I would not think of killing you while we are looking for the Russian. But if I choose to kill you, Julot will never know it was not the Russians, or an accident, or however I choose to set it up."

He sat back and let me think about it. Whether he was still playing the game, or whether he was now deadly serious, the problem was I couldn't see him as a hit-man. And yet he must be. I'd sort of put him in the 'arrogant little shit' category and I could be very wrong there. Antagonising an arrogant little shit was one thing. Making an enemy of an assassin was maybe another.

But there was nothing I could do about it for the moment and if he was serious, then I was still safe enough while we were working together, if we ever managed to work together. At some point I'd think this out better, or even talk direct to Julot, although I had to realise that I was just the hired help, however friendly Julot appeared. Michel was the full time protégé and I shouldn't have any illusions about how the cards would fall on that one. So for now, we should just get on with the job and that was what I suggested to him. He shrugged in that way that Europeans seem to be able to do, which Englishmen never even attempt. The movement managed to tell me that he had complete contempt for me and anything I said, while agreeing to go along with my idea, because it happened to suit him at the moment. For the second time in ten minutes I thought of punching his lights out, but I resisted the temptation.

"So where do you think we should start?" he asked, "at one of the houses, or the restaurants?"

I shook my head. "We've no way of knowing where he is at the moment, unless you have other info you haven't shared yet, so hanging around somewhere could just be a waste of time."

"We could call the hotel and the restaurants, see if he has a booking at any of them."

"If he's booking in his own name and if they'll give out that information to someone who doesn't have a Russian accent. We can try it, on the basis that you never discount the obvious, but I don't think we'll get far with that."

He looked blankly at me and I realised that I'd spoken a little too quickly with some words that maybe he hadn't fully understood, but that was tough. I wasn't here to help with his English tutorials.

"We'll try calling the restaurants later maybe," I said again, "but even if he is there, we can't just walk in and take him out. He'll be tucked away somewhere and his bodyguards won't let us get close. Not if they're any good, they won't. We'll have to go there first and see what the layout is, if there are any vulnerable points maybe."

"You are telling me how to do my job?"

"No, I'm explaining how I'm going to go about doing mine."

"You just get me to him, I will only need a small amount of time and opportunity."

Great. A bloody ego as well.

"What I want to do," I said, controlling my reply, "is have a look at the places he runs, see what sort of people are around him, get a feel for what we're walking into."

He almost became human for a minute while he considered this.

"You really think this would be useful to do?" he asked.

I took a swallow of my drink.

"Yep," I said, "gives us a view of the people we might come up against and how he runs his businesses. Look, he's not going to be sitting around waiting for us to come for him. Anything we can learn is going to help and we might also pick up some information on where he's going to be at a specific time."

Michel thought about this for a few seconds. Perhaps he'd thought we'd just walk into Lysenkov's hotel and shoot everybody till we found him. I had no way of knowing whether he was the sort of killer who was able to take a project and work out his own access, method and escape for a hit, or whether he was literally a blunt instrument, a man who when given a set of instructions would follow them to the letter and get the job done. I was beginning to think it was this last

84

option, that I'd credited him with too much intelligence and mistaken raw animal cunning for actual tradecraft. Then he asked:

"Will we not lose the surprise that we have over him now?"

Okay, that was at least a sign that he was thinking.

"I don't think so. He doesn't know who we are. If his guys are any good, then they'll notice anyone too close or just hanging around and then any surprise is gone anyway. We want to be in and out, so we're going to have to know where to be in order to do that."

He nodded, which from him was a major sign that I could be talking any kind of sense.

"So, where first?"

A struggle, but he was ready to follow me.

"East London. I think we should start at the bottom, the place where he's least likely to be himself, but where we may pick up something about the Russians he has working for him."

"The drinking place?"

"Yes. But we're not going to drink. We're not going to get in anyone's face. We're not going to draw attention to ourselves in any way."

He smiled at me and got up.

"I will be invisible. I will not speak. I will not be - " he struggled for the word and then gave up " – in anybody's way." Then he leaned down towards me. "Unless of course, by some chance he is there. If so, I will kill him cold dead."

Nice, I thought, as I got up and followed him out. I'm going to the East End with someone who's looking for a fight. He'll probably feel right at home there.

*

We drove to East London and Michel got a view of the non-tourist side of the city. Not that we talked much, but he was taking everything in. Past the financial 'City' type buildings by Liverpool Street station and then, within a couple of minutes, turning into Bethnal Green Road and straight into the graffiti covered industrial units that start there. Then there are some small typical East London traders, small shops in little parades, surviving next to the estates. I'm sure Michel had seen similar in European cities, but there's a despair about the London estates that is immediately recognisable. Maybe it's not just London. Maybe it's all over the UK, but it's there and it's a living thing.

We pulled up in a side street off the main Bethnal Green Road, well before the shopping section where Tescos and Boots had taken up residence and a few minutes walk from the Russians' place. I then did what I never like to do and left my gun and bullets in the car. I was fairly sure Lysenkov wouldn't be there and we might be searched at the door on the way in. If we got in. I didn't know what we would be walking into, but I didn't want anyone finding a gun on either of us. It would slightly ruin the image of two mates out for a quick drink.

I also didn't want any kid joyriding the car especially with my gun in it, but you can't have everything your own way. We'd have to take a chance, so I put mine in its carrier bag and after some explanation and argument, Michel took off his shoulder holster and we locked everything in the boot.

I had no idea what this place would be like and I was half expecting some darkened pub with blacked out windows, but it was even less than that.

On a rubbish strewn street, there was an open doorway and some steps going down. No-one on the door, but then no-one was going to go down those stairs without a very good reason. In fact, I found myself stopping at the doorway and I had to remind myself what that good reason was. But I reckoned that two guys wandering in off the street for a drink would get away with it for a few minutes at least. Michel wasn't so sure. I asked him if he was scared, to wind him up a bit, but he had a point. If this was trouble, we should weigh up whether what we might gain would outweigh what we could walk into, but I'd done that already and I was, if not happy, then at least prepared to go in.

"We go in, get told to piss off, make a joke of it and if we don't get to stay, we leave. That's all. They want to be anonymous, they're not going to want to have trouble and police getting involved, so most of it's going to be threat, not ABH."

I had to explain what that was and reminded myself he was Belgian. And then I reminded him of that.

86

"Not a word down there that anyone can hear. You're English, right? No European connection at all."

"Do you think I should walk a little more uncultured then, as well?"

I didn't answer, just started down the steps. Red stone steps with worn edges. Good for camouflaging the blood if it soaked in I thought, but that was just reaction to walking into somewhere unknown. This was going to be no worse than half the pubs in London. The only difference was just that I might not be able to understand what they were saying when they were throwing me out.

Door on the right at the bottom and as I pushed it inwards, the smoke filled air hit me. There's that cigarette ban almost everywhere now and this was like a throwback to the seventies. I didn't know whether Michel smoked, but if not, he was about to start.

I was expecting every head to turn as we walked in and they did, even if some of them had a little trouble moving their necks to do it. The room was just a big cellar with a bar running along the far wall and some tables and chairs. The floor was concreted, the walls had some old torn and curling posters of what I assumed were Russian places and the atmosphere, if you could call it that, was quiet, dead even. There were maybe two dozen men, only men, leaning against the bar, or the walls, or sitting at the tables. They fell fairly neatly into two categories. There were lean, hard looking men, with sunken faces and shortish greased hair and dark circles round their hard eyes and then there were large, hard looking men, with heavy faces, skinhead cuts and those heavy rolls of flesh at the base of their necks. The smoke was so thick you could hardly see the other side of the room. There was some music playing quite loudly, which strangely, sounded like eighties pop, something that made me like the place even less.

But no-one had gone for us yet, so I walked in, trusting that Michel would be moving with me. Bearing in mind that I wouldn't usually want to let people get either side of me, my psyche was screaming, but I shut it up and walked to the bar. There were only two beers on tap, but I didn't want to drink here and a short would be an easier drink to 'lose', than a full pint. And there was only one drink to ask for.

"Two vodkas."

No 'please'. These guys wouldn't say please.

The barman was about eighteen stone. He wasn't a bodybuilder, but you could imagine him carrying a barrel of beer up the stairs under each arm. When he spoke he leaned forwards on the bar in front of me and I thought I heard it creak. His voice was thick with an accent that I only knew from films, but it was unmistakeably Russian.

"This Russian drinking house."

"I know. I'm descended from Russians." I gestured with my head towards Michel. "He isn't, but I am. I had Russian grandparents."

I didn't think it would last for long, but I didn't need long. I wanted to see the sort of people that Julot thought Lysenkov would be using. Either for low level work, or to train up for working closer with him. If Julot was right and this was the recruiting ground, then we were seeing the people we would be coming up against when we went for Lysenkov.

The barman shifted his weight slightly. His hands were huge and there were tattoos on his arms and also tattoos of stars and diamonds on his fingers. He said:

"First generation Russian only."

The voice was guttural, harsh and I had no illusions that if they wanted us to leave, they'd throw us out. But I also thought that if we went voluntarily, they wouldn't push the violence. Lysenkov would want this place below the radar level. Somewhere the police would know about, but would leave alone as long as there were no problems.

I leaned forwards on the bar as well and got a whiff of personal body odour that I could have done without.

"Are you telling me, that your children will not be allowed to drink in here when they're older?"

That confused him a bit, but I didn't want him angry, I just wanted to keep him on the back foot. I put a twenty pound note on the bar.

"I understand," I said, "we're in the wrong place. So one drink for me and one for my friend and one for you and then we will go straight away."

He flicked a glance at the twenty and I realised I wouldn't be seeing any change from it.

"One vodka," I said, "just to drink to the memory of my Russian grandfather."

The twenty disappeared and three almost clean glasses took its place. Vodka splashed into them.

"One drink and then you go." It wasn't a request.

I nodded, picked up one of the glasses and moved to lean against a side wall, assuming Michel would be following me. The heads slowly turned back to their own conversations. We hadn't been accepted, but for the moment at least, we weren't going to be lynched.

"Very smooth," Michel said under his breath.

"Yeah, but just you stick to saying nothing. Someone will report back higher up the chain that there were two English guys in here and let's make sure they know we're English and not European."

I took a sip of the vodka, which hadn't been chilled, but which was still enough to strip the skin off the inside of my mouth and throat and then looked around at the people. Not too closely, just casually to take them in. They were without doubt a hard looking bunch and unlike English thugs, they were quiet with it. There wasn't an air that there would be trouble, just an attitude of meanness that hung everywhere.

"They're a tough lot," I said to Michel, who was also looking around him. "Do me a favour Michel, don't go for the eye contact, all right? I don't want a fight in here."

"We might learn more then."

"Don't be stupid, we'd get ourselves kicked to pieces and we've learned enough from this already."

He looked at me.

"What? What have we learned? Except that I now know that you can talk your way into a place."

I tried not to sound patient. I didn't want him blowing up at me in here.

"We know that here at least, they're not expecting any problems, or we would never have been allowed to stay. We know the types of people he employs at least for the grunt work and we can get an idea that they're not dancers, there are enough genuine hard nuts here for the man to have his pick."

After I'd explained 'grunt work', 'dancers' and 'hard nuts' for him, he seemed to get the point.

"But we have not progressed. We are no nearer knowing where he is or how to get to him."

I gave up and concentrated on not making eye contact with any of the inmates. That's what it felt like, a place of convicts and suppressed violence, set, weirdly, to rubbish electro pop.

We stood for a few minutes longer and then I said we should go. Michel wanted to wait for a few minutes more, which surprised me, but I thought if he was realising the value of being here, so much the better.

One of the lean, hard types in a sleeveless T-shirt to show off the muscles and the tattoos, hard-eyed us as he walked past to go to what I reckoned was the gents. No reaction from me and thankfully none from Michel either, although without his gun, I wasn't sure that he'd want to start anything with these guys.

"Okay, ready to go," he said and I started away from the wall, with my now empty shot glass. I'd managed to drip most of the vodka onto the floor without anyone noticing.

"Wait," Michel said, "where that man went, that is the toilet, right?"

I shrugged. "Looks like it."

"Okay, I will return in a minute."

I should have known. I really should have known, but what could I have done, told him not to go?

After three or four minutes had passed, I realised that not only was Michel still in there, which in itself was maybe okay, but that the Russian who had passed us before, hadn't come out yet. I didn't believe an unarmed Michel would start trouble here after all I had said to him, but the fact was he was still in there. I looked around the room. No-one was paying me any attention any more, so I put my glass down on a nearby table and pushed through the door to the corridor behind. Ten yards down, there was a short flight of steps up and another door with a word in Russian, or what I took to be Russian on it. It could've said 'Ladies', but in this place I doubted it. I pushed it open and saw Michel with his hand on the Russian's throat, pushing his head back against the wall at the far end of the short run of urinals and with a four inch knife against the man's neck.

"What the hell are you doing?" I nearly shouted and then stopped myself from being so loud. If anyone heard us, we'd be torn apart by the guys in the cellar.

"Asking a few questions of my new friend."

The Russian didn't look scared, more resigned and definitely angry. His hand was on Michel's shoulder, but he wasn't resisting. I guessed he had some experience of being in 'situations' and felt he had a better chance of survival by keeping still.

I didn't know what to say to Michel.

"Are you mad? We didn't come here to start a war."

"You think I will listen to you? This man can give us information if he chooses to. So I ask him questions."

"And have you got any answers?"

"Not yet, but I have not begun to hurt him yet."

We were talking in stage bloody whispers and I could see the tension in Michel's hand, the one holding the Russian, although his other hand on the knife seemed completely relaxed. There was a trickle of blood starting from the side of the man's neck where the knife was slowly cutting him and as he felt this, his eyes became angrier and I wondered how long he would stay still. How long Michel could hold him still.

"We have to go," I told Michel.

He just laughed. "This man knows where Lysenkov is."

He used the name. The idiot used the name.

I felt myself getting angrier, aware that at any moment the door could open and one or more Russian thugs could walk in. And they might be armed with at least knives as well. I could get killed here in a Russian bloody toilet in the heart of East London.

Easy, Garron, think your way out. Persuade Michel to leave now.

The two of them hadn't moved now for the minute that I'd been in there with them. Michel was not a big man and he would, he should, be getting tired soon. The Russian wasn't fighting, but as soon as he felt Michel weaken, he would explode into movement and there wasn't a lot of room in here.

"What makes you think he knows anything?" I asked.

"The tattoo. On his shoulder. The tattoo of the skull."

"So what?"

"I do my homework. It tells that he is a murderer. Someone that Lysenkov would want to use."

"You stupid shit-head! They all have bloody tattoos! You think Lysenkov uses them all? Has he told you anything? No. This guy probably knows less than we do about the man. How the hell would he know anything about our man's movements, where he'll be? Does he look like he's at the top of the tree?"

Michel slightly lowered the knife so that it wasn't cutting into the Russian's neck anymore, but he kept the grip on the man's throat.

"He might have heard something," he said, but the certainty had gone. "We need some information from somebody," he added, louder this time.

And I got it. He was frustrated. He was, in fact, a blunt instrument. Nothing more. This wasn't his sort of game. I could see why Julot wanted someone with him now and I didn't like it. He might be fine in action, but when he couldn't function, he got mad about it.

"If he heard something, do you think he'd tell us? In the amount of time you have to work on him before someone else walks in here? What do you think his reputation, his life would be worth in this place?"

The knife lowered further and the Russian's eyes changed. He still hadn't said a word, but he relaxed slightly.

"Come on," I said to Michel, "we need to get out of here. He now knows more about us than we do about him and I don't want to hang around while he tells."

Michel didn't so much as flick a glance at me, but he said:

"Yes. I have made a mistake. He now knows we are looking for Lysenkov. And he knows I am not English. Or Russian."

"That's right, so let me crack him one that'll slow him down for a bit and we'll get the hell out."

At which point the knife flashed and the man collapsed clutching at his throat and choking. Blood appeared, that's the only word for it, *appeared* everywhere across his hands and down his chest, but not on Michel, who had removed his left hand from the Russian's throat in the instant of cutting it open.

"A few seconds," Michel said, "only a few."

I guess I was in shock of a kind. Which is a strange thing for me to admit. But the whole thing had been so unexpected, so unnecessary...

"You killed him."

Michel turned slightly to me, but he was still looking to see that the blood didn't run towards us and get on his boots.

"You," I said. "You killed him."

He reached into a cubicle and tore off a wad of the toilet paper. Used it to wipe his knife clean, threw the paper in the toilet and using another piece, either to keep his hands clean, or to avoid leaving fingerprints, flushed the chain. He still hadn't answered me, so I grabbed him and pulled him round to face me. The knife flashed again and I found myself in the same position that the Russian had been in, hand against my throat and knife against my neck. It had been a neat move and I could believe that he'd practised it a thousand times and used it a hundred.

"Yes," he whispered into my face, "I killed him. I made a mistake and I gave him information he could have passed on. Now he can't. And if you ever put your hands on me again, I will kill you straight away."

He held the position on me for a few seconds more while I realised that although I could move one of my arms, he was inside that arm and the speed that he had and the position of the knife meant I'd be cut whatever move I'd make. Would I be dead? Maybe. But not now. He needed me now, so I kept still until he let go and moved back.

"We need to move him somewhere," Michel said.

"Not unless we're hanging around to clean up the blood as well," I replied and I was pleased to hear my voice was firm, no shakes. Maybe that was because I hadn't really thought he was going to kill me.

"You are correct," he agreed. "But I was correct that it is better he is dead than alive to talk."

He was probably right about that. I just didn't like it. And I didn't like leaving the Russian here. And I didn't like walking back out through that cellar.

"Go through his pockets," I said.

"What? Why?"

"Make it look a little more like we were going for his money, not anything else."

"He probably has none."

"Yes, Michel, but if his wallet is empty, no-one will know if he had any or not. Geddit?"

He quickly turned out the wallet, which had a tenner and a few coins in it and we took them.

"Now out," I said. "You first, don't rush, walk easy round the side of the room to the stairs and out. I'll be a minute behind you."

"We could go together."

"What, you scared of them?"

He looked at me.

"Never mind," I said. "Look, you went in before me, you go out before me."

Michel smiled: "But he went in before both of us."

I think he considered that was a joke.

"Get going," I said and he did. "No eye contact," I whispered after him as he went through the door, but he didn't answer and I could only hope. I didn't have too much confidence in his self-control. But he was right. From our point of view the man was better dead than talking. It was just that it should never have come to that. I took a look back at the body lying in its own blood a few feet away from me and I felt sick. But now wasn't the time to throw up. Control it until you're safe. And then, stupidly, I noticed how I'd thought of the man's body as lying in 'its' own blood, not 'his' own blood. I'm becoming like them, I thought as I opened the door, went down the steps and turned right, into the corridor.

Not yet, I told myself, not yet.

It was a long walk through that corridor and longer through the cellar. I thought we were already lucky not to have been challenged, or had anyone interrupt Michel's little killing, but the luck held and twenty-five minutes after walking in, we were back in the car. Twenty-five minutes and one death.

"Where to now?" Michel asked.

"Home," I said. I still had that sick feeling in my gut and throat. "I've had enough for one night."

I thought I saw the edge of a smile on his face.

"And, Michel," I added as I put the car in gear and moved off, "if you ever pull a knife on me again, you make damn sure you do kill me. Because if you don't, I will take it off you and cut you wide open with it, professional or not."

I was facing forwards, but out of the corner of my eye, I saw the smile fade.

*

I dropped Michel near to his hotel. He didn't want me to know exactly where he was staying and I didn't want to know. It was standard security and it suited me fine. I just wanted him out of the car and well away from me. There was no point in pretending that I hadn't seen people die before, I'd been responsible for people dying before, but the suddenness and the pointlessness of what Michel had done had got to me. I hated to admit it, but it had shocked me and that wasn't a word I was used to applying to myself. I still had that nauseous feeling in my stomach and the tightness in my throat and I hadn't even begun to think about the possible effects the killing might have on what we were trying to do. Maybe nothing. Maybe it would just be seen as a mugging. Maybe they'd think we'd tried to proposition him in the toilet. Maybe they wouldn't even call the police, just clear him out. Either way it was dawning on me that this was a different game to the ones I'd been involved with before. Hillier and even Smith killed people, but not so randomly, not so pointlessly.

I took a couple of deep breaths. Wound the window down, got rained on, wound it up again. Switched the radio on and found one of the talk stations, I didn't want music right then. Not that the subject matter was any better than my own thoughts. Another knifing in London. Another teenager dead or dying. More, in fact, pointless, random murders.

And the difference between the two?

I wasn't even sure I could work that one out. Was there a difference? The fact that Michel was older, was employed in effect to do what he did? That the gang kids were amateurs in comparison? Or maybe that at least with Michel the people he targeted were in his way of life. The gangs would attack anyone that crossed their path.

The old Ben Siegel line popped into my head. 'We only kill each other.' Or do we? Would Michel stop at only killing his own kind?

What if Julot directed him at someone random. Would he stop and think about that?

What had I just done thinking that line? 'We only kill each other.' Was I one of them now?

I switched off the radio and tried to blank my mind. I could deal with this, with the doubts, even with Michel's stupidity and its consequences. I could deal with it.

- *What does that say about you, then?*

- Nothing. Not a damn thing.

- *If you say so.*

- It just means I can get through this. That's all I have to do. Get through this.

- *If you say so.*

- Shut up.

- *If you say so...*

I parked up a few streets away from the flat. Not because of any security risk, just because finding a parking space in Camden is a rarity. Stuck the gun back in the loop in my jacket pocket hanging down where the lining of the pocket used to be and grabbed the bullets in the carrier that Michel had delivered.

My head was still working things through as I walked to the flat, but I wasn't so out of it that I didn't see the group of kids hanging out again by the service road at the back of my block. Just what I needed. Another bloody confrontation today. I was close enough to see that it was the same gang as I'd tangled with before and by that time they were close enough to recognise me. They'd not been hanging around every night, but they were back in force this time, maybe a couple more young thugs than previously. The lead man himself was turning towards me now and squaring up.

"Told you I'd be coming back for you."

It was a sneer. The contempt of youth for anyone and anything that dared to stand in its way.

I stopped a good fifteen feet away from them and looked at the group. Confident in themselves, in their numbers. And I wondered, as I was about to dent that confidence, if I'd actually have to shoot any of them and realised that if that was the case, I wouldn't hesitate.

- *Just like Michel?*

96

- Self defence. Besides, these aren't humans. They've forfeited the right.

"Nothing to say to me?"

The leader again, working himself into it and playing to his audience. His followers.

"Yes," I said. "I thought you'd be back, so I came prepared." Half a glance around the area, but there was no-one near us that I could see and anyone starting to get close would see this lot and move away, so I pulled the gun out of my jacket and keeping it close, to shield it from anyone who did come round the corner straight into this, pointed it, not at the leader, but at one of the newcomers. He went white.

"Anyone still here after I count five gets shot. Then I wipe the gun and stick it in one of your grubby little dead hands and walk away."

There was silence for about two seconds. Then I began to count.

"One."

It's never a good idea to do this, to set a limit on yourself, because then you give yourself no way out. Once you reach your limit, in this case the number five, you've got to carry out whatever the threat has been.

"Two."

The other point is that the people on the receiving end of the threat, know when you're going to have to do something and can tailor their reaction to that timeframe. Unless you cheat, of course.

"Three."

I hadn't changed my aim and the kid at the end of the sight had gone from white to transparent. I knew the leader would have to say something and it was now.

"He's bluffing. He won't shoot anyone in the street like this. It's just a bluff."

I smiled at the teenager I was aiming at and keeping the gun perfectly still, shifted my weight very slightly.

"Four."

"Shit!" the kid screamed and bolted.

I shifted the aim to another one of the gang and he too ran. As I shifted aim again, they scattered away from me and the leader, realising that his support was gone, started backing away as well.

"It's not over," he shouted as he picked up speed after his troops and for a second I thought about making it be over, of shooting the little scumbag dead there and then, but instead I lowered the gun, another image entering my head as I did so, another time, another place, where I'd held fire, where I'd not become like Michel.

Then they were gone and I pocketed the gun and let the tension ease out of me as I checked that they were out of sight and walked down the service road at the back of the flats. As I climbed the fire escape to our back door, I looked for the cat. I wanted to tell him that round two had gone our way, but he was out somewhere, past battles forgotten and only tonight's confrontations to consider.

- You see. Not like Michel.
- *No.*
- He would have shot one of them dead straight off.
- *Not used the threat, which could have gone wrong.*
- In which case I would have shot someone. But it wouldn't have been first choice.

I reached the landing on the fire escape and realised how tired I was, mainly the release of tension, now I was home. I looked around at the night and all that was in it. Life went on. The lights were mainly on now in the bedsits and the flats and the houses around me and none of the people in their safe little homes with their own life affirming problems knew how close I'd come tonight.

Save it, Garron, there's nothing in these thoughts for you.

I unlocked the back door to my little flat. Just like all the others.

Home.

Safe.

*

It wasn't that late, but the flat was dark when I entered, although she was awake.

"Where have you been?"

She didn't shout it, or raise her voice at all. It was just a question out of a darkened room. A question I didn't want to answer.

"Go back to sleep," I said.

She sat up on the mattress and put on the side light that sits on the floor there. Blinking in the light she said again:

"Where have you been?"

Straight question, straight answer.

"In a Russian drinking den."

"Christ," she said softly, "you're getting involved with it then."

It was a statement, not a question and I didn't answer. I wasn't in such a good mood myself.

I took off my jacket and let her see the gun as I took it into the kitchen and put it behind the cereal boxes in one of the cupboards. She'd once asked me why I kept it there, why I didn't hide it properly and I'd told her the truth. There was nowhere in this place I could hide it that a professional wouldn't find it. So I might as well just tuck it out of sight and make sure a professional wasn't looking for it.

I poured a drink of water for myself and took it back into the main room. She'd seen the gun, I knew that. I suppose I was hoping she would just leave it then, but that wasn't going to happen.

"Can you at least tell me why?" Her voice was louder now, "why you have to do this?"

I leaned against the table and looked at her. Tried to see it from her view. Maybe tried to understand it myself. But I wasn't sure I wanted to understand it. Certainly I didn't want to think about it now.

"Can we talk about this another time? In the morning, maybe?"

"Jesus, Garron," she said quietly, "you can't even talk to me about it. You just want me to be quiet, to leave you alone. To let you get on with it. I was expecting you back. You didn't say you'd be out and I've been sitting here waiting, no answer on your phone, just waiting and then you come back and say 'leave it till another time'.

It would have been better if she'd been shouting. The quiet voice made it worse.

"I'm just tired, Jenny, that's all."

"Tired? Why what did you do tonight? Kill half the Russian immigrants in London? And then come back here as though where you've been isn't important, doesn't matter?"

She sat up straighter. It was quite cold in the flat and she was wearing a black T-shirt in bed with a line drawing of a lion on it. I always liked her in that T-shirt.

"Garron, I learned to live with what you do when you're working the jobs. I tell myself it's not too dangerous and that you're looking after people, it's protection, stopping people getting hurt."

I started to interrupt, but she stopped me

"Yes, I know that may be naïve, but that's what I tell myself. But then something like this comes up and it's like it was when that stuff happened with Hillier. It's different from your work. And you give yourself excuses and reasons and maybe you even manage to fool yourself, but it happens. Somehow it happens and you go out with that gun and I don't know if you're coming back. So no, we can't leave this until the morning, I want to know why you're doing this and I want to know why I'm not enough of a reason to stop you."

So there it was. She wanted me to live the way she wanted. For good reasons, so I wouldn't be hurt, but also for selfish reasons, so that she'd know that she was enough for me. Or was I just projecting my thoughts onto her? I took a deep breath and started badly.

"We've been through stuff like this before, Jenny."

"No," she said, "not like this."

"I have to help Mick. If I don't, then his life is in danger and if he stays out of sight, then sooner or later, my life, our lives will change because my work will dry up and we'll run out of money."

"And you'll have to get a proper job."

"We've been through that. I've tried before to get a job that would suit you - "

"No, you tried and then you gave up. For you, this is easier. You don't want a normal life with me and I don't understand why not."

I sat down by the table. It had happened. She'd finally come out with it.

"Tonight," I said, not looking at her, "I've faced down an eighteen stone Russian bruiser and a ten stone Belgian assassin. I've seen a man pointlessly killed three feet in front of me and stepped out of the way of his blood. I've been threatened by a gang of teenage thugs who seem to be targeting me and I've forced them to back off." Then I looked at her and there was incomprehension on her face. "Welcome to my world, Jenny. This is it."

After a moment she said:

"But it doesn't have to be."

"I had my chance. It didn't work out. This is what I do now. This is what I am now. And you know that. You knew it when I met you. And you recognise it, because you grew up the same way I did. There's no real line that separates what I do looking after a client, from what happened tonight. You choose to think that there is, but you know that who I work for is not always down to me, who they are and what they've done is not something that I know, or try to think about."

"But you do. You do think about it. I know you do, because I know you by now. You're not a thug and you're not a killer. For Christ's sake, Garron, you care about people!"

And she looked at me then, this woman who loved me, who I loved and I knew that she saw it then in my face, in my eyes, as others had seen it before. I had to deal with what I had been through this night and with what I would have to face before this was over and to do that I had to draw in on myself and I knew that what she was seeing now was a colder, harder edged version of the person she knew. I felt it, but could never see it. But others had and I knew it was there now.

But this was Jenny, not anyone else and she was tougher and had more guts than most.

"Yes," she said, speaking quietly again, "I can see your world, but what that is, is just part of you, it's not all of you. What you've done, what you've seen tonight and other nights, is where you have chosen to be. And you can choose to move from there if you want to. But only if you want to. Only if you can see a future for us and not just be looking at the next five minutes. Only if I'm enough for you. For you to want to change."

There was quiet as she sat back on the mattress, her back to the side wall. The challenge was there now and I didn't know what to say. But I could see where she'd come from on this. Why she was tying what I did so closely in to her. I wasn't sure I could explain it to her though, without hurting her too much.

"Jenny, do you see a pattern here?"

"With what?"

"With what you've said. With you looking at what I'm doing and making what I do depend somehow on what you mean to me."

"I don't understand what you mean."

Her mother had committed suicide after Jenny's sister had overdosed and died and Jenny had taken that as a personal rejection of her, rather than as an action her mother had taken on her own. To me, there seemed to be a pattern with what was happening now.

"What I mean, is you felt that when your Mum killed herself she was rejecting you. Now you think that if I carry on with my life, the things I do, I'm also rejecting you. But it isn't like that."

After a second she replied.

"That's a bastard thing to say" and her voice was tiny, "you're turning the fact that you don't want to change, that for some reason you want all this violence, into a discussion of me. You're saying that I'm paranoid, so it's my fault."

And suddenly there were tears in her eyes and running down her face and I didn't think that I was being that hard, but again I'd got it wrong and I stood up to go to her, but she said:

"No, don't come here now and say you're sorry. Tell me you're going to change, tell me that you care enough about me to have a future, but don't just put your arm around me and say it's going to be all right."

So I stood there and I tried to work it out, while she faced me, the sobbing unchecked, the despair real.

"Jenny, I don't know what I'm doing next week, let alone next year. I've never looked more than five minutes ahead, because I've never needed to and I've never really thought that I'd be around to have a future, but I do know that I love you. I need you. I've spent my whole life on my own and I'm trying now to adjust to not being on my own, to including another person, but it's not easy. And I can't just change overnight."

"I'm not asking you to change overnight, but this is not overnight. And this is not something like gambling, or alcohol, this is being involved in violence, in killing! Or maybe it is like gambling, maybe it is an addiction."

I sat down nearer to her on the floor.

"Maybe it is. Maybe I need it."

She reached out to me and gripped my arm hard.

"But why? What are you trying to prove? You're not a fool. What is it?"

And there it was again. The same question that I could never answer, that most of the time I tried to avoid thinking about. And somewhere, Al looking at me, asking me that same question, but maybe knowing the answer. Maybe having seen in me the thing that I could not recognise, or admit to recognising, in myself.

I backed away from it again.

"I'm not looking to prove anything. I don't want to prove anything."

"No? How about not making it to the top as a boxer and trying to prove you're still up to the fight now?"

There was a silence, while she realised what she'd said, but I didn't move away.

"It wasn't my fault I didn't make it as a fighter."

"I didn't say it was, but it still happened."

"And I'm not…making up for that somehow. Boxing's a sport. This isn't." I felt my temper rising slightly, which hadn't happened for years. "I'm not out there mugging old ladies, or defrauding single mothers. Anybody in front of me is a criminal, is a violent person with a history." I heard my voice rising and fought to control it. She'd touched a nerve and I hadn't realised it. "I don't want us to break up. I don't know what our future is. I don't know what will happen tomorrow. I don't know whether I'm doing this for Mick, or for Al, or for me, but I'm doing it and I'm going to see it through. And then if you want me and you want a future with me, then after that we'll talk about it. If necessary we'll clear out of London and talk about it. No promises, not from me, nor from you, but we'll try."

"If you're still alive," she said in the silence that followed.

I took a deep breath. Saw the abyss in front of us and held my control to step back from it. To keep us alive. After a few moments I replied to her.

"Oh, I'll live. I couldn't give you the satisfaction of looking at my grave and telling me you were right."

It was poor taste humour, but it helped stop the tears a little and although we weren't finished with this, not by a long way, neither of us wanted to walk and there was an unspoken agreement to pull back from the brink enough for tonight, to allow us to ease off.

But a lot of things had been said. A lot of feeling had been shown.

And there was no going back from that now.

*

The next morning would have been difficult, with both of us treading carefully around each other, but Jenny was on a college day morning and I took the coward's way out and stayed more or less in bed until she was ready to leave. She kissed me goodbye, but only just. And from my point of view, I didn't push anything either.

When I did surface, I fed the cat. Well, I put food in his bowl and left it there and then eased into the day gently. I was still having trouble thinking about what had happened at the Russian drinking cellar and the conversation with Jenny wasn't helping any either. I knew that if I thought about the Russian thing too much, I would realise that it had been my insistence on going there that had started the chain of events leading to the man's death. I shook that thought away. Michel was responsible for that, not me. But I knew now what he was capable of. There would be no more leaving him on his own. Next time, if he wanted to pee, he'd have to have a chaperone.

I needed to sit and work out the next move to get to Lysenkov, but Mick called before I'd got started. I was worried straight away, because we'd changed the agreement to text messages, but he told me he was okay, but needed to meet me as soon as we could arrange it. I hoped it was some kind of information, but no such luck.

"I'm running out of money, mate," he said "and you've got a week's rent that I could use as a stake and the cash from that last job I gave you with the jeweller. I don't think I can wait for the next week's rent, so whenever suits you, we can meet up."

Which is what we agreed to. I had a little difficulty getting my head around going to pick up weekly rents for someone when I was engaged in trying to stop a Russian Mafia boss kill the same person, but I reckoned Mick had to have the money and that was the end of it. I said I'd call him later when I'd worked a few things out and we left it at that. I didn't tell him about Michel and the dead Russian, or he might've insisted that I bring him the money straight away, in case I didn't make it through another night.

I'd arranged to call Michel by three in the afternoon, give him time,

I'd said, to get his tourist shopping done in the West End, which had only produced a sneer from him. The truth was, though, that although I'd learnt a lot from the previous night, including a lot more about Michel, I still wasn't sure how to get closer to Lysenkov. Maybe we would have to stake his house out and start plotting his travel patterns. That would be the professional thing to do, but I couldn't see Michel wanting to wait for as long as that would take. And Julot would have to pay for more manpower.

Michel's idea had been to phone Lysenkov's restaurant, based I think solely on the idea that if Michel had a restaurant, he'd eat in there often. He might be right, but I doubted it. Problem was, I didn't have any real ideas of my own. I was a bodyguard, not a detective. I couldn't rope anyone else in either, maybe use a legitimate detective agency for the legwork, because the moment we saw this guy we were going to kill him.

I got up from the table and went into the kitchen to put the kettle on. Standard British reaction. When in doubt, have a cup of tea. On the worktop next to the fridge was a photocopy of one of Jenny's work papers. 'Social work and policy course: Assessment and planning - intervention and review.' It was subtitled: 'The study of the differing views and opinions around how and in what way social issues and questions can be understood.' Under that there were some numbered points. I read the first two. 'What is the nature of the relationship between citizens and the state?' and 'How might social issues such as inequality, discrimination and crime, be understood?'

Then I gave up. It felt like an unfair view into another world and I suddenly realised that I was losing her. Not that she didn't love me, but that she was moving on from where she'd been when we'd met. Then she'd needed me. Now she was understanding that there was a world out there beyond our four walls and that maybe the fact that I wasn't changing could keep her locked in. I looked at that last question again. 'How might social issues such as inequality, discrimination and crime, be understood?' I could bloody answer that! I switched off the kettle and went back into the main room. I'd lost my thirst suddenly.

*

I was getting nowhere, so I went round the corner to the phone box that had been working a couple of days earlier. By now, of course, it had been vandalised and I spent another ten minutes looking for one that not only had the handset attached to the main box, but actually gave a dial tone as well. I didn't like the look of the bit I had to put against my ear, but after a quick wipe down, I reckoned it was as good as it was going to get.

I'd had no ideas, so although I didn't think it would work, I called the restaurant as Michel had suggested. A European, but non-Russian voice answered with the name of the restaurant and a 'how can I help you' that made me feel I was worth a hundred pound tip. I decided to go for broke.

"I am meeting Mr Lysenkov this evening at your restaurant, but I've misplaced the time of the reservation. Could you tell me please, what time we are due to meet there?"

"Mr Lysenkov has no booking for this evening, Sir."

But the tone had changed straight away. I'd tried to speak with less of a London accent, but maybe that wasn't enough. Or it could have been the fact that I'd added the word 'please' into the mix. Maybe people who went to this restaurant didn't say please. But we could play the game some more.

"Oh, I'm sorry," I said, "perhaps I have the day wrong. Could it be for tomorrow night?"

"It is not our policy to give out details of our clientele's bookings."

The 'Sir' had gone now.

"Very commendable," I said and hung up.

What had I learned? That he wouldn't be at his restaurant tonight and that he owned a place which probably wouldn't let me through the door. Which left what? The night club and the hotels. He wouldn't be staying at his own hotel unless he had meetings or a mistress set up there and I couldn't visualise him at the nightclub, so we were stuck. I needed a proper detective who'd know what to do now. I needed a partner who would come up with some good ideas of his own. I needed to buy some more milk so I could have breakfast and at least that one I could do something about. Other than that I was stumped. I went back to the flat and called Mick. There was nothing else going on. I might as well give him his money now.

*

We met up in Wembley at a coffee shop. I have no idea why Mick picked Wembley, I assumed it was reasonably near to where he was staying and not a particularly Russian inhabited area. I guess it was in a coffee shop and not a pub because pubs had the possibility of somebody he knew walking in on him. I don't think anyone Mick knew, or might have any contact with, would be seen in a coffee shop. Maybe in a greasy spoon, but not in a brand-name, on-every-high-street coffee shop like this one.

He was already there when I arrived, looking the same as ever, but I still did a double take as it was so odd to see him out of his natural environment, his flat or the local pub. And drinking coffee!

I collected a cup of tea, very boring by the standards of what was on offer in this place and sat down opposite him. Mick was never overweight, but now he looked more drawn and thin than I'd ever seen him.

"Didn't know you were a coffee drinker, mate," I said as I sat down.

"I'm not," he replied, "I'm trying to blend in."

I wasn't sure if that was meant to be a joke or not, so I let it go. He didn't look like he was in a joking mood.

"You keeping out of trouble?" he asked me.

"Nope." I had decided not to tell him what had happened the night before, but looking at him now, I changed my mind and gave him a cut down version. I thought that if I had to go through this for him, he should at least know what it was I was going through. When I'd finished, he shook his head.

"You should clear out, Garron, don't get involved for me. Maybe if I just fade for a bit…"

He didn't finish the sentence, because he knew and I knew, that he couldn't just fade. If he wasn't working his areas, he couldn't live without benefits and if that happened, he'd be found sooner than he could collect them. It was a gesture, but it was good of him to make it.

"I'll be fine," I said. "Besides which, if you vanished for too long, I'd have to find someone else to work for."

"You'd manage," he said and then with a bit more of himself in it, "you know what they say, as one door closes another one opens."

"Yeah, but with me, they usually close on my foot and open into my face."

I passed him an envelope with the rent cash and the job money less my take. I had thought of leaving my cut in, but then if this went on for a while, I was going to start running short, given most of my jobs came from Mick. I had the money from Julot, but I might have to use most of that to vanish myself and Jenny at some point.

"Cheers," he said, pocketing the envelope without opening it. "What's your next move?"

I had a quick, I would say automatic, glance around, but the place was fairly empty. I still didn't use names, but I told him that I had no real ways forward. I just had no information. I told him about my pathetic attempt at conning the restaurant into talking to me and he managed a smile.

"Never going to get information like that, mate, best thing you could do for info from somewhere like that is pay for it. Get yourself to one of the low paid guys there, kitchen porters, cleaners, whatever and throw some cash at it."

"That's what you'd do, is it?"

"As good as anything in this situation." He drank some more of his coffee, holding it like the street guys do in winter when they're trying to keep their hands warm as well as drink and I suddenly got a vision of what Mick would be like if we didn't sort this out for him. For as long as I'd known him, he'd lived the same way. He'd built up a set of walls for himself and within those walls he functioned. Without them, it wouldn't be long before he didn't.

He put his cup down and looked at me straight.

"I know this could all go very wrong, very quickly. I want you to know that I feel really bad about it. I know you and your girl are trying to stay out of trouble and this could be as bad as it gets." He paused for a moment. "I just want you to know that."

I wasn't used to emotion from Mick and I wasn't quite sure what to say to him and as I was about to tell him not to worry, not to talk about it, he carried on.

"I think I ought to be able to get some idea of where this guy is, though. I've got a couple of people I might be able to screw some information out of. If they don't think I'm too hot to talk to."

"That's good, Mick, I need anything I can get."

"Leave it with me, then," he said and there was a slight spark back in him. "I mean, I can't make it any worse for meself, can I? I'll see what I can do. I'll keep the texts coming as well, okay?"

"That'll be good, let me know you're still around."

I got up to go. I hadn't drunk my tea, but then, I didn't think it bore much resemblance to my idea of real tea. This stuff probably came from an actual pot, or something.

"How's she taking it all?" he suddenly asked.

Jenny, he meant.

"Not too good," I said, "but we'll sort it out."

"I hope so, I wouldn't like to be the cause of you two having problems."

I looked down at him, suddenly older and smaller than I was used to seeing him, a fish out of his pool and struggling to breathe.

"You're not the cause, Mick," I said to him, "believe me, you're not the cause."

*

Given I had no other ideas, I went with the thought that Mick's approach would be the best, if not only way forwards, so I picked up Michel later than I'd arranged and we drove down to town. It was after 6:30 pm, so the bloody congestion charge wouldn't apply, but it still meant the car was photographed and filmed. But I parked up where I couldn't see any CCTV cameras and we walked for a while into Kensington. Could've been two mates out for the night, except for the fact that we didn't talk and just about stayed on the same side of the street as each other. I left my gun in the car boot again, but Michel refused, 'just in case', he said and given the fact that I didn't expect much from this, I let it go.

The restaurant was upmarket. It was more than upmarket, it was top quality, but all restaurants have to throw out their rubbish and it's always the lowest paid grunts who get to do that. I didn't think Michel would be useful talking to the staff and I managed to get him to agree to stay outside on the street at the front of the place and a little way up the main road. He wasn't happy, but brightened up at the realisation that if Lysenkov was going to show, it would be through the front door, not the back yard.

The question for me now, was how to get around to the back and talk to the staff. There was a wine bar next door to the restaurant and I started to walk in there and was immediately stopped at the door by a polite bouncer. Firm, but polite. Obviously been to one of the new Doorman Charm Schools, or maybe you just get a better class of bouncer at these places than I was used to. And then for the first time in years, I had a stroke of luck based on my old life. The bouncer was about my age, but shorter and heavier than me and with the regulation skinhead cut and thick neck. But after he'd put his hand forwards and shaken his head and told me I wasn't 'complying to the establishment dress code', he looked closer at me and then said:

"Bloody 'ell! Garron, ain't it? I ain't seen you in bloody years!"

I tried hard, but I had absolutely no idea who the man was. 'Course, I wasn't going to tell him that, but he must have seen the hesitation in my face, because he carried on:

"Jimmy Bellamy," he said, sticking out his hand, "I'm a mate of Tony Hicks. You sparred with him before the British title eliminator. You remember, I used to come with him to the gym when he was working with you."

There was hope in his voice and given I needed his help, I certainly wasn't going to tread on it.

"Jimmy! Of course I remember. Sorry, I just went a bit blank there for a minute."

I still had no idea who this guy was, or whether I'd ever seen him before in my life, but Tony Hicks I remembered as a workman-like light-heavy who I danced around and picked off easily enough in the build up to my last fight. The one where my wrist went for the second time, and the hand broke and the bones split and we knew it could be all finished.

But Jimmy Bellamy I had no recollection of. But what the hell. I'd got sod all out of my boxing career, the least it could give me was

110

entry to a poncey wine bar in west London.

So I shook his hand and made the conversation and listened to him tell me as others had done how I could have been the best, how I should have been a title holder and how he was there the night I took someone or another to the cleaners and eventually he asked me what I was doing now and I thought, in for a penny, go for broke.

"Listen, Jimmy, what I'm doing now is a little bit of background work for a security job I've got coming up. That's what I'm into now and I've got a bloke coming to the restaurant next door who is quite high profile, if you know what I mean. I wanted to have a check on the back exit from there, just in case there's any hassle or he wants to leave and avoid any press, you know and the buggers won't let me back there to have a look. Now you know how it is, Jimmy, how can I look professional if I take him there and I don't even know the back way out. He wants to leave and I lead him into a broom cupboard or something?"

He nodded at me and I took that as a good sign, so I leaned slightly in towards him.

"So I thought maybe I could nip in here and see if anyone would let me have a sight of the back yard and what it's like over the wall their side." I straightened up again. "Didn't know you were here of course, Jimmy and I wouldn't want to land you in any shit or anything, but…"

"It's no problem, mate," he said. I'd become his 'mate' now and I didn't care as long as it was going to get me where I needed to be. "I'll get you out the back of our place, no trouble, just leave it with me."

He called inside to one of the staff who was walking past, a good looking girl with a tray of empties in her hands and told her I was from a security company looking at possible camera placement and that she should show me out to the back yard. Then he clapped me on the shoulder and I said I'd see him on the way out and followed the girl through the noisy bar full of trendy, flashily dressed twenty-somethings whose round of drinks would cost more than a week's rent for one of the tenants I collected from. But I wasn't here for social comment, I was here for comments of a different kind.

We reached the back door of the place and I said thank you to the waitress, who turned on her heels, ignored me completely and went back to the bar. I shrugged, though probably not as elegantly as Michel would have done and pushed through the fire door to the back of the building. There was a small rectangular yard with large wheelie rubbish bins lined up against the wall to one side. It was quiet out there after the noise of the bar and there were a couple more of the staff, obviously on a break, leaning against the back wall and smoking. I made a pretence of looking at the walls and angles for the non-existent cameras and then, when they'd gone back inside, pushed one of the wheelie bins to the opposite wall where the restaurant yard was, climbed up on it and looked over to the other side. The yard was a mirror image of the one I was in and there were two staff on that side, also on a break, sitting on the steps outside the back door of the restaurant and also smoking.

I watched them for a few seconds until they noticed me. Neither looked Russian to me, the girl was a young Asian woman, mid-twenties I would have thought, although I'm lousy at ages and the man maybe about the same age, but white and from the accent, more Mitcham than Moscow. They were both moaning a bit about one of the managers in the restaurant, which was just about what I wanted them to be doing. Contented employees don't rat on their bosses so readily. When they did see me leaning over the wall, the man looked quickly over his shoulder back through the partly opened doorway, while the girl called over to me.

"Oi, what are you doing up there?"

London accent, but not hostile. Made a change from most people who shouted at me.

"Looking to lose a couple of tenners," I said back to her.

She laughed at that and got up to walk over to me. The man stayed where he was though, more suspicious, or less willing to get involved.

"You paying them out, or just dropping them over the fence?"

I thought about pulling myself over to their side, but for the moment, I thought that might be invading their space a little bit too much, so I just leaned further over and started my pitch. I'd had a couple of possibilities worked out in my head, but given the way this girl had got up at the mention of the money, I reckoned she was easily corruptible and certainly open to a bit of bribery. The man I

112

was less sure of, so I kept the conversation going with the girl.

"Well, I'll tell you what I'm interested in, but after you tell me your name. Unless you'd prefer not to."

"I don't mind," she shot back, "I'm Priya, that's Daniel," there was a gesture to the man behind her, "but he's always worried about upsetting people, so he'll probably just stay sitting there."

"I won't," Daniel said, with a touch of annoyance and he got up to walk over to us.

"So do you always hang over walls to talk to people?" Priya carried on and I realised that she was flirting with me, which didn't happen very often and which I wasn't really prepared for. Maybe she had a thing for guys with scar tissue, who hung around in back yards. Or maybe she felt she needed to earn her money.

"No, Priya, I only hang over walls when I'm not allowed inside the building whose walls I'm hanging over."

"What do you mean?" Daniel asked. His voice was a little whiny and a bit nasal as well. Not a great combination.

"I mean they won't let me in."

"Why not?" Priya this time. "Did you bounce a cheque or something?"

I smiled down at them.

"No, nothing like that. They won't let me in, because I work for a lawyer."

"Plenty of lawyers in here," Daniel said, "whole place is full of lawyers."

"You don't look like a lawyer," Priya added.

It was taking time, but I was at least drawing them into a conversation. Take too long though and someone might come out and drag them back in off their break. I also had a quick look behind me in case anyone from the wine bar had come out and was about to interrupt and ask what I was doing on top of their wheelie bin.

"I didn't say I *was* a lawyer, I said I worked for one. I'm supposed to serve papers on the owner of this restaurant."

"Blimey! The old Russian guy?" Priya's face was a picture. "You'll never get near him."

I didn't comment on the 'old' bit. Lysenkov wasn't ancient. Not unless I was middle aged.

"Yeah," I said in reply to Priya, "that's what I'm beginning to find out. I don't even know where he is."

"No, I didn't mean that," she said, "I meant you'd never get close enough to hand him anything. He's got minders and everything. Can't you post the stuff to him?"

Daniel cut in. "Don't be silly, he's got to hand them to him. In person, you know?"

"All right," she snapped back, "I didn't know that."

There was a slight pause, and Daniel said:

"Come on, break's over. We've got to go back in."

Priya didn't so much as look at him.

"In a minute, haven't got the money this guy's throwing away yet. You go on inside if you want to."

Daniel muttered something, but he stayed.

"He's right, though," I said to the girl, "I need to hand the papers to the man. What I'm after, is knowing when he'll be here next. Score in it for you, if you can tell me."

I'd never have got away with this with anyone who had any kind of security feel whatsoever, but these guys just didn't think like that. I guess maybe a lot of people don't.

She started to speak, but I carried straight on.

"'Course, if you just make it up, I'll be turning up here again for nothing and then I'll just have to hang around until you leave and take the twenty back off you again."

That shut her up for a moment and then she admitted:

"I don't know when he's going to be in. It's just every now and again. The manager always knows and then they keep a table for him, but it could be anytime."

Not what I wanted to hear, but at least it was the truth.

"Could you find out? For a larger payout, of course?"

But the answer was no, she couldn't and by now Daniel was tugging at her sleeve and I was giving up.

"I can tell you who would know where he is though," she said, almost as an afterthought. "That big guy who's always with him. He must know where he is and where he's going to be."

"Who's he?" I asked her. "What does he look like?"

"Big blond guy," she said.

114

"Looks a bit like the big, bad guy in the first Die Hard film," Daniel chipped in, "not the Alan Rickman one, the other guy." Then he added: "But with shorter hair."

Thinking about the photo I'd seen, I realised he was right and that was why he'd looked familiar.

Kirilenko.

"And he always has a glove on one hand," Priya said. "Weird."

Definitely Kirilenko.

But it didn't help.

"Well, that's all very interesting," I said, "but not very useful unless I can find this big guy."

"Oh, that's easy enough," Priya said. "He'll be at the nightclub his boss owns. He told me he almost always goes there after he's finished with the old Russian guy. He's asked me loads of times to go there with him after work, but I haven't gone. He's a bit scary really, like if you went with him, he might never let you go again. And that glove thing. Suppose he *never* takes it off?"

After a second I said:

"He's at this nightclub regularly?"

"Oh yeah. He said he always goes there. I think that's where he picks up his girls."

"If he has girls," Daniel said, a little unnecessarily.

"Wouldn't say that to his face would you?" she flashed back.

He shrugged and after a moment's silence, he said: "Come on now, Priya, we've got to go back in," at the same time that she said: "Is that enough dope for the money, then?"

I took out another twenty and held the forty pounds out over the wall. I didn't think I owed Daniel anything, but it would be worth it to keep him part of our little group. As she reached up for the money, I pulled back slightly.

"Just one thing, guys, not a word to anyone that I was asking, all right?"

"What?" Priya said "and get beaten up by that big guy? Not a chance, mister."

I handed twenty to Priya and held out the other twenty to Daniel. He was almost reluctant, but not quite. As they pocketed the money and headed back into the restaurant, I dropped back into the wine bar's yard, pushed the wheelie bin back into place and got a very strange stare from a young guy with a Kurt Cobain T-shirt who was now standing with his obligatory cigarette in the doorway to the wine bar. Obviously not waiting staff, 'cos he wasn't dressed right and he had an attitude as well.

"What were you doing over there?" he asked with an Aussie drawl.

"Looking into the restaurant's back yard," I answered, truthfully.

"Oh," he said. And then recovering with as much sarcasm as he could muster: "Was it nice?"

I looked at his T-shirt.

"Nirvana," I said and pushed past him.

I made my way through the bar to the front door and my newfound friend, Jimmy Bellamy. He wanted to chat. I wanted to get going before Michel found something to shoot.

"Er, Garron, this security stuff you do, there isn't any extra work you need someone for, is there?"

I cursed myself, because I should have seen this one coming.

"Well, it's not my company, Jimmy, you know and also, it's not regular work, so if you've got a steady gig here…"

"Yeah, but I've got to move on a bit, haven't I? If the opportunity comes up?"

I looked at him. Jimmy Bellamy. A man who I couldn't remember, who'd been a hanger-on to a fighter who hadn't made it. I corrected myself there. To a fighter who'd made it even less than I had.

- *Wasn't your fault. You were good.*

- Shut up.

"All right, Jimmy. Let me have your number and if anything comes up, I'll get the boss to bell you. But no promises. There might not be anything for weeks, not even for me."

"Ah, thanks, mate. You got a mobile to key it in?"

"No," I lied, "you'll have to scribble it down."

Which he did. We shook hands and I turned up the street to where I hoped Michel still was. Forty yards up the road, I glanced back. Jimmy was back in his doorway and out of sight. I tore up the mobile number and chucked it in a bin nearby.

Michel was loitering in the entrance to an office.

"Anything?" he asked with that Belgian lilt, which I'm sure could sound cool, but from him sounded like a sneer.

"A start," I said. "Hope you've got your dancing shoes on. We're going clubbing."

*

But although I was dressed reasonably in case I'd got into the restaurant, with a shirt that actually had a collar attached and a pair of trousers, Michel was still in jeans and his shiny new leather jacket and since it was still too early for Kirilenko to be at the nightclub, I dropped Michel back near where he was staying and went back to the flat. It did occur to me that even dressed reasonably I still managed to be scruffier than Michel was in jeans. I wasn't sure if that was a comment on Europeans as opposed to Englishmen, or just a comment on me, but it wasn't the sort of thing I was going to lose sleep over.

Jenny wasn't at home when I got there, but there was a note. She could have phoned, or sent a text if she hadn't wanted to talk to me, but instead she'd left a note. It said: 'Don't know where you are. Am going out. Don't know when/if you'll be back. Will probably stay with a friend tonight. Need to sort my head out. So do you. Don't call. Jenny.'

I called. Straight away. It went to voicemail on her mobile and I left a message. That I was home. That I had to go out. That I'd be back much later. That I loved her.

I hoped she'd listen to it, but there were no guarantees. If she did, what did I really expect her to do? Come running home to wait here for me? I wasn't worried about her staying with 'a friend'. It would be one of the waitresses from her work, possibly even one of the girls I'd met that she knew from the college. But I'd had to call. I couldn't *not* call. I had to tell her that she was the most important thing to me, but even with that, that there were still things that had to be done. Not that I'd said exactly that, but she would know. I guess we were both also realising that sometimes when people begin to change, in her case maybe begin to grow, things can get lost along the way. And sometimes, those things are other people.

Then I suddenly wondered how much of what was happening

between us was actually down to me and what I did, what maybe I was and how much was due to Jenny changing and needing more than me. More than I was, whatever I did.

Or maybe that was just a way to make me feel like this wasn't all my fault.

I found myself shaking my head slowly.

- *You'll drive yourself nuts like this.*

- That's great, coming from a part of me that's talking to myself.

I killed some time by having something light to eat – out of a packet it has to be said and by feeding the cat who wasn't there to appreciate the gesture. I used to be good at waiting, I'd got used to it before the fights and even before jobs for Mick, or way back when I worked some of the time with Al. The easier jobs he used to say. By which he meant the ones where he wouldn't be worrying too much about me. Sometimes I thought he only had me there as a test, to see how I acted, or reacted, but in the end I never found out, I just learned how to do the job. I'd learned even more since then.

- *And where has it got you?*

I looked around the flat. It wasn't much.

That's a lousy thought, Garron, leave it alone. At least until you've seen this through. You're alive, you don't owe anyone money, no-one is actively gunning for you at the moment and you're not cornered as yet, by police, thugs, or anyone else. Be satisfied with that for the moment.

- *And Jenny?*

- Leave it for now. Concentrate on the job in hand.

I stuck the telly on for a bit, switched off after the ten 'o' clock news headlines and put a couple of CDs on. At about a quarter to eleven I checked over the gun and speed-loader, called Jenny and got the voicemail again and got myself ready to leave. As I switched the CD player off, Beth Rowley was singing to me, telling me that if I should die and my soul was to become lost, then it wouldn't be anyone's fault but mine.

I guess she was right about that.

*

I picked up Michel and we headed out to East London again, but this time Wanstead way, rather than the East End. He'd changed into better clothes and still looked like a slim-line male model type. Bloody Europeans for you. I'd expected Lysenkov's club to be in the West End, but this location was pretty good, with what I guessed would be a wide catchment area. It wouldn't be just for Russians though and I didn't think we'd stick out in the crowd.

The first argument was about weapons. I told him there was no way he would get into a nightclub with a gun or a knife, unless the doormen were really poor and I guessed they wouldn't be, given who owned the place. Eventually he agreed that he'd leave the weaponry in the car again, although I could tell that he was hoping for Lysenkov to actually be there, or at least to be able to have a go at Kirilenko.

That was the second argument.

"The idea, Michel, is that we check out that Kirilenko is there and then just follow him back to wherever he goes. If he has a home near here, then we have a starting point for him for when he goes to link up with Lysenkov tomorrow, or even the next day."

"That is an idea with many problems. Maybe he does not go home tonight, maybe he goes back with some girl, or somewhere else."

"Yes, but maybe he doesn't and we don't have too many options at the moment. We can't get close to Lysenkov, so we're tracking the person who sooner or later will take us too him."

"And can you track him? In this car? Do you know how to do that without being seen?"

His confidence in me was obviously growing by the minute.

"Well," I said patiently, "I've done it before and it's worked, so no guarantees, but we'll give it a go, eh?"

He was silent for a while. Probably working out how best to kill me when he'd done with Lysenkov, Kirilenko and half of the rest of the London based Russian Mafia.

"Another thing, Michel, very important. We don't confront Kirilenko. We need him to connect to Lysenkov, we don't want him alerted to the fact we're interested in him."

More silence and I thought again of the Russian that he'd killed and said it again.

"Do you understand, Michel? We keep away from Kirilenko."

"I understand."

But he didn't like it and he hated the fact that I was right. And I found myself wondering if I should ditch him and do this part on my own. It might be easier to manage, but then I doubted that Michel would stand for it and the last thing I wanted was him turning up there on his own because I'd pitched him out of the car.

He was still quiet, so I used the time to go over in my head what could go wrong. I thought the chances that anyone from the drinking cellar would be at the nightclub were remote. It was too different a place and this wasn't a Russian hangout. If the club was empty it would be more of a problem because we would stand out, but as long as there were a few people around, we'd be okay. Too many and we might not get in. Or worse, Michel would get in and I wouldn't.

All we needed to do was establish he was there and then track him when he left. Or, if he wasn't there, establish ourselves in the place over a few nights and sooner or later he would come in.

Thin, I thought to myself, but all I've got right now.

I drove once past the club and there was a small group of people going in, which was a good sign. The two doormen were large, but luckily not anyone I recognised, although I hadn't recognised Jimmy Bellamy either but he'd still known me. We parked up on a parallel street, a couple of hundred yards away from the club and I took off my jacket and put it in the boot along with the gun in its carrier bag which for form's sake I tucked in the well where the spare tyre would have been. At least if someone sprung the boot, they'd nick the jacket and hopefully miss the gun. Michel got out after me and reluctantly handed over his gun, a knife, a strange piece of twisted metal and what looked like an extendable spring loaded baton.

"Anything else?" I asked him.

A box of extra bullets dropped into the boot as well. As a punishment, I didn't tell him that they'd probably take his pens away from him if they wanted too. A minor point, but I was sure it would annoy him.

We walked towards the club and joined the short queue to get in.

"If they search you on the way in, don't get angry. Just take it."

He nodded. Professionalism taking over. I hoped.

I looked over the outside of the building. It was large enough, could have been a department store or something like that before becoming a club, although at four storeys high, I wondered what they used the top floors for. Maybe Lysenkov and his partners only owned the club part, or rented it, but if he owned the whole building, it would be good cover and legitimate business to rent out the rest of the space.

We were searched reasonably well on the way in, although I guessed that if I'd wanted to, I could have got something in with a little thought, although nothing bulky. I'm not a nightclub person, but I've been in a couple and some where they only let you in after you've handed over everything except your money and credit card. We paid our cover charge, cash of course and went inside. As we went down the stairs and through double doors to a cellar dance floor, the music hit me as a wall of sound. I was going to make the comment to Michel that we'd moved up a class in cellar, but that would have been too friendly a gesture and besides which, there was no way he would have heard me. The place was obviously popular, on a weekday night it was nearly full, although not completely rammed and it was the usual East London mix of young people, although what the hell the music was, I couldn't make out. Garage? House? Techno? At which point it struck me again, that although I wasn't past it yet, I certainly no longer qualified as young.

Looking up, there was a higher floor, which must have been at ground level and a middle section of the ceiling of the cellar had been removed so that there were punters looking down on us over railings from that floor. There was even another part above that where the ceiling again had been taken away. That would make it the first floor and I'd reckoned four storeys, so three above that, for offices, meeting rooms, whatever. It even occurred to me that Kirilenko might live here, or at least have a place to sleep here, in which case we could be stuck all night waiting for him to leave.

I gestured 'drink' to Michel, who had also been checking the place out and we moved to the bar. Non-alcoholic for both of us and I paid. I was technically the host, after all.

Above the noise - I couldn't call it music - I told Michel we should start to circulate and try to spot Kirilenko. He suggested we split up and meet back here in 15 minutes, but I wasn't happy about that after what had happened the last time I let him go off on his own, so we agreed to stay within sight of each other, but move separately.

It wasn't easy to see who might be around, given the number of bodies moving. It looked like random movement to me, but I reckoned that someone with no sense of co-ordination and a lot of energy might have called it dancing.

All the way around the basement level and nothing, just a lot of effort and sweat from the dancers and a lot of volume from the PA system. Put that together with the lights flashing and the bass thumping through your head and it was a nightmare trying to locate anyone. There had to be a DJ somewhere, but I couldn't even see him. Maybe he was higher up, where he had a view of the dance floors. Maybe Kirilenko was too.

We completed a circuit of the floor and I gestured upwards to Michel. The Russian might not be here at all, but we had at least two more levels to check out. There were spiral stairways going up and through our ceiling, which was the floor of the next level and I went first, Michel hanging back and as I looked down, talking to a couple of girls. Either good cover, or stupidly asking them questions. I hung around half way up the staircase for a few moments, but I was presenting an image, standing out from the crowd, so I had to hope for the best and leave him down there.

Emerging onto the higher level, the noise volume didn't change, but the décor did. On this floor, there were sofas and barstools and you could lean over the railings and spill your cocktail on the masses gyrating below. Probably the only thing stopping you was the price you'd had to pay for them. Given the reason for this floor was the view of the one below, there was less of it, the middle piece missing, but it was still a substantial area and I moved away from the spiral stairs towards one of the bars, not to drink, I still had my mineral water from the basement, but to park myself somewhere and wait for Michel to arrive. It took him a while, which didn't make me very happy. I hoped he'd just been practising his continental chat up lines, not asking questions about Kirilenko.

As he looked around, he spotted me and moved off in the opposite direction. I was torn between thinking it was the right thing to do and being pissed with him for making me follow him, just because I didn't trust what he might do. I shifted away from the bar and someone, a dark haired girl, said something to me as I walked past her, but I gestured that I couldn't hear her and moved on. Maybe she'd recognised me because her boyfriend, or more likely her father, was a boxing fan. Or maybe she wanted me to buy her a drink. My ego wasn't quite big enough to assume the second, but either way, I wasn't interested.

The lights weren't flashing on this level but it was darker overall, which meant equally poor conditions to be looking for someone. As the volume continued and seemed to me to increase, I began to hope like hell that the Russian was here. I wasn't sure how long I could simply hang around inside this place. The gigs I'd been to over the years must've been as loud as this music, but somehow this seemed more invasive. Maybe it was just the type of music, stuff I didn't like or want to hear, but it was driving me mad.

I'd lost sight of Michel for a few seconds and I scanned across the place looking for him. When I spotted him next, he was again chatting up, or at least talking to, a girl by one of the pillars that supported the next level. He was stationary and so I moved towards the side wall and leaned back against it and took stock of the place again. I really was out of it here. Too old, too badly dressed, too grumpy. The few nightclubs I had been to in the past, sometimes only because I'd been working at them, hadn't grated on me as much as this one did. Had to be the music. Or the dancing. Or the price of the bloody mineral water!

There was a doorway in the wall ten feet along from me that said 'Gents' on it, so fixing where Michel was in my mind, I pushed through and as the door closed behind me, the noise dulled slightly. There was a short corridor, but I didn't go down it, just took ten seconds to clear my head. Of course the problem with that, was that when I went back in through to the club, the music hit me again like a heavyweight's hook.

Michel was still there, but as I watched him, he turned away from the girl and moved on. He had his back to me and I saw him stop short. No movement. No movement at all and I wondered if someone had pulled a gun on him, before I remembered that this was a legitimate club, not a gangster hideout. And then I started moving as my brain, dulled by the insistent thumping of the bass beat, kicked into gear, because of course it could quite easily be a gangsters' hideout and the only ones with guns then, would be the gangsters.

There was a small knot of people not moving now and I walked faster to cover the twenty yards or so, pushing through the crowd and angling automatically to come in from the right because I was right handed and as I was approaching from behind Michel I would be facing whatever had made him stop still.

Ten yards and comments and shoves from those I was pushing past, but something was wrong and the whole thing would go to pot if Michel blew it now, but as I got to five yards I could see it wasn't Michel causing the problem but the huge, short haired, blond man who was now just standing up from his seat where he'd been drinking with two blonde women.

Kirilenko.

I hadn't seen him as I'd approached, because he'd been sitting, but as he stood, I could see he was about six four at least, with a breadth to his shoulders that was scary and that hard look about him, the same look that Al had, which said he was quick and lethal.

I saw the two other dark men start to close in either side of Michel and I realised that the bodyguard had minders, he had his own damn minders and then I caught the slight glint of an inch of steel, half hidden in Kirilenko's huge gloved left hand, the damaged hand that was still flexible enough to hold a blade and certainly big enough to almost conceal it and so I carried straight through with my momentum, coming in on the blind side of one of the dark haired men and over the top of Kirilenko's left hand, my right fist slamming through onto the side of his jaw, going for the front near his chin, which from the side like this, should've given the maximum disorientation as the jaw shifted and the brain stayed stationary for a split second longer, but missing it slightly and landing higher on his jaw, side of his face really, but with enough power that he fell sideways, his left hand still clutching the blade, but no threat now, no threat as he crashed into the people to the side of him and fell through them onto a small table sending it over to the floor.

But he didn't go out. It took him down, but not out. And even as a part of me registered that, the fact that an ex-pro had hit him a good shot and that he was still there, I was instinctively stepping forwards to kick into his head when the peripheral vision noted the two minders moving and the one nearest me with his hand already inside his jacket and close to me, too close to me and the brain automatically measured the distances, calculated that it was no go, changed my movement to go for the nearest minder and I body checked him backwards into the crowd.

Michel was moving now, forwards to the fallen Kirilenko, but the second man had his gun almost clear and I grabbed Michel by the shoulder and the front of his belt and hauled him sideways away into the people around us where the minder couldn't get a clear shot.

There was chaos surrounding us, but no shots had been fired and it would calm soon enough if no-one else got involved, so as we pushed away from the Russians towards the nearest exit, I shouldered one large guy into the back of another in the hope that they'd start a ruck.

There was no chance for the exit though, as there was another man, hell, a third man, same dress, same stance, probably the same type of gun, covering the door and I shot a backwards glance to the scene behind us and although there was no blond head showing, the two heavies were pushing their way fast through the clubbers towards us.

"Staircase! Up!" I shouted at Michel and we shoved through to this level's spiral steps and although we could make a target for the men behind us, I couldn't believe they would shoot in this place and besides which, we had nowhere else to go.

"I could have taken him then!" Michel was screaming at me, once, twice and then again, until at the foot of the staircase, I turned on him for a half second, grabbed him by the throat and from six inches in front of his face yelled at him:

"The other one was about to shoot you!"

I turned straight away and started up the stairs at a run. This was crazy. Russian Mafia chasing us and I'd just wasted maybe three seconds on Michel's stupidity. Or maybe I was stupid for responding to him. Three seconds that could kill us both. I should have known better and it was no use thinking that the subconscious had measured the distance and the risk, the fact that it was a risk at all should have stopped me.

But it had shut him up and we raced up the spiral steps, braced for the shots that didn't come and I thought about the fact that if this had been Moscow a few years ago when the mafia had been untouchable, they would simply have cut us down there and then, bystanders or not. But again, this was London and the ruthlessness had to be tempered with some recognition of that.

I'd half expected someone at the top of the stairs, but there was no-one, we'd been too quick, or they'd had no radio contact. This level was a narrower, circular floor, with bars running most of the way around the walls and standing room only to the rails that overlooked the two floors below. It was almost a viewing gallery, but we didn't stop for a look at what was happening below. There was a customer lift, but the last thing we wanted was to get trapped in that, so we just went for the nearest doors set into the side wall, crashing through them and onto the exit stairs. Up was a dead end for us, so we turned down, but had only got a dozen or so steps towards the next landing, when we heard Russian voices from below. There was no other way out and I already knew Kirilenko's men were armed, so I turned straight away and went back up, trusting Michel to follow me. I'd only just reached the point we'd come from, when the door from the club burst open and the two heavies that had been with Kirilenko ran full tilt into us.

One of them was slightly ahead and he was really too close to use his gun easily, so I slammed my left hand down on his gun wrist and rammed my forehead into his face. I wasn't aiming, anywhere would do and I heard the gun fall as the man folded in front of me and I lashed a kick out sideways at the second man landing with the edge of my foot, the hard edge of the heel of my shoe catching him somewhere near his knee. His gun went off and for a second the noise deafened me and I had no idea whether I'd been shot or not, but I was still moving and as he'd fallen slightly forwards, his right leg giving way, I grabbed his jacket and pulled him further into me, smashing my left knee into his upper leg, then his groin, then his gut as he fell. His gun had fallen somewhere as well and as my head cleared from the sound of the gunshot, I could hear the noise from down in the stairwell again, so I twisted round and shoved the man head first down the stairs.

The first man was on his hands and knees, blood dripping onto the floor from his face where I'd nutted him, but he was still there, so I stepped in and kicked him as hard as I could through his side ribs, hearing the cracks and as he screamed, pulled him sideways and pitched him down the steps as well.

I was breathing hard and looking up I saw Michel halfway up the next flight of steps with a gun in his hand.

"His," he gestured downwards. "Seven shots left. We could go down now. Through them. Not up."

And thank you for helping there, mate.

I could hear the Russian voices closer now as they came up the stairs. They must've heard the shot and were taking slightly more care, not running full tilt, but either way, their two damaged colleagues on the next landing below us wouldn't delay them more than a second.

"And if there are more than seven of them?" I croaked out at him.

A split second's consideration and he turned on his heel and ran upwards. We could have stood and fought, but I had no gun and they would just have to take their time. If they got someone above us as well, it would be over.

"Why didn't you shoot one of them?" I gasped after him, meaning the two I'd sent down the stairs.

"You were in the way. And you took them out quickly. Waste of the bullets."

That was it then. And stupidly, it made sense. But there was no thanks for saving his life, or for disarming the man so that Michel could get to the gun. But right now I didn't care about thanks, I just wanted to survive.

I knew the door to the next level would be locked. These were private floors, whether offices, or storage, or whatever and there was no way any of the punters would be allowed to wander up here. Even so, I wasn't expecting a full double door built across the bloody staircase landing as we turned on the stairs and the next level came into view. There was no point in talking about it, so I flat kicked straight against the middle of the two doors, just above the Chubb lock, working on the idea that they were there to discourage curious or drunk people, not violent action. The doors moved, but they didn't go and there wasn't enough space to step into the kick properly without stepping down a couple of stairs which didn't help.

The lock would go eventually, but we didn't have time.

"Hold them up," I said to Michel and kicked again.

More movement of the doors, but we could hear the running feet below and Michel went a few steps down to the turn and fired blind into the stairway, knowing he wouldn't hit anyone, but causing them to stop and think about it.

Deafening noise again from the shot and I looked up and there was a camera pointing at whoever would be in front of those double doors, so now they could know exactly where we were and there could be a dozen guys on the other side of the doors, but we couldn't stay here, so I kicked again and twice more and the bloody doors splintered inwards slightly and the next kick broke the lock casing away from the wood and they were open.

Michel seemed fairly calm, especially compared to how worked up he'd been inside the club and I guessed it was because he had a gun in his hand and so had his confidence restored. Another difference. Put a gun in my hand and I start getting nervous.

We were through the double doors at what, if I'd got my bearings right, was the second floor overall from the ground level. Not surprisingly, it had a locked door and I was aware that the higher we got, the fewer options we would have. We were literally running out of places to go.

Just to put some space between us and them, we ran up to the next level, but at the next landing which should have been the third storey, the door into the corridor was also locked. But there was no point in just running up to get trapped at the top. I thought about kicking in this door as well, but it was a single door here and I'd be kicking against the jamb, so I told Michel to shoot the lock out.

"I have only the six bullets now," he said.

"You better make sure you only take one shot to open it then."

Again the split second's thought, as though evaluating what I had said in order to find some reason to refuse and then he aimed casually and I moved back in case the damn thing ricocheted.

The pursuit had slowed following Michel's earlier shot, but they could afford to slow down. As far as they were concerned, they had us cornered.

The wood around the lock exploded and it only took a fairly easy kick to splinter it further, get two hands around the door edge and wrench the bloody thing open. We moved into a corridor the other side. After the space of the club, I'd been expecting a large area, not a passage with rooms to either side of it, but I didn't care. There had to be another way into this corridor from the other end and that is what Kirilenko's Russians would be making for, to cut us off. I was just hoping it was a way out as well.

The rooms were all locked as we moved along the passage, but they had narrow glass panels in the doors and I glanced through a couple. In one of them, there were mattresses all over the floor and I realised you could sleep half a street army here if you needed to. Not a good thought in our position, I didn't want to meet an army and we ran on towards the other end of the corridor.

I was hoping for a fire exit, or at least another staircase at the other side, but we weren't going to get there in time before the guys behind caught up close enough to get a straight line shot at us along the corridor. I hit a couple of the doors as we raced past them, but everything was locked and we were still thirty feet, twenty feet from the door at the far end when Michel swung around, flattened himself against the side wall and fired almost the full length of the passage and I heard the cry as someone was hit.

He swung straight round again and fired past me into the lock of the single door at this end and as I ran on and flat kicked through it with momentum and with the direction of the door this time, my mind registered that he was good enough. Not just the shot itself to take the lead guy out, which in poor light was a marksman's kill, but also the instinct to know when the optimum time was to turn and fire.

And the shot that had whizzed past me to break the lock.

Although that was easier. He might not have been worried about whether it hit me or missed me.

We were out onto the next staircase now, a mirror image of the one we'd left, but they knew where we were, they had the cameras and the manpower and probably radios and somebody wanted to let us know that, because there were shouts from below almost like this was a hunt, like the hounds were on our trail and they were close to us now, very close, so we bolted upwards again and the next floor, the fourth maybe, was also locked.

Time, we had no time and this was the top floor, so I gestured to the roof hatch that was above us on the landing and Michel covered anyone coming up as I went up the steel rungs in the wall and pushed at the trapdoor.

Also bloody locked and I had no purchase and a moment of pure panic as I couldn't see a lock before I realised that it was bolted on this side to stop anyone getting in, not locked to stop someone getting out. They could have someone already on the roof, but I doubted it and again there was no choice, so I pulled the two bolts and slammed the door up on its hinges, reached up and pulled myself through into the night and the rain. Michel was right behind me and I kicked the hatch shut again after him and although there was no way to lock it, no-one was going to put their head through there in a hurry, knowing that we were armed and with one man of theirs already shot.

Of course, they didn't know we only had three bullets left.

A few moments respite and the adrenaline slowed slightly as we tidal breathed and the rain cooled us down before we both realised that we were still trapped, just in a slightly better position than inside the building. I looked around at the roof as Michel said:

"We have to stay close to here. We cannot allow them out of there."

"Yeah," I managed to get out as I took in the surroundings. "We're stuck on a damn roof and we're going to hold them with three bullets."

Michel shrugged and started to take note of where we were as well. The night was dark and it was raining, not tipping it down, but the sort of steady drizzle that London excels at and which makes everything seem even greyer, but the roof had spotlights set in the ground, not many, but maybe three pairs that I could see and that meant that we weren't going to be stumbling around in the dark. For as long as we lived, anyway.

I was beginning to hurt and it took me a moment to realise that it was my right wrist again, probably from the punch at Kirilenko, but it was a dull ache, not a scream and so bearable and besides, there was something else buzzing around in my head and it had to come out, whether this was the right time and place or not. I straightened out from my knackered crouch and asked him.

"What the hell happened down there? What did you do that made them go for you?"

He shook his head.

"You will not believe me, Garron, I know, but I did nothing. I did not see Kirilenko until I was by him and I said nothing. I did nothing. But when he looked up and he saw me, he knew me. I do not know how, but I saw it in him."

I did believe him. Partly because he didn't have to lie to me, he was independent and arrogant enough to say whatever he wanted. He didn't feel that he had to justify anything to me at all.

The second reason was worse. We'd been naïve at the least. Julot had wanted me to get Michel close to Lysenkov. I was an unknown to the Russians. But we'd just paraded Michel in front of their top bodyguard. Lysenkov had made a pitch at Julot. It stood to reason that they would know enough about Julot to know who his right hand man was in the same way that Julot knew about Kirilenko. Hell, Julot had photos of Kirilenko! There was no reason why the Russians wouldn't have shots of Michel. And I'd walked him straight in here. Some bloody bodyguard I was! We'd just blown whatever element of surprise we might have once had. If we did manage to get out of this in one piece, we would probably have even less chance now of getting to Lysenkov. We were guilty not just of being naïve, but of being downright stupid.

Looking around the roof, there was a little cover, a couple of large air-con ducts at either side, several aerials, some Sky dishes and a couple of brick posts which seemed to serve no purpose and were only a couple of feet high. And, of course, the hatch leading downstairs, which was now opening back slightly on its hinges. Michel put a bullet into the opening and there was a shout and it fell closed again.

"There's got to be a way down from here," I said. "Have a look round for a fire ladder or something."

He shook his head.

"You look, I will stay here with our friends."

131

He had a point and it grated that I hadn't automatically caught it.

But there was nothing, no way off the roof. I checked behind us where there was a four storey drop to the side road and then the front and the back, which had the same drop to the street or the car park and I was jogging to the far side looking for anything, any possible exit, when I heard a burst of what could only have been automatic weapon fire from behind me and when I looked around the hatch had been shot off its hinges and Michel was the other side of it, flat down on the roof as a hand holding a sub-machine gun poked out from the hole and sprayed bullets in a semi-circle towards him.

It took me a second to realise that the other side of the semi-circle would be next and that it would be pointing at me and sure enough the gun turned and I hit the floor as bullets flew a few inches above me. Whoever he was, he couldn't see out to aim, but he didn't have to.

I was pushing myself into the ground with the side of my head flat against the wet stone facing the gun. I couldn't turn away, because the movement would momentarily lift my head higher, but it didn't matter which way I was facing, except that psychologically, I was looking at the thing that was going to kill me and I didn't want to see it. If the gun angled lower, if the hand shifted position...

I could feel the grit and the rainwater against the skin on my face and the collected rain on the rooftop soaking through my shirt and I suddenly got that pull in my stomach, that ice cold grip inside you that tells you that you're scared and in danger of losing it. I'd been shot at before and for some stupid reason, maybe because I'd also had a gun, or because I'd been moving and had a chance to survive, I'd not frozen. I'd reacted and fought back. But here I was unarmed. I had no cover. And I'd never been shot at by a weapon like this before. All I could do was lie here and wait for the bullets to hit me. And the knowledge that any one of those small pieces of metal that were flying towards me would just stop me short, that there was no way to counter it, that knowledge hit me and I wondered whether even if I had anywhere to move, I would actually be able to.

We were outside and the noise of the shots was less than in the confined space of the building, but that was cold comfort when I was waiting for the sting of a bullet to hit me. Or maybe it would be immediate pain, or just the sheer force of the projectile ploughing into me.

Then I saw Michel get up, walk towards the hatch and fire one shot down into the hole. I heard no shout, but the firing stopped and there was quiet. The gun had been facing away from him towards me when he moved, but it would still have taken nerve to do that. Or maybe that was the point. In these situations, he had no nerves.

He walked past the hatch to where I was still lying on the floor and looked down on me.

"Now we are even."

Meant he'd saved my life.

I breathed out, unaware that I'd been holding my breath.

"I didn't know we were keeping count," I muttered.

"Come on," he said, "we have only a few seconds to move."

I got up carefully, feeling that my legs were unsteady, but not wanting him to know that.

"Move to where?"

He gestured to the far side where I had been heading. One of the air-con ducts was there and it would at least give us something to put between them and us. We jogged to it, squatted down behind it and it was then that I heard shots from somewhere else on the roof. It took me few moments until I realised what that probably was.

"The other staircase," I said, "on the other side of the building. There must be another trapdoor to the roof from there."

Michel just shrugged and I was torn between admiring him for his calm and thumping him for it.

"It makes sense. Two places to come from. Soon they will organise themselves better and then they will come for us again."

"And what are we going to do?"

Again the lift of the shoulders. "We will die," he stated.

"Well, that's bloody reassuring."

The feeling that I was about to die had in fact faded a little, I guess because no-one was actually shooting at me at that time and although it was an illusion and Michel was probably right about what was going to happen, I wasn't ready to sit here for that yet.

We were about thirty feet from the far side of the roof and because we were squatting low behind the duct, we couldn't see what was beyond the edge.

"Try not to let them shoot me," I said to Michel, "I want to have a look over that side."

"How should I stop them?" he asked.

I would have said he asked with sarcasm, but I'm not sure he extended to that. Maybe contempt was the nearest he got.

"Oh, I don't know, song and dance, read 'em a story, shoot them, one of those ought to do it."

"I have one bullet left."

That stopped me short. I hadn't been counting. Michel, of course, had.

"Well, if you need to use it, then use it."

He shook his head.

"One bullet, my friend. If we do not get away, that is for me."

"What?"

He turned his cold, young eyes on me.

"Do you think I am going to let the Russian Mafia take me alive? Do you know what they would do to me, to find out where Julot is?"

Cold again in my gut, but this time I was in control of it. So far, with the exception of Kirilenko himself and the two heavies I'd tangled with on the stairs, the Russians had been faceless, just 'the Russians'. But to Michel they were more than that and I should start thinking of them in the same way.

"Okay. You sit tight then, but don't shoot yourself just yet."

There had been no more firing since the second trapdoor had been shot away and I sneaked a glance at both of them. There was silence, but I reckoned that was only while they were on radios to each other, co-ordinating their next attack.

I scuttled in a crouch to the far edge and looked over. It was too dark to see clearly and there were no lights on the roof of the next building, but it was possible. At least I *thought* it was possible. I could see Michel, but I reckoned the spotlights' range didn't include me at the edge of the roof, so it was no good beckoning him over and I didn't want to call out loud, so I ran in that half crouch back again.

"All right," I said. "We can maybe get out. There's a gap of about seven, maybe eight feet to the next roof, but I think we can jump that. It's a bit lower as well, so that helps. We haven't got long, though, we have to go now."

He didn't move.

"Come on!" I hissed at him.

"I do not think that I can jump."

"You what?"

"I do not think I can jump," he said again.

His voice was perfectly calm, the tone even. Just discussing whether he could make it to tea, nothing about escaping Russian gunmen.

For a second I couldn't answer him. Then it just kind of came out of me.

"Great. You've got enough guts to put a bullet in your own brain, but not enough to try to get out of here."

His pride must have been hurt by that, but he said nothing and fear is irrational. I knew this because two minutes earlier I'd been lying flat on my face, scared to my bones with the bullets flying above me. Now with something to do, something to act on, I could move. But he couldn't.

"Look," I tried, "at least come and see how far the gap is, see if it's possible."

How close. I should have said 'how close' the gap is, not 'how far'.

There was a burst of fire again, this time co-ordinated from both hatches as I'd feared, but not yet in our direction and it helped Michel decide. We scrambled low along the roof to the far edge, getting deeper into shadow the further away we moved from the central spotlights. At the edge we both looked over. It seemed a hell of a long way down and as the ground was probably a side alley between the buildings, it was unlit, at least at the point where we were. Somehow that made it seem worse.

The gap was, as I'd said, seven or eight feet, it was difficult to be exact in the dark, but it could be jumped, I was sure of that, especially with the extra adrenaline that was flying around at the moment. I glanced at Michel. Mr Cool. Maybe he had no extra adrenaline to help him fly.

In our favour was the fact that the neighbouring building was a little lower than ours. Against us was the rain, which would make the jump more dangerous, plus not being able to see what we would be landing on, or even if there would be any way out from the next roof.

But it was a chance and staying here we had none.

"Right. Let's go," I said.

"I cannot."

"It's this or die here, Michel."

"I cannot."

So I grabbed him by the throat and stuck my face two inches from his. Role reversal.

"You are going to fucking jump this gap, or I am going to break your neck here and now. You're going to have to shoot me with your last damn bullet to stop me and then you'll have nothing to kill yourself with before those Russians cut you up piece by piece."

I didn't stop to think about the stupidity of threatening to kill a man who was about to kill himself. Instead I dragged him up off his heels.

"Now we're going to shift back ten paces and then take a run at it."

He moved with me as I scrabbled backwards a few yards. Then I realised that from further back I couldn't see the edge of the roof we were jumping from. If we jumped too soon, we could fall short. If we overstepped, that would be it. On top of that, if we slipped in the wet, that would be the end. I also realised that I was still shaky from nearly being shot. Not the best time to rely on your legs, but none of this could be helped. We just had to do it.

"You go first," he said.

"We go together. Same time."

I took a deep breath and was about to say go, when the firing started up and something hit one of the low stone posts near us. Michel went flat again and I was a moment behind him and for a second time the bullets sprayed around me as we lay on the rain soaked stone, but this time, maybe because I had a possible way out or maybe because this *was* the second time, I kept control better. I still thought I could die, but I knew that if I didn't, then there was a chance to survive.

"As soon as they stop," I said to Michel.

He didn't answer, but nodded slightly.

They would have to stop firing at the point, at least briefly, when they wanted to come out onto the roof. We'd have maybe two or three seconds then and we would have to use them.

More noise, more gunshots and then it stopped.

"Go!" I stage whispered to Michel in the sudden silence and I pushed myself up into a run. I couldn't babysit him now. Either he was with me or he wasn't.

Four, five paces and the edge was there, push out hard, no real slippage and a feeling of nothingness, nothing there, of panic as the vision caught sight at the edges of how high we were and falling, dropping, arms flailing as the psyche took over and tried to force the body to grab for something, anything, as it fell and impact, hard impact on my feet, knees, legs, as the roof opposite came up to meet me, bend at the knees to absorb some of the force and roll with the momentum, protect your head and roll, once, then again, losing it into a sideways sprawl, feeling the wet stone straight through my clothes and impact again against my side and my shoulder as I pitched up against something, some kind of brick post, chimney, or something.

Half second to take stock, to recognise that I was here and not broken at the foot of a four storey fall, to check the pain in my side from the post, but the head okay, knee hurting, but not badly, legs and ankles okay, then scramble behind the post because these Russians had automatic weapons and if they hadn't actually seen us jump, they'd work it out soon enough.

No sound from Michel and I wondered if he had jumped at all, but then there was movement and he crawled towards me. It was darker here than on the other building, but close up I could see pain on his face and the effort it was taking him to move quietly. I pulled him round behind the post.

"I have landed badly," he whispered. "I have hurt my ankle."

"Broken?" I asked.

"I do not think so, but painful if I move it. I do not know if I can stand on it."

"Okay, stay here." There was no time for sympathy, even if I'd been inclined to any. "I've got to find out if there's a way off this roof."

He nodded and I was about to move, when there was another burst of fire towards us from the top of the other building. Then a voice with that unmistakeable Russian accent.

"You have nowhere to go to. Stand up and walk towards us. We will not shoot."

I didn't even bother to look at Michel. We both knew what would happen if we gave ourselves up. I took a quick look around the post and saw a couple of outlines lying low on the roof opposite, indistinct, but definitely shapes against the light glowing from the spotlights on top of their building. I wondered if the shots could be heard from the streets below, but even if someone had heard them, recognised them for what they were and called the police, it wasn't going to help us overall.

"Why don't you come over and get us?" I called back.

"They won't," I said to Michel. "They know we're armed. Anyone jumping that gap, even if they wanted to, would be a sitting duck."

"A what?" he said.

Bloody foreigners.

"An easy target," I explained.

"Ah, I will remember that one."

I almost hit him then. Two minutes earlier he'd been ready to blow his own brains out and now he was taking lessons from me in English phrases.

There'd been no answer from the Russians.

"What will they do now?" Michel asked and I noted how he was deferring to me at the moment, whether because of the pain in his ankle, or the embarrassment of having been scared to jump, I didn't know. Or maybe he simply saw this as my show now.

"They may try to get into this building from below, maybe even break in, although I would guess they wouldn't want to do that unless they have to. More likely they'll get some torches or even floodlights up from the nightclub and light the place up. Then covering fire when they can see where we are, while they send over some shooters. Then that'll be it." I paused for a moment. "If we're still here by then, which I don't intend to be."

With the rain and the lack of light on this roof, I couldn't see a thing further along the top of this building. I couldn't even see where it ended.

"Stay here and out of sight," I said to Michel and crawled further along the roof until, when I was deeper into the shadows, I turned to the right and moved carefully to the side. I was already soaked to the skin, crawling in the puddles wouldn't make any difference.

Right at the edge, there was six inches of stone 'lip', so as you knew you'd reached the limit, just the right height to trip you up and send you four storeys to the ground floor. There was a quick burst of gunfire from the other rooftop and I kept low. I didn't think they could see me, they just wanted to keep us scared and pinned down. As a tactic, it was at least fifty per cent effective.

I started working my way along the wall away from the nightclub and about twenty yards further down, I found what I'd been hoping for. I crawled back to Michel.

"There's an old fire ladder, or access ladder, or something, over there."

"Does it go all the way down to the ground level?"

He had a point and I had no answer for him.

"Only know that it goes at least part way. I couldn't see all the way down. Question is whether you can make it on that ankle."

"I will have to," he said.

I started to lead him back and the Russians fired again. Every sixty seconds, it seemed to be and for about a three or four second burst, so when it was over, we moved single file in a straight line into the darkness behind us and then across to the side.

At the ladder, Michel was going to go first, but I thought it made more sense for me to. That way, I could support him if he needed it and he could use the last bullet upwards if someone was to follow us. As I swung over the wall, I tensed up automatically for the shots. I thought I might be silhouetted against the sky behind us, but nothing happened. The ladder was old and rusty and wet, but it was holding and that was all that mattered. Michel followed and I heard the intake of breath as he put weight on his damaged ankle.

"You all right?" I hissed up at him.

There followed a line of quiet French, or Flemish, or whatever it was that he spoke, which I assumed was him cursing his leg, the ladder, Russians in general and certainly me as well.

After a few more rungs, he said:

"I am not sure I can continue. It is not like walking."

Which of course it wasn't, but I couldn't help him. If he couldn't get down, he'd just wait for the Russians to come for him.

"Try to take more of the weight on your arms," I told him. "Spend less time on your right foot, like you're limping down."

There was no answer, but he carried on.

We were about half way down, with only a couple of half slips on the wet rungs, when the roof above us exploded into white light. They'd brought up floodlights of some kind. There was more gunfire and I knew we had little time left before they came across, found the ladder and fired down at us. Michel knew this as well and we hurried on. And then there were no more rungs beneath me and I looked down and called to Michel to stop.

I think I'd really been expecting this. These ladders never go to ground level. The bottom section is always removed, otherwise every petty break-in artist and local lad would be up it. The lowest rung was maybe a little over fifteen feet above the pavement. I went hand over hand until I was hanging from the bottom rung. That made the drop about nine or ten feet. So I dropped. Landed well and got up. Couple of pains from my right knee and the side I'd hit making the jump between the buildings, but I was okay.

But Michel wouldn't be able to do it.

"Get down to the bottom rung and hang there."

"What are you going to do?" he called as he worked his way down.

"I'm going to break your fall," I said.

There was no way I could catch a full grown man from a ten foot fall and hold him, but I could get into a catch position and absorb some of the impact for him.

He was hanging now and it occurred to me that I didn't like this guy and if I just let him drop, I could take his gun, shoot him and get away from the Russians safely, but the thought went away. I tried to keep it, but it went away.

"Swing your legs slightly, get your bad foot out of the way and let go."

He wouldn't want to. Anybody dropping wants to drop straight, not swing and maybe land on his back. But he had to trust me. And he wouldn't want to do that either.

He was still there and we heard shouts from the roof above and he swung a little and let go. I half caught him, almost the way you'd carry

140

someone across the threshold and felt the jar into my back and my hip, bent my knees to take the weight and then felt them buckle and went over, but at least in a half controlled way until I hit the ground, half his weight landing across me and taking the breath out of me, but survivable and he was down and there were more shots from above as I pushed him off me and we moved for the car. But I had to slow down and support him, he couldn't run, could only limp fast and I was torn between going for the car where we were headed, or for the front of the club which was nearer and would have people around. But Michel was too conspicuous, being unable to walk properly and a crowd might not stop them attempting the kill or being able to isolate us, so we carried on for the car, aware that they would be on the radios to others on the ground and that they would be moving much faster than we could.

"You should have left the car closer," Michel panted at me and I wondered at the fact that we were working like this together to survive, when I would have been quite happy to knock him cold and he would no doubt be pleased to kill me.

"If you'd told me you didn't know how to jump, I would have done," I snarled back at him.

But now we were in the street where the Mondeo was parked, moving at a sort of limping run, with me supporting Michel, taking his weight.

Fifty yards only to the car on a quiet street at gone midnight, the nightclub obscured by other buildings and people's homes and there were only a few distant calls from clubbers leaving which carried to us and I should have been able to hear anyone running behind us but there was no-one and at twenty-five yards I started to think that we were going to get away with it, when something hit a parked van a few feet away on our right and I glanced back and saw them running. I couldn't believe they'd taken a pot shot at us on a residential street, but they had and there had been little noise, some kind of silencer, so they wanted us bad. And with me right next to Michel, holding him up, we made a big enough target to make it worthwhile trying a long range shot.

The last few feet and they were gaining ground. I was supporting Michel on his right side with my left arm, which made it easier for me to reach for the keys and hit the central locking, but I still had to get him to the passenger door.

"My gun. It is in the trunk," he said, but there was simply not enough time to open the boot and get the damn thing out, they would have been on us, so I left it and got him to the door and then went over the bonnet to the driver's side to cut a second and Michel had been thinking enough to have leaned across and pulled the door release.

We were facing away from the pursuit, standard procedure if you might need to get away quick from a location and a definite advantage. As I scrambled in, I could see the Russians, four or five of them, running like hell along the road and only forty or fifty yards away and I wondered what they'd been promised if they got hold of us, or what they'd been threatened with if we got away. Either could make the difference as to how hungry they were to keep running.

Ignition first time and I botched into first and swung out, clipping the edge of the bumper of the car parked in front of us, but it was his own bloody fault, I'd been here first and he'd pulled up too close and if that was the sum total of the damage tonight, we'd be laughing.

More shots, again silenced, but no damage and then as we pulled away something hit a parked van closer to us, closer because the Mondeo had been shielded to some extent until we'd pulled out. But we were moving now and for a second time I thought we'd made it, when in the mirror I saw a car pull up in the road and the diminishing figures get into it. It was moving before the doors were closed.

"They're not giving up," I told Michel, "they're coming after us."

Michel twisted in his seat to look behind.

"They are going to keep coming. Can you drive away from them?"

Intelligent thought from a Belgian under stress, but I knew what he meant, so I bit back the put down and said:

"I can have a bloody good try."

But he couldn't leave it.

"Trying will not be good enough."

"It's English understatement, Michel, just put the seat belt on and go with it."

I was up to forty-five now and had just managed to clip in my belt and a good job, because now there was no time for anything like that.

I was having to concentrate because the street was a rabbit run and if anything moved or stepped out from behind the cars that were parked on both sides of the road then there would be no way we would miss it and that could be it. We'd crash, roll, or burn and lie there waiting for the Russians to catch up in their own sweet time, walk over and put a bullet in each of our heads.

Lights in the mirror and I tried to think of where we were and where we needed to be. I had to lose them and to do that I needed distance and I couldn't get that on these streets. They were too narrow and I would have to slow too much to take any turn and be able to use it to lose them. Turn at any speed and I'd simply hit something and stop myself.

So I had to get out to a main road, which meant a couple of turns and they gained on us into the turns and lost it a bit out of them and I thought I could get to the roundabout out of Wanstead and on to the bigger road up past the Whipps Cross hospital.

Red pedestrian lights before the roundabout – what the hell was anyone doing walking at this time of night – but it was clear and we went through them fast and I saw the headlights again and another set further back. Had to be a coincidence, they couldn't have had two cars, but there had been four or five men chasing and with a driver they would need maybe two cars to get all the gun hands in.

Then we were onto the roundabout, red lights again and traffic on it, too much bloody traffic and simply no way through to go all around and out to Whipps Cross, so I hit the horn and swung it left through the red light and onto the A12 dual carriageway which suited me, but I made a couple of cars on the roundabout brake as I cut across in front of them and they hooted as well, which pissed me off, couldn't they see I was in a bloody hurry? I've got Russian Mafia on my tail, for Christ's sake.

Into the underpass and Michel sprawled across me a bit from the turn and I realised he hadn't put on the seatbelt, even though I'd said to, so I swore at him and told him to do it now, before he made me lose control.

Car in the right hand lane and I shot past it on the inside, got another hoot for the manoeuvre, but there were lights already in the mirror, what were they driving, some kind of 4x4? A Range Rover, or something else with power, because it was rocketing after us. Two cars ahead covering both lanes in the tunnel and I hit the horn with my left hand and kept it there as I raced up the far side of the underpass behind them, the one on the outside seeing something was up and accelerating away and I followed him, passing the inside car and then swerving left in front of it as the idiot ahead of me slammed his brakes on. Why the hell did he do that?

Speed camera and it flashed as I went through the forty mile an hour limit at about seventy-five and something registered in my brain that Tony wasn't going to like this.

Slight gain as the Range Rover was held up by the cars behind me, then broke free and stormed after us. More powerful and gaining and yes, a second car, saloon of some kind following it up.

Streetlights flashing by and the brain only just registering them as a blur, seeing nothing consciously now but the road ahead and luckily few cars about and those that were there could be passed, but then suddenly rows of brake lights ahead and a roundabout, the one at Redbridge underground and a moment of pure panic, never going to stop in time and a brief stab at the brakes, till I remembered the feed left and then saw it, the feed onto the North Circular, the blessed three and four lane North Circ, which could give me a way out.

Braking hard to take the left curve on the feed road, but that brought the Range Rover dangerously close and something hit the back window and missed me, striking the roof above my head and bouncing, dammit, ricocheting somewhere in the car.

Michel swore and I didn't know if the bullet had hit him, but I couldn't ask and I couldn't go any faster, I was in the left hand curve now and just holding the wheel against the pull of the Mondeo, its weight trying to force me out of the turn and through the thin dividers into the structure of the flyover I was joining. It was trying to throw me, the bloody car was trying to throw me and I could do nothing except fight it, nothing except hold onto the turn, right on the edge it felt, right on the edge of losing it, losing the whole thing and then the turn straightened at last and I could take a hand off the wheel for a second and change down gears and floor the accelerator and we arrowed into the faster traffic of the A406.

Rear lights and brake lights as we moved up in speed and passed other cars, more of them now on this major road, all making their way easily from East to West unaware for a few moments more that there was a struggle to the death going on among them.

Feed to the M11 almost immediately and I thought of the possibility of the open motorway and then realised the speed of the Range Rover and of the other car following us. On an open road they'd catch us too quickly. What I needed was to get off the big roads and lose them somewhere. Exactly the opposite of what I'd thought at the beginning of this. I needed a little bit of a gap and then a way out.

I sat in the Mondeo in the M11 turn off lane, the back window cracked and with a hole in it on the right hand side, but still able to see through it and watched the two cars close in behind me. At the last second I wrenched the wheel over and crossed the divide to where the North Circular continued. It was too much to hope that they wouldn't make the switch, but it might have made one of them lose control slightly and give me some time.

The saloon further behind reacted quicker, the Range Rover swung across and side swiped a large hatchback, the weight of the off-roader shunting it out of the way and sending it across three lanes before the driver got some of the control back. I couldn't see how it ended, but with that, the police were going to be on the case pretty quickly, if they weren't already aware of the chase. Even if they thought it was just joy riders, they'd be after us now.

I'd slowed the Range Rover, but not stopped it and the saloon was now right up besides the bigger vehicle, the two of them taking up two lanes next to each other and growing again in my mirror.

Speed limit down from fifty to forty on the flyover and I was at well over ninety and accelerating, the car roaring, the wipers on double speed and my grip on the wheel immense, the tension in my arms huge, trying to make myself relax, stupid thing to say to yourself, relax, you're in a high speed car chase in the wet with people shooting at you, but hey, just try to relax.

Michel had been silent, gripping the handle on the inside of his door and turning a lot to see how close they were. Lots of cameras and another speed one, Tony was going to love this, the lines on the road just a blur, another shot and this one missed, I think and then another that hit the bodywork at the back, they really didn't care, they just wanted us dead, rolled, crashed, whatever.

"They are shooting at us again," Michel shouted, which I thought was about the dumbest thing he could have said, but I let it go, I couldn't say anything, I was only just controlling the car, felt like one slight error and I'd splatter us all over the place and besides, he was just scared, nothing he could do, totally at the mercy of the fates and whether or not I could hold it together.

A104 exit, but I couldn't take it, I'd have to slow at the top and they'd be too close, already the shots were close and a car like that Range Rover could just shunt into me and it would all be over bar the shouting.

How the hell was I going to get off this road? But I had to get off, they were just driving us down, they were too fast and on top of that, the police would be here soon, had to be here soon. I kept expecting blue lights in the mirror, although they could intercept in front, of course, why did I automatically think they would come from behind and I wondered what the Russians would do then.

Couple of cars getting out of our way and another one in the outside lane staying there and I cut inside him and hit a stretch of water and no control, just a slide forwards and slightly to the left, an aquaplane for two, maybe three, terrifying seconds until the traction caught again and I slewed right where I'd been trying to correct the slide and nearly lost it trying to straighten up.

Closer, they'd gained while I'd had no grip and the shots came and the windscreen in front cracked and the wipers started to catch each time on an edge and I wasn't going to be able to drive through this with no wipers, so I hit the windscreen with my left palm and it cracked some more and Michel got the message and pushed his seat back and got his good leg up and kicked hard at the screen and it went at the second kick.

Wind-rush and noise and glass flying in with the rain, couple of pieces stinging my face, but I could see properly again although I had to squint against the weather and try to breathe against the wind. Bloody huge Costco flying past on the left and I wouldn't take much more of this and neither would the car. We had to get off this road and hide in the back streets, but there was no time, no bloody time, possibility to try for the industrial estates, but I couldn't slow to exit, and if I stayed on, they were going to shoot us into bits piece by piece.

"Can you shoot the driver?"

I had to shout above the noise of the car and the force of the wind, but he heard me.

"I cannot see him properly, I could shoot the windscreen and maybe miss, or only wound the driver."

"That might be enough, it would shock them, slow them down."

I was struggling to speak against the wind buffeting in and I wondered how he could, until I realised that he didn't have to face the front as I did, that he could turn away from the wind and the rain.

Overpass and right hand curve and they were closer still.

"It is a dangerous shot to try," he said, "I have only one bullet." A pause and then: "I should instead shoot the tyre."

"What?"

"The tyre would stop them."

I couldn't believe he'd said that.

"You'd never hit it."

Left hand curve now and I could see no way out. The saloon was hanging behind, backup in the unlikely event that the Range Rover didn't make the kill and now a flash of blue lights, far behind and time running out.

"They could use that car to move Lysenkov, it could have block tyres," I shouted.

"In that instance, it may also have a bullet-proofed windshield."

"Right, but it's a Range Rover, it's built to take a blowout." And then I added: "you know, punctures - flats," in case he hadn't understood.

"Punctures," he said, "but not a bullet."

Point made and no more time, so I told him to do it.

He wound down his passenger side window and unclipped his seat belt.

"I will need space, er...the angle to shoot past the back of our car."

"Okay, doing it now, but you won't have much time."

He wrapped the loose seat belt around his left arm and shoulder and turned himself around to face behind us. I shifted the car right

147

and then counted him down.

"Three, two, one, now!" and as I turned the Mondeo left at an angle of about thirty degrees, hoping it would give him enough space, he leaned out of the window, holding himself close to the car with the belt, using it to steady himself and hunching in against the window frame, aimed the borrowed gun at them.

It was probably the best shot I would ever see. A marksman on a clear day with a laser sight couldn't have fired cleaner. The distance wasn't huge, but the size of the target, the movement, the conditions...Whatever else I thought of Michel, he was, in fact, a dead shot.

There was a noise I hardly heard above everything else and the Range Rover suddenly slewed to the side, turning almost around on itself. Cars like that survive blowouts, but as Michel had said, this wasn't a blowout but bullet damage, maybe even through and out the other side of the tyre and with the speed and the rain, the driver just could not control it. The car span. A beautiful, vicious, circle and a half, slowing, it's true, but with too much momentum to stop before it slammed into the side wall and rolled.

I didn't see how many times it went over, maybe only the once after the wall had broken its spin, but I didn't care. The saloon was fifty yards further back and braking to avoid the Range Rover, the police might stop for the crash and we were at the A10 turn off with the time to ease off and make the roundabout at the top without getting shot.

I slowed to forty, then thirty at the end of the exit, through the first lights twenty yards before the roundabout which were green, and almost stopped at the red lights onto the roundabout itself. But in the mirror I could see the headlights of the saloon coming again, already at the bottom of the hill behind us and further back several police cars in the distance and that made me push through the stop lights, swinging across the traffic coming from the right and impact, bloody impact, as something hit us at the back on my side and shock as it pushed us sideways and I thought we'd lost the wheel maybe, couldn't really see who'd hit us, but it was a glancing strike, not at speed and the car picked up again and I forced it around the turn to the right hand exit up the A10 towards Enfield. There was an immediate left that would have taken us out of sight into some quieter streets, but I'd swung off the roundabout too fast and I couldn't make the turn.

We were soaked now, the rain no stronger, but with the speed of the car, it had been hammering in through the gap where the windscreen had been.

Michel was seated back in the car now, belt clipped back on as we gathered speed again and maybe he wanted some acknowledgement of the shot he'd made, or maybe he was too professional for that, but all I said was:

"We've got to get clear of this car right now, before the police get a helicopter up. Once they do that we're finished. They'll track us until we dump the car, then they'll carry on from there. And you can't even walk, let alone run."

"So we leave the car."

Understatement from him this time. It wouldn't be so easy. I could see the saloon again and the police would still be there further back. Another speed camera flashed and I thought they were going to have a field day putting together all this data on us and then there were more lights at a crossroads, but green and we shot through them, but their saloon was very fast, screaming up behind us. I was at over eighty already, but they were doing way more than that and I floored it, asking more of the Mondeo, when another intersection appeared and this time the lights were against us and I had to slow, I *had* to, as a car passed in front and there seemed to be a gap, couldn't judge it properly, not at the speed we were travelling, but I hit the accelerator again, through the lights and over, horns blowing at us, but through and noise, huge bloody noise as the saloon crossed behind us and something hit it, glance at the mirror, a transit van or something, at speed and the thought that, Christ, they've had it, whoever was in that van has had it, but no going back, the saloon thrown to the side and we were away.

Police lights there again, further behind the crash and we were up the hill and over the top, suddenly out of the line of sight and I slammed the brakes on, slowed before we got to the next speed camera, got it under forty and there was no flash, then even slower to the bottom of the hill and into the first turn, sirens I could hear now, but no lights yet and this was a tight left, Trinity Road, the sign caught my eye as we turned and a religious man would have taken this as a sign, but not me, I just wanted the darkness, the quiet.

Regulation speed down this road, we couldn't hide if someone saw us, the state we were in they'd remember us, but we didn't have to attract attention. Keep it quiet. No roaring engines. A local all-nighter still open at the end of the road and right turn there, looking to ditch the car, driving blind now. We were near Enfield, I knew that, but not where exactly and I didn't care. This was quiet here, driving easy, nothing now in the mirror.

Right again at the end, no choice, dead end to the left and then flats, low council flats and a burnt out car. Sign saying Roman Way and left, pull it into a gap and cut the lights and cut the engine.

Silence.

Blessed, bloody, silence.

Just the rain falling on the car and on us.

I couldn't take my hands off the wheel, they'd been there too long. I just couldn't let go of it, until an effort, a physical bloody effort and I did and the shakes came as I knew they would.

No comment from Michel for a time and I wondered at that, wondered if it was professional courtesy and then as I began to get my hands back under control, he said:

"We have to go, we cannot stay here."

"Yeah," and my voice was strange in the quiet night, a storm still raging in my head, in my ears. Then getting it back together, the brain kicking in again. Things to do. We couldn't just leave.

"Wipe the car down," I told Michel, "tissues, cloth, your shirt, anything, but try to wipe everything we touched."

I pushed the door open as Michel got started and swung my legs out. Stood up and found they were weak and shaky as well and I had huge muscle ache down the front of my right thigh.

We needed to clear the boot and I tried, but it wouldn't open, the side was bent inwards from where it had been hit when we were on the roundabout. So I opened the back door, pulled forwards the back seats and got into the boot that way. My gun and jacket were still in there as well as Michel's weapons and spare bullets. The look on Michel's face as he took his gun back could have sunk a thousand ships. I was just pleased to have my jacket back, not only was I freezing, but I was soaked and the jacket was dry which made me look a little more respectable.

Nearly done, a quick job and it needed to be, some nosy neighbour could be watching. There was nothing we could do if the police really went to town on the car with forensics, but that depended on when they found it and whether the locals had stripped it down, had the plates off it and burnt it up before then.

One more thing and I pulled the cowling off the steering column and messed with the wires under the ignition. There was no immobiliser and no alarm fitted, it was an older car, so it was possible to make it a joyride job. At least at first glance. The window could have been slightly open for us to get into the car, or we could have forced it, but we'd have needed petrol, so I opened the fuel cover flap, which had no lock anyway and then just unlocked the old style petrol cap and took it away with me. I had nothing to make it look like I'd broken it open without a key, so I just had to take it and make it seem that we'd broken it earlier and I raided a nearby recycling bin and took out a newspaper, folded it and rolled it tight and jammed it into the fuel opening as hard as I could. Closed the flap partially over it and that was the best I could do. Again, if one of the local lads got an idea in a couple of days time, he might open the flap and set light to the paper, but that would be a bonus and it wouldn't do for us now.

I thought of breaking the side window to make it look more like a stolen car, but it would be noisy and besides, if the police got to the point where they checked their cameras, they'd see it wasn't broken until after the chase.

A look in the wing mirror at my face and I tried to pick out a couple of bits of glass that had stuck there from the windscreen, but I wasn't bleeding much and I wiped away what little blood there was.

Michel was limping around the car, holding onto it for support and I helped him as we moved away. A quick glance back at the thing that we'd wrecked. No windscreen, buckled at the back on the driver's side, bullet holes in the body and most of the back window gone.

But it had got us here.

Michel started to say something, but I waved him quiet. Voices carry at night and though someone might sleep through a car door closing, they'd wake at the sound of voices under their window.

We moved slowly, like a pair of drunks, looked like it too, probably, with me supporting him and after we'd made some ground and turned some corners, I told him to wipe down the Russian's gun and we'd ditch it. He cleaned it off and I borrowed a black bin bag from a front yard, untied it, stuck the gun down in the middle of the rubbish, retied it and dumped it back where I found it. With a bit of luck it would simply vanish along with yesterday's milk cartons.

Two more streets, everything quiet still and I called Tony at his home number. He wouldn't appreciate being woken up, certainly not for this reason but it couldn't wait. His voice was indistinct when he picked up, but at least it wasn't his wife answering.

"Car's been stolen, understand?" was all I said and I got a garbled yes and cut the connection. I wondered if he'd call me back when he woke up properly and realised what that meant, but he didn't. I thought he'd probably wait until morning before reporting it stolen, it would be more natural, but he might go to the lot now, say he was driving past and saw the car missing.

Another fifteen minutes walking and limping and we reached a main road that led on the right towards the A10 and left into Enfield town centre. I didn't want to see the A10 ever again so we turned left to the town.

"We get a cab?" Michel asked.

I shook my head.

"We'd be remembered this time of night and the state we're in. No, we get the night bus. I'm going to leave you at the first stop we get to and I'll walk on to the next one. That way we're not seen as being together. Don't get on a bus until I call you that I'm at the next stop, okay? Stay separate on the bus, but you get off where I do. You understand?"

He nodded and we limped on to the stop, which thankfully had no other people waiting.

"You'll get on all right with that ankle?"

He looked at me in surprise that I'd asked.

"Of course."

"Okay. Don't get on any bus until I call and don't talk to anyone either. They have cameras on these buses, but it can't be helped. Just keep your head down."

I walked off towards the town centre, trying to blank all thought of what had happened and what could still go wrong until I was home and safe.

Home. Where Jenny was. But, I remembered with a jolt, not where she would be tonight.

And safe. A strange idea at the moment.

Reached the bus stop, called Michel and fifteen minutes later a big, red, N279 pulled up and we rode it, me and the Belgian assassin, ten feet away from each other, all the way to Euston where we both got off. He made no comment about me helping him to his hotel and I left him outside a modest guest house. No goodbyes, ours was a working relationship and it had moved on tonight, for better or for worse, with a realisation from both of us of what the other was capable of. I thought that he might still want to kill me someday and I had no doubt now that he could, but he wouldn't take it so lightly.

I thought about walking to Camden, clearing my head a bit, but I was dog-tired and it was still raining, not that I could get much wetter, so I took another night bus the few stops back.

Surreal.

The chase seemed an age ago, possibly even unreal, yet it had happened. We had killed men tonight, me and Michel, men that had been trying to end our lives, it's true, but –

- Except for whoever was in that transit van.

Yes. Except for whoever was in that transit van. Because in the end, it isn't true that we only kill each other, is it? We kill whoever happens to be there. In the way. Stopping our progress, or our survival, or whatever.

- He might not be dead. People do walk away from crashes.

- And many don't.

So it was different this time. Instead of absorbing what had happened and dealing with it, my mind kept coming back to the van. I knew I'd have to check up on what had happened, it would be reported somewhere, but in the meantime I had to live with it. It was no longer just me and Michel and the Russians. We'd affected someone else. Someone wasn't going to get home tonight. Somewhere, someone could be waiting for somebody who wasn't going to come home.

- You weren't the one. It wasn't you driving.

- It could have been. Just as easily, it could have been.

- But it wasn't.

- Sequence of events. I'm just as responsible.

So I kept working on it, the rest of it, the rest of the night's events, feeding them through my system, working through the fear and the tension, in a way that would allow me to carry on. To move on.

Except for the van. I had to put that away. Lock it away until I found out what had happened to the driver and could face the thought of what I had done.

The flat was dark and it hit me again as I entered that there was no need for me to be quiet. It seemed like days ago that I'd read the message from Jenny, but it had only been earlier this night. She had no idea what had happened. And if she had been here now, would I have told her everything? Or just expected her comfort, just leaned on her and taken her support? Her unconditional support.

It was conditional now.

She wanted more and I had no right to think she should expect less.

I switched on the small side light by the mattress and the cat disappeared through the flap in the window. The emptiness of the bedsit, which is what it was, struck at me for the first time since I'd originally moved in.

Empty because she wasn't there.

I went to the kitchen, reflex action and took the whisky out of the cupboard.

- You going to drink all that?

- Piss off.

- It won't help

- I nearly died tonight. Believe me, it'll help.

I thought about showering, to get rid of the cold as well as the dirt from the roof of that building and the sweat I'd been drowning in during the chase, but in the end I just sat down on the cold mattress, my back to the wall and felt the aches in me from the last few hours take over. Tried to ignore what was going on in my head as well as the physical pains and wondered whether I'd crash out before I finished the bottle, or what I'd do if I finished the bottle before I crashed out.

*

But as ever, if you survive, the next day comes. Meaning different things to different people, but there just the same, demanding to be acknowledged, refusing to be set aside, having to be faced.

I'd eventually dozed in spurts, but another text from Mick, letting me know he was still okay, finally woke me properly when it was daylight and the thoughts came in.

Jenny isn't here.

An innocent man was hurt, maybe killed, last night.

We blew it with the Russians.

Michel is as dangerous as he thinks he is.

I'm going to have to speak to Julot today.

I'm going to have to explain to Tony today.

All of this made me feel even worse and then, when I began to move myself, the aches of the previous night started in.

- *But you survived.*

- I don't feel like I did.

- *Al would be proud of you. You survived.*

And for maybe the first time in my life, the first time since I'd met Al way back when I was a scrawny teenage junior welterweight prospect, it struck me that Al's approval wasn't what was important to me.

I started to think about that and then leant painfully on the empty bottle of whisky that had kept me company all night, which stopped any kind of rational thought for a while. But that was fine. I didn't want to be confusing myself with Al in my head, when I had a whole list of other things to deal with.

I called Jenny. I didn't know whether she should be at college today or not and I should have known, but the call went to voicemail and I hung up. Then I called back, got the voicemail again and asked her to call me. It was all I could do for the moment. I wasn't even sure what I was going to say to her that could make a difference, but I couldn't not call.

I put off phoning Tony and Julot and Michel, who I would also have to speak with and had a shower instead. In the middle of that the mobile went and I jumped out of the shower and grabbed at it, thinking it was her, but it was Tony's number and he was understandably upset. He had a right to be, but he was also interrupting my wash and I was dripping all over the floor, so I told him I'd be around later and he just about settled for that.

I should have called Julot, but I decided on breakfast instead. Not much of a breakfast as there was no milk even though she hadn't been here, but I had to eat something, I was running on empty. But there was no bread either and not much of anything else except the cat's tuna, which I wasn't interested in for breakfast, so I gave up, settled for a cup of tea with no milk and then got dressed to go to the shops and stock up. Well, not stock up, but bread and milk were essentials.

On the way, there was a payphone, so I killed the two birds and called the number I had for Julot. He answered it himself, the deep, rich voice unmistakeable. I didn't want a long conversation, partly because I'd screwed up and he'd know it and partly because it was raining almost as hard as last night and I was getting soaked again. At this rate I'd drown before locating Lysenkov.

Julot knew all the details about the previous night, Michel had obviously briefed him in full.

"I congratulate you, my friend."

That surprised me.

"For what? Showing our hand so brilliantly?"

"For surviving. For disrupting their organisation. For, er…lighting the fire beneath them."

I thought he was taking the idea of looking on the bright side a little too far.

"But they'll close up, go to ground."

"Only to a point. They must still function. They are not fighting an enemy that they know, that they can find. They are limited in what they can do. They will not be able to locate me. He might consider hitting some of my businesses or my contacts, but he would no doubt want to have a smooth transition in taking them over, so that would not be what he would choose to do."

"But we still have to get close to him."

156

"That is true, unless he begins to look for you."

I understood that and I didn't like it. Lysenkov had found Mick easily enough and they must have CCTV footage of me now from the club last night. No name yet, but it wasn't impossible that they could get that. No location either, but maybe eventually friends, associates. Those that were left.

"Can you find anything out?" I asked Julot. "Anything at all about where he is, how to get to him?"

"If I could, I would already have told you and Michel, But I will listen again."

There was nothing else to say, although a lot for me to think about, but as we closed the conversation, Julot said:

"You were very good last night, I understand, very professional I was told. From my source, that is high comment."

"Yeah, well, I kept him alive, which is what I'm supposed to do." And then for some reason I added: "I guess he impressed me as well."

"I am glad that the two of you are beginning to respect each other as you work."

"Respect is a big word, I said he impressed me, but not with everything. He's very good at what he knows, he just doesn't know everything yet."

The response was quick

"He is the best weapons man I have personally seen. And still he will learn more."

If I hadn't known better I would have said there was almost a touch of pride in Julot's voice and I noted it, because for the first time it was a little out of character for the man. Perhaps he caught that in his tone as well, because he added:

"But of course there is always someone better, somewhere."

Yes, I thought as the line went dead, there's always someone, somewhere.

*

I'd gone off the idea of breakfast, so I went back to the flat to pick up my car keys and head off to where I'd left the Saxo at Tony's. He'd

157

have to be faced at some point and it might as well be sooner.

I had to take public transport round to his car lot, as I'd left the old Saxo there when I'd picked up the Mondeo. That gave me enough time to think about what Julot had said and I didn't like it any more for thinking about it. What it came down to, was that the best way for Lysenkov to get to Julot now, was to come for me. Which was why he was quite happy about it. He thought that we wouldn't have to look for Lysenkov anymore, because the Russian would come to us. Or more specifically, me. If they could get someone who would recognise me. Only of course, he wouldn't be able to find me, so if he found anyone and I wasn't underestimating his capacity to have contacts who would chase that down, it would be someone I knew. Tony, or Sean, Mick was already on his hit list, or even just the barman at Mick's pub. Maybe through one of them, even Jenny. Someone would get hurt. And Julot didn't care, because it would bring Lysenkov one step closer to me and Michel would be there with me waiting.

Except I couldn't let that happen.

I didn't know how, but I couldn't have anybody else getting hurt for me. So far, Mick had just about got away with it, but couldn't surface, that van driver who I didn't even know had been hurt or worse and now through my stupidity, someone else might be targeted. For a second I wondered if Julot had realised that, had thought it through. It had been my idea to go to the club and track Kirilenko, but Michel would certainly have relayed what we were going to do to his boss. And Julot would have worked it out, the possibilities, the likelihoods, the angles and this could have been one of them. It was only me who couldn't think ahead.

- *Al would have thought of it.*

- Piss off.

I didn't have to think any more on that because the mobile rang. This time it would be Jenny. But it wasn't, it was Mick. Poor substitute, but a friendly voice at least. He'd seen on the news about the chase and the shooting on the North Circular and that there were Russians involved. Organised crime warfare, the police were saying, but he was thinking the worst, that it could have been me. I told him that it was me, it was crime, but not organised and it could definitely have been worse. But he was genuinely worried and still thought that I should leave it and disappear. When I told him about Lysenkov having my picture now and knowing my link to Julot, he went quiet. Given that I had nothing to add, there were a couple of expensive silent mobile minutes chalked up before he said:

"All right. We don't know where to find him, but he has to go somewhere to meet people, to work, to run his bloody empire. The fact that it's not known, doesn't mean to say that it isn't there."

His voice sounded stronger than the hesitant Mick I'd met in the café, more like his old self.

"Unless he sits tight for a bit, until his lads catch up with me."

He didn't like that thought.

"So you can't stay doing nothing," he said, "waiting for that to happen. Someone must know something about where he is."

"Yeah, someone, somewhere, but that doesn't help us."

"It may do, if I put the feelers out even harder. Call in all the favours."

"It'd put you back in the frame, though, wouldn't it. Right now, you're vanished. This would bring you out again."

"I know, but if you don't find him for this Michel bloke, then I'm going to be vanished for a long time and in the end that's going to be difficult to keep going."

I tried again.

"Whoever you use, Mick, could sell you on to the Russians. If not where you are, at least what you're doing."

"I'll have to be careful then."

There was another thing and I told him.

"If you do find something out and I get to him and Michel takes him out, people are going to know you were looking for him. They'll think you were involved."

"Look, mate, what are you trying to do, put me off completely? I'm trying to pull myself back here and you're trying to stop me."

It was true and I wasn't sure why. God knew I needed Mick's help if he could do something.

"I'm just letting you know what could happen, that's all," I said.

"I've been in this shit for more years than you can add up, son, I'm well aware of what can happen. If I do nothing, then either they'll

159

catch up with you, or I'll stay in this half life for a hell of a lot longer."

I gave up.

"Okay, Mick but if you're going to do this, let's make it quick. They won't be wasting time at their end."

He said he'd call later, but just before he rang off I asked him:

"Mick, on the news, did it say anything about a white van? Driver of a white van caught up in it on the A10?"

"Yes," he said. "He died."

*

I got to the car lot trying not to think about anything at all and braced myself for Tony's onslaught. It wasn't as bad as I'd thought it would be, although that might have been because I just stood there and took it and didn't argue. And then, in between telling me what a useless pratt I was for losing his car, he seemed to notice the bruising and splits on my knuckles and the few slight cuts on my face where the glass from the windscreen had gone in.

"Wait a minute," he said, "you didn't lose the car did you? You wrecked it."

We were walking back to his small office from the edge of the lot, where he'd pointed out the spot he'd carefully dropped a splash of petrol to show where the 'thieves' had spilt some when they'd filled the car up to nick it. I thought that was a little over the top. This was a stolen car, not a murder and the police probably wouldn't come anywhere near the car lot, which was why I'd been happy enough to come back here to pick up the Saxo. I thought they'd just take the vehicle details and give Tony a crime number for the insurance, but then it struck me that when they pieced together the fact that this car was the same one that had stormed around north east London last night, they probably would take a look. Tony didn't know that yet and I wasn't sure whether to tell him. If he didn't know, then when the police turned up his reaction would be genuine. But I couldn't do that to him and besides, he'd go completely berserk with me afterwards, so I tried to explain. I hadn't got very far before he got very angry.

"So there are going to be police all over this place looking for anything to connect to a high speed chase around half of London!"

It wasn't a question, so I didn't answer.

"Well, say something, you stupid sod! How the hell did that happen? Especially in my car! Who were you after?"

I thought it was a bit much that he'd assumed it was my fault, that I'd been the one doing the chasing.

"I wasn't after anyone, Tony, I was trying to get me and my client away from some people who were trying kill us. In the process, the car was photographed, went through speed cameras and got damaged. So I thought it was better to dump it as stolen than to bring it back."

The look on Tony's face was a mixture of anger and shock. I'd like to have thought there was a little bit of concern in there for me as well, but I couldn't be sure of that.

"Jesus," he said, "that wasn't you then on the news this morning?"

"Don't know, haven't heard it."

"Bloody chaos on the roads, because there's lanes closed on the North Circ and the A10."

I shrugged. Part of Michel's Gallic temperament rubbing off on me.

"And people dead. People dead and you stand there like nothing happened."

"I'm not standing here like nothing happened, Tony, I'm tired, I'm hurting and I didn't ask for last night to happen."

For a second or two I stopped, thinking about whether or not that was really true. In a way, I'd made it happen. I'd provoked the reaction by going there. But they'd forced me to that by targeting Mick. Tony was talking again, the voice of sense in an insane world.

" – got yourself into, man? How did you get to this?"

We were at the office now and I sat down on one of the two chairs in the cramped space.

"I tried to get these guys off Mick's back. He's done a runner until I can do that."

"You told me you had a job, that was why you needed the car."

"I did. It's just the two jobs got linked together."

It sounded weak, even to me. There was a long silence as, still standing, he stared down at me. Then he said:

"If you can't tell me the truth, if you have to lie to me, then what have you got left?"

"I didn't lie to you, Tony, I just didn't tell you everything."

"That's lying, mate, no two ways about it."

Another silence. He was right, of course and I nearly said something about protecting him by not telling him what was going on, but that would've been a lie as well. I hadn't told him because I thought he might not have rented me the car.

"Look," I said, "I know you're upset about the car, but - "

"Sod the bloody car! I'm not even thinking about the bloody car! I'll get insurance and you've paid me as well and it's a hunk of metal! But you, hell, you my oldest mate, don't trust me enough to tell me the truth! I don't know whether to be angry with you, or feel sorry for you."

I shouldn't have followed him into the office. There was nowhere to go, no room to move and I had to just sit there with him standing over me.

"I'm sorry," I said.

"What?"

"I said, I'm sorry."

He sat down at the other side of the small table.

"Okay," he said, "that's a start."

"Don't get your hopes up, I'm not going to make a habit of apologising for everything."

"With a bit of effort you wouldn't have to."

I sighed out loud.

"What do you mean by that?" I asked him.

"I mean you need to change some things around."

All I needed. Friendly good samaritan advice.

"Ah, piss off, Tony, I've had a hard couple of days and nights. I've said I'm sorry. I was wrong. I should've told you more of what was happening. Now let's leave it, okay?"

Heavy silence and after a few moments he said:

"Jenny came round to see us last night."

So this is what he'd been leading up to. Well he'd have to work for it. I was annoyed now and I didn't say anything.

"She wanted to talk about you," he went on, "said she didn't understand what was happening to you both."

"Great, that's all I need. My girlfriend and my oldest friend trading secrets. Was Marie there?"

"Yep."

"Christ, that really must've put the final nail in."

Tony's wife has never been comfortable with me. Her talking to Jenny was something I didn't want to think about.

"Actually," Tony said, "Marie spoke up for you. She said she liked you, you even make her laugh sometimes, which God knows is difficult enough and that if we ever had trouble, you would be the first person she'd go to because you're a hundred per cent reliable and she trusts you and you wouldn't let us down."

I'd started listening for the 'but', because Marie, as far as I knew, didn't like me and didn't like me being around.

"Where's the catch, Tony, what else is there?"

"There's no catch, Garron. Jenny was upset. She doesn't know what to do. You can't lie when someone comes to you like that, you have to tell them the truth."

"And what was Marie's truth?"

He shot a look at me that told me to back off and he had a point. This was his wife I was talking about and she was probably worth about ten of me.

As was Jenny.

"Okay," I said, "I'm sorry. Again. What else did Marie have to say?"

He waited for a moment so as I would know he'd noted the apology. Then he went on:

"That you being around scared the hell out of her. That she was worried when she knew you were around me. Not because you'd do anything, but because you're trouble. You attract trouble and the people around you get caught up in it."

"She believes that, does she?"

He shrugged.

"She sees Al dead, Pete dead, Mick on the run and you on your own."

"It's bollocks, Tony and you know it. I wasn't even really in touch with Al when he died. Pete was a crackhead and Mick picked his own life."

"But you're the thing they all have in common and that's how she

163

sees it. You make her nervous."

"And she told Jenny that?"

"Yeah."

"Great. Bloody great. You agreed with her, did you?" I was getting a bit angry now, them all sitting around discussing me like that.

"No," Tony said, "I didn't think she was being fair. It was their way of life that caused their problems, not you." Then after a second he said: "But I also said that you're in that life as well."

I shook my head.

"I don't mean to be."

"I think part of you does."

"And that's what you told Jenny?"

"I told her the truth. I told her that there was no-one I would rather have as a friend. I told her that she wouldn't find anyone else like you, no matter what, but that she has to understand what she doesn't want to see in you and what you won't tell her. What I think you won't admit to yourself. That you're not just some ex-boxer, but that you've moved on from there. That now you're a bodyguard. Not a part time rent collector with an occasional right hook, but a genuine, professional hard nut."

I shook my head again.

"You shouldn't have said that to her, Tony, I wish you hadn't said that to her. It's not true and you don't realise it. You haven't seen the guys out there, the way they act. The things they do. I'm not what they are and you're painting me like I am."

He said: "And you're too close to see yourself now."

"I'm not like them."

I was insisting now and I think it was what he was waiting for.

"No? Then do something about it and keep the most worthwhile part of yourself. Her."

I looked across at him.

"I know, mate, I know it," I said, "but I have to finish this. I can't just leave Mick hanging out there on his own. I just can't do it."

After a second he said: "I know you can't. If you could, you wouldn't be the same person anymore."

We let it rest there for a minute. I wasn't sure whether to talk to Tony about the rest, whether to tell him that I wasn't sure, in the end,

164

how much was for Mick, or even Al and how much might just be for me. I couldn't think about that for long myself, let alone discuss it with anyone else. So I let it go and wondered if again, it was another lie.

"What are you going to do about her?" he asked.

I took a deep breath.

"I don't want to lose her, Tony, I don't want her to go. I'm going to have to ask her to hang on until this is over. And then try to change for her. Try to leave this stuff behind." I thought again about how sick I'd felt when Michel had cut open the Russian's throat in the toilet of that cellar and how that sickness had stayed with me. Thought now, about someone's father, or child, someone's partner in that van, broken on the A10. "I can do that," I added.

"It'd be worth it," he said. "She's trying to make a life for herself and you could be in it. She wants you in it. It's a way out for you. A chance."

"I know," I said, "but somehow it's not easy."

*

I left Tony with a word of warning. If anyone, anyone at all, was to contact him about me, he should play it straight, tell them that he knew me, not try to hide it. If pushed even slightly, he should give up my mobile number, or call me himself if they asked him to set up a meet. Or maybe I should say, to set me up for a meet.

Lysenkov could already be on to me and there was no way I was going to let anyone else get hurt over this. He protested, but not too much. The fact that I'd told him to do it, together with the attempt on Mick, made him realise how serious this was. We agreed that if he had to call me because someone was standing over him, he'd use my name in the call. I took my Citroen, or rather, his Citroen and drove home.

I'd hoped Jenny might be there when I got back, but the flat was empty. She could have been at college, or on the lunchtime shift at the restaurant. Or just avoiding me.

I was still tired and aching, so after I'd tried to call her and got voicemail, I lay down on the mattress and tried to rest.

It wasn't easy.

The van driver was dead. An innocent man was dead. A man who I'd never known, would never know, was dead because I had taken a particular course of action. His family had had their lives changed forever, not because they were in conflict with me, not because he'd threatened me or mine, but because I'd chosen a path and followed it through. And yes, I knew it wasn't just down to me, I knew others had caused what had happened, but it had been my choices that had brought us to that crossroads at that time and passing the buck wasn't going to make me feel any better. This was going to sit with me for a long time and cause me a lot of pain.

But not as much as the man's family.

And for what?

It had been a serious misjudgement, taking Michel to the club when he could have been and in fact was, recognised. It was true that he'd been at fault as well, but it had been my idea, my responsibility. It was the sort of error that separated people like Al and Julot, possibly Lysenkov even, from people like me. Al wouldn't have taken Michel, probably without even thinking about it. The fact that there was a possibility of a problem would have been something he'd have instinctively known and subconsciously noted.

And yet, as Julot had said, we broke out of there. We survived it. Not just because of me and my actions, but certainly Michel wouldn't have lived through it if I hadn't been there.

So maybe I was no better than Michel. Maybe I too, needed to be pointed at something and given instructions.

Or maybe it was just that I was still learning. Michel might become better technically, but he'd never get beyond hired assassin status. I was out of my depth and making mistakes, but if nobody killed me, I'd learn from those mistakes.

Which was a crazy way to be looking at it.

From one side I was trying to change. To have a life with a woman who loved me. Sickened by what was happening around me. Scared by what else could be in store for the people I did care about.

From the other side, I was assessing how to improve my professional know-how and how good I might get to be at this stuff.

Too much going on in my head and I was too tired. Sleep was what

166

I needed and eventually, despite the images that I could not control, sleep came.

*

It was mid-afternoon when I was woken up by the phone ringing.

Not Jenny, but Mick again.

"I know where he is."

Awake instantly, with the lurch in my guts and the sudden heightening of the senses.

I want it to end, but I don't want it to happen.

But the information was there. The time frame was set. And we were off and running.

*

I called Michel and drove round to his hotel. There was no pretence between us now. Not about me withholding my mobile number, or him keeping his hotel and which room he was in from me. We had a lead and a short period of time to work in and we both knew that when this was over, my mobile and number would be discarded and his stay at the hotel, under whatever name he was using, would leave no way for me to contact or follow him.

So he'd given me his room number and I went straight up. On the second floor and basic, but comfortable, like the rest of the hotel. There was one straight-backed chair which I sat in. Michel sat on the bed.

Mick had told me that Lysenkov kept an office in West London. Or more precisely, he rented the whole top floor of an office block under the guise of a real and legitimate company name. Much of his 'quiet' business was conducted from there. Occasionally, if he wanted to see people away from his more flashy enterprises, he would set up a meet at these offices. The company was run by a manager, a legitimate manager and since Lysenkov didn't own the block and his rents and rates were always paid on time, there was no interference from the landlords. They probably thought he was a model tenant. If you're being paid on time, you're not going to worry about the occasional body disappearing in a car from the back of the building, especially if you genuinely don't know it's happened.

Apparently Lysenkov even arranged for his own cleaners, which for a business was ridiculous, but of course for him made perfect sense. I thought maybe that would have drawn some attention to his operation, but Mick said that it could be easily explained. All he had to do was say that his company worked irregular hours and didn't want interruptions and would pay for the cleaning himself, and so on. So he rented the entire top floor and he was left alone.

I'd always suspected that Mick must have a contact, or maybe more than one, inside the police itself. Someone who would keep their ear to the ground for him. I nearly asked him about it this time. After all, it was me that was going out on a limb for him, but in the end, I didn't. For one thing, it was a question too far and second, given that Mick knew we were going for a hit on Lysenkov, it didn't make too much sense for him to have more or less told someone inside the police that we were interested in where he was.

Or maybe it did. That person wouldn't be able to make too much of it, if the information had in fact come from him.

I gave up. Mick had survived for thirty odd years with his strange mix of goods and insider knowledge. In that time, he'd have built up God only knew how many contacts and in which areas.

His last words to me were that he'd rocked a lot of boats getting this information and getting it this quickly. The implication was there. If we didn't get to Lysenkov, the Russians would have even more reason to start ripping up the floorboards to find Mick.

So we had a building and a problem. Mick's contact thought that Lysenkov was there now. Or at least had been there an hour ago. There was no way of knowing how long he might stay there, or whether, if he left, he'd stay away for a while, or be back the next day. Since he now knew Julot was looking for him, he might retreat to his fortress home and stay there until Kirilenko and his men had flushed us out.

Starting with me, I thought.

But we had no idea of what this building was like, no photos, no plans, no idea of the security, the layout, nothing. If we went in, we'd be going in blind. If we waited, we might lose the first and possibly only opportunity we'd have.

Part of me wanted to be careful.

Part of me wanted to get it over with.

Michel wanted to wait outside and shoot him from the car as he came out of the building. That was a stupid idea and I told him so. Lysenkov could come out of the front, back, or side exits from the place and even when he did, he knew there was a threat against him. He was likely to have four guys close in around him and take less than a few seconds to get from the building to the car. And we had no idea if it was possible to park and sit easily in a car outside the office block, or what the area was like.

After batting that one around for a few minutes, Michel conceded. Then he pulled over a laptop and asked me for the address. Looked it up on an internet site which had zoom satellite pictures of the Earth and we got a look at the building from above and the street layout around it. It was no substitute for being there, but it did mean we now knew that it was on a reasonable size road to the front and that there was a small street by one side of the building with what looked like an external fire escape stairway going from the top floor to the street level there. There was an alley, or tiny service road on the other. From the angles, I couldn't tell whether the back was attached to another building directly, or whether it was a covered car park that I was looking at.

I wondered if we could follow Lysenkov when he left. If we got there before he left. But then I only had the old Saxo to drive which probably wouldn't keep pace with them and even if it did, the odds were he'd be in a car with bullet-proofed glass and bodywork. I wasn't sure that Michel could get his hands on a rocket launcher at short notice. If we did manage to follow them, he'd probably simply drive straight into the sealed grounds of his mansion. Even if the car could do it, I wasn't up to another car chase and if they spotted us following them, assuming they'd have two cars, the principal and a blocking car, they'd just stop the second car and shoot holes in us.

So we were left with entering a building we'd never seen, getting to the top floor, dealing with however many men Lysenkov had with him and then getting out again.

I could see Michel was fired up for it. I had to be the voice of reason. The problem was, I couldn't think of any other way to do it. This was the first possible sniff of the man that we'd had. If we didn't take the chance then we might not get another. The bodyguard in me was screaming that it was dumb. No preparation, no plan, no contingencies. But the part of me that was turning against this whole life, wanted it. It was the wrong way around, but that part of me could only see Kirilenko coming after me as the known face on the CCTV footage from the club. Coming after me and using Tony to get to me. Or putting me together with Mick, since they knew about Mick already, asking at his local and getting Jenny's name. "Yeah, she's with Garron. Doing some social workers' course or something at that college…"

I couldn't think about it. I couldn't let that possibility even exist as a thought. Whether it was money or muscle, the connection could be made. I couldn't let that happen and I'd walk into a thousand Russian shooting galleries to stop it.

- *Even if she's leaving you?*
- Even if I never see her again.

We were edging to a decision here, but I was still worried about Michel's ankle. If he couldn't move, he'd be no use at all, but he showed me about three yards of strapping on his leg and told me he'd had pain killing injections, so I had to trust him on that. Then he made a call asking for some equipment. Whether it was to Julot or not, I didn't know, but he said forty minutes and I checked the time and if we left then, we'd be at the offices after business hours were over and he could be gone by then, but even Michel wasn't dumb enough to go in there without some kind of edge, so we waited for the delivery. A part of me wanted the delivery to never arrive, but that was the wrong way to be thinking and I looked at Michel and wondered at the fact that he didn't feel that way at all.

We spent some more time thinking through possible scenarios and it was going okay until Michel told me I was just support. He wanted both Lysenkov and Kirilenko. I asked him if he was going to go in with one hand tied behind his back as well, but he missed that one, told me that would be both stupid and unprofessional. So much for British humour travelling well.

Then there was a knock on the door and we took delivery of two ski masks, two pairs of thin gloves, two stun grenades, which I wouldn't have recognised if they'd gone off there and then and a small amount of plastic explosive, which I desperately hoped Michel did actually know how to use. I had my gun and speed-loader and he had weapons already in the room here and we packed things away in pockets and for him, a small waist bag that looked as though it had been originally made for the beach.

As we got ready to leave, I was struck by another thought.

If Mick's source was that crooked, how well could Mick trust him? Or put another way, it was bloody quick work to dig this up this information on Lysenkov. Unless Lysenkov wanted it fed back to whoever was asking for it.

I looked at Michel, happy as a kid with his new toys and didn't voice my worries.

We'd find out soon enough.

*

Grey London.

Grey skies, grey buildings.

The threat of rain yet again as we neared the end of autumn and the stop-start city driving, through the same scenery, across different areas, reflected the mood. Different houses passed, different places, yet the same feel mile after mile, the same greyness.

Or maybe that's just the way I see it.

There's a park, a place for kids to play, yet I see a place where you have to avoid the smashed alcohol bottles and the used syringes. The council block which should be a home and therefore a refuge, is now a gang-ruled, no-go area. The expensive house with security gates, just a slap in the face to those for whom it is out of reach and will always be out of reach.

Cynical she'd called me, and it had hurt because it was true. Because I was in a place where whatever I looked at was becoming twisted to suit that view. But it had also hurt because I didn't want it to be so, because I wanted to live differently. Because this was the only life we have and I was throwing it away. And because, in the end, I didn't know how to stop that. I didn't know how to change. I was

171

losing her, maybe had lost her already and without her, I wouldn't be able to change.

We sat in silence while I drove until my phone rang, jerking me out of my thoughts and back to reality. I looked around the area before I answered. All I needed, to be pulled for talking on a mobile while driving when I had half an arsenal and an assassin in the car.

Again, not Jenny, but Tony's voice.

"Had someone round asking about you, so I did what you told me, said I didn't have a number for you, but that next time we spoke, I'd get you to call him."

So they were pushing already. Very fast, but it didn't sound right for the Russians, not heavy enough. Tony was still speaking.

" – text you through his number, you can call him and get him off my back. Name of Dayton, Detective Inspector."

Jeez. I'd told Tony to give me up if he was pressurised in any way, but I hadn't meant him to pass my name on to the Old Bill. Especially Dayton, who was no fool.

"What'd he say?" I asked Tony.

"He seemed to be sure that we knew each other, so I went with that," he answered. His voice went muffled as he bit into something. Probably a home made snack made by his loving wife in her family home kitchen and wrapped by one of his two intelligent, clean cut kids.

Not that I'm bitter, or anything.

"I told him we knew each other from way back and you did a few odd jobs for me around the lot every now and then."

I'd got most of that in between his chewing. I'd have to ask Jenny why she never made me snacks. If I got the chance.

"What else?" I asked him, "if you can pull yourself away from your tea and cakes."

"I told him I didn't know when you'd be in next, but you called in regularly and next time I'd tell you to call him."

So I had a little time.

"And they found my car," Tony continued, "back of Enfield somewhere, in a right state."

Or no time at all. That was very quick and I didn't like it. What did Dayton know that I didn't, that linked me with that car. Or had someone seen us dumping it and called the police in. Either way I wasn't happy and the choice was to contact Dayton now, as an innocent man would, or to just leave it and fade. Which might put things back onto Tony and at the least wouldn't look good.

"All right, Tony, I'll call him. Put you in the clear. But if he comes back, then I wasn't around yesterday and all I do is some odd jobs and driving for you, like you said. Make out I'm a bit of a charity case if you like, helping me out for old times' sake, stuff like that."

"Won't be difficult," he mumbled.

"And what are you eating there, when you're trying to talk to me?"

"Oh, it's a pork pie, one of the dodgy ones from that mobile van at the end of the High Street. I'll be here a while tonight and Marie's told me she's not cooking up two dinners if I'm late."

So much for domestic bliss. I rang off and started looking for a phone box, one that wasn't near a traffic camera. I wasn't using my mobile to call Dayton and if he could pinpoint the number I was using at a payphone, which I knew he could, then with the time I called, he might be able to see me on film getting back into my car, pick up the number plate and then he can look for that on other cameras and suddenly I'm in the frame if I go anywhere near a certain office block in West London which might well be in the news tomorrow.

I finally found a phone I was happy with and which amazingly looked un-vandalised, parked up quite a way off and walked back to it. Michel was furious, he wanted to get straight to Lysenkov, but I took the keys, not that he knew how to get there anyway and walked off.

This was important, not only to find out what Dayton was up to and to cement in his mind my non-involvement in the car chase the previous night, but also to protect Tony, which was something I had to keep sight of. No-one else was going to get hurt over this because of me.

It also wouldn't be a bad idea to establish in Dayton's mind, if I could, that at least at this point in time I was nowhere near an office in West London shooting gangsters.

It was a mobile number, so I put a fair bit of change in and he picked up quickly.

"DI Dayton," he answered, the voice quiet, but with an edge to it. Probably because he'd clocked the incoming number and hadn't recognised it.

I didn't introduce myself, I just said:

"I was told you wanted to talk to me."

There was a pause and then he got it.

"Garron."

"Yep. You've been to see my old mate, Tony and he said you were looking for me."

"He's right there." Neutral tone, almost friendly and he sounded older on the phone. "I'd like you to come in and we can talk properly."

"I don't have anything to tell you, Inspector. I haven't seen or heard from Mick Lennox since I spoke to you outside his flat and as far as I know, neither has anyone else. I haven't been around that area, I haven't been to his local there, I haven't heard anything about him at all and yes, I'm still worried about it."

I was laying it on a bit thick, but it was all deflection against what I knew was coming.

"Is that a roundabout way of saying that you won't come in to talk to me voluntarily?"

I started to reply, but he cut me off.

"Because I can issue a warrant for your arrest and start looking for you right now."

"You don't want to arrest me, because you know I haven't done anything you can arrest me for and you don't have to look for me because I gave you my address."

"You gave my officer a wrong address."

"No, I didn't. He must've copied it down wrong."

There was an almost theatrical sigh from the other end of the line.

"Don't piss me off, Garron, where were you last night?"

"What?"

Playing it straight back.

"You heard me, where were you last night? With someone who'll swear for you of course?"

I thought of Jenny.

"No, I was crashing at a friend's place, listening to CDs and unfortunately for me, he wasn't in last night to back that up."

That stopped him for a second, so I thought I'd rub it in a bit. I was a little surprised at myself. I've never been very good at lying and here I was, lying outright to an experienced police officer. Maybe because it was over the phone, it was easier. Or maybe I was just getting better at it.

"What's happened, Inspector Dayton, have you found Mick, then?"

I could almost hear him weighing it up. He wanted me in front of him in a police station, but he knew that wasn't going to be easy to arrange unless I agreed to it, so he was toying with how much to let me have. In the end he went with it.

"No, we've not found Lennox. What I have got, is a high speed car chase around North East London, two car smashes and another wrecked car dumped in Enfield, which just happened to belong to your friend the car dealer."

The payphone wasn't one of the old style boxes, it was open, with just a small weather shield type plastic covering at each side. I looked at the houses and the trees and a couple of cars went by as I left a gap in the conversation and then I said what he expected me to say.

"What has any of that got to do with me?"

That almost patient tone, the one that British police do so well, appeared in his voice.

"Well, Garron, it could be just a coincidence that you are a known friend of the car dealer whose vehicle was dumped last night. But when I then learn that the two other cars involved were carrying Russians, some of them now critical in hospital, others of them dead, but all of them with criminal connections and in possession of weapons, my poor old policeman's brain connects those Russians to the fact that when your friend Lennox disappeared, one of the witness statements said there could have been Russians there. Now that in itself could be a coincidence, but the link in both sets of circumstances is you. Friend of Lennox, connection to the car. Do you see where I'm going with this?"

"I wasn't there," I said.

"Prove it to me."

"How the hell can I prove I wasn't there, if I was on my own somewhere else?"

"Come in and have a DNA swab. That'll help to rule you out, if you weren't in the car."

It was maybe true, but also a way to get me into a station to work on me. But I had thought this one through.

"Inspector, if that car really is one of Tony's, then my DNA is probably all over it. I test drive almost all of Tony's cars for him, it's part of the work I do for him. But whatever you say, I still wasn't driving that car last night."

Suddenly the cat and mouse was over. His tone changed and hardened and it was like he was going to reach out of the phone itself and pull me in to him and although I knew he must have done this many times before, used this trick on a thousand suspects, it was still effective.

"Stop the bullshit, Garron. I'm not saying you know where Lennox is, or even whether he's alive or not and I'm not saying that it had to have been you driving that car last night, but you're the connection. You lied to my officer before and you're lying to me now, so I want you in and face to face with me."

The outburst had taken me by surprise, but I had to carry on talking back to him. Totally straight. Totally innocent. I could go for anger or distress and in the end I went somewhere in the middle.

"I don't know where Mick is, if he's still okay even and I haven't seen Tony in days. And I'm not coming in to a police station to have you hold me for ages, just because I drove one of his cars three months ago, or whenever it was." I felt my anger growing now, as I got into the part of the wronged citizen. "I didn't lie to anyone and I'm not getting stuck in some police cell while you find out someone else is the bad guy." I paused for a moment. "Now, I've got to get the bus and go to work and no, I'm not going to tell you where that is, 'cos it's bar work, cash in hand and if you barge in there and pull me, it'll be the end of the job."

I put the phone down as he started to speak and went back to the car. It had been worth making the call. I hadn't learned much, but I now knew a little of what he thought was going on and, for what it was worth, I'd protested my innocence and planted a little misdirection. I could only hope now that he wouldn't connect a down

176

on his luck ex-pug on his way to a low grade bar tending job, with a fully armed assault on the Russian Mafia.

Although, of course, if I didn't survive the night, it would have been a fairly pointless exercise.

*

Michel was in a sulk when I got back to the car and asked if there were going to be any more delays. I told him to shut up and we drove on in silence. I'd like to think he was silent because he was nervous, as I was, but he didn't appear to have anything resembling nerves when it came to this stuff and that worried me, because although Al had never shown it, he'd always told me it was good for you to be nervous of trouble.

As long as you didn't freeze.

There he was again, getting into my head. But Al would be turning in his grave, knowing I was about to do this.

- *Tough shit. Your decision. He's not here.*

The voice was right. I was my own person here, not Al's stooge and I had to realise that this was the way it should be.

Another twenty minutes and we were close, in an area a little south of Acton and I thought that this was a strange place for Lysenkov to place himself. But then these were his private offices. The public hotel and restaurant were prominent, this was tucked away, not far from the centre, but not in the limelight.

I told Michel we would drive past once as a basic check and to look for cameras. I wasn't going to turn the Saxo down the side street, or take it past too many times. I might get away once with one of Tony's cars turning up near Russian criminals, but twice and Dayton would have a field day.

As we drove by, I could see cameras covering the front of the building and Michel, who had more time as he was the passenger, said there were another two, each side of the building, one pointing at the side road and one at the alley. There were lights on in the offices on the top floor and Michel saw movement behind the windows there. The lights were also on in the foyer and there was a security guard, almost certainly from the building's owners, not the Russians, sitting behind a desk. That was okay. We weren't going in through the front anyway. There was nowhere to park nearby and that suited me as well. If all went according to what passed for a plan, no-one would be following us out of there, so we wouldn't be running for the car.

I eventually parked up about a five minute walk away and along a street that had no CCTV and as far as I could see, no reason for anyone to look at an old car that didn't have a residents' parking permit. It was late enough that we wouldn't get a ticket for being there and in as much as I was happy about any of this, I was happy to leave it there.

We then loaded up to kill.

Which was weird.

I'd taken my gun with me before to places when I'd known I was looking to kill someone. But then it had just been me and the gun. It had taken me a while to get used to carrying it, but there was never a ritual with me. Check if it's loaded, check the speed-loader and leave. Now all I did was stick my gun in my right hand jacket pocket and the speed-loader in the left and watched as Michel systematically looked twice through the contents of his bag and then re-secured it around his waist. He then checked his gun, which was in a shoulder holster under his left arm and after that the short automatic machine-gun type weapon which he had tied in what was almost a sling under his jacket. Then he handed me one of the ski masks, nodded and got out of the car.

So that was how the professionals did it.

I had only one other thing to remember and I deleted the call records off my phone, the few recent texts I'd had from Jenny, who was the only one who sent me texts and the handful of saved contacts. I knew Jenny's number off by heart and Tony's and I'd memorised Mick's new number and Julot's, since I didn't want to store it, so I didn't need to keep anything. And what I didn't want, was to die in a Russian mafia office leaving my phone here with immediately obvious access to contacts on it.

Actually, I didn't want to die at all.

I got out and opened the boot. Since I didn't want to die and I was leaving my phone here, I didn't want it to get nicked by some casual street punk, so I put it in the well with the spare tyre. If the car went, *c'est la vie*, but if some toe-rag just did the window to check what had been left inside, then I should at least still have a phone.

And wouldn't you know it, it started to rain slightly again.

We split up and walked on different sides of the road towards the office block, Michel's limp almost unnoticeable to me. As we approached I took in as much about the building as I could. I was coming from the left and I could see the fire escape going up the side of the offices in short diagonal turns. I counted nine floors above the ground floor, so we'd have a bit of a climb up to where we could get at the Russians. The camera on the side of the building would see us, but although it might be recording, we weren't so worried about that. We would be covered up.

Our thought was that this was a small enough office that only the guard down in the front lobby would be looking at the screens and probably not that often. At the same time, we couldn't risk the off chance that he would spot us too soon and either alert the Russians, or call the police, or possibly both. So we'd planned a minor distraction, not anything that would set off all his alarm bells, but something that would get him up off his chair for two or three minutes, enough for us to get into the building. We hadn't, of course, known for certain that we would be able to use the fire stairs, although we'd seen on the internet that they were there, but they looked okay. We might have had to get in through a back door, or the service entrance at the ground level. But we were going to blow out the locks of whatever door we needed to access and we knew that at that point, it was probable that an alarm would go off.

From then on it was a matter of speed. Would the guard simply call the police, or check the problem himself? Were his CCTV cameras pointed at the doors in such a way that he would be able to see the damage to them, or would he have to go and check? We had no answers to these questions, it was all down to chance and how good the security man was at his job, but I did know that given the choice, I'd rather enter the building at the top where we needed to be, than have an alarm go off when we entered at ground level, meaning we'd then lose time getting up nine floors.

Michel was on the other side of the main road which still had an irregular flow of traffic. He was a little ahead of me and I gave him the signal to get the guard off his seat and then we'd leg it, or in his case limp fast, up the fire escape.

What he did next was what we had discussed, but it still seemed crazy to me. On the other side of the road, out of the range and the angle of the building's cameras and on a diagonal to the front windows of the offices, Michel knelt down on one knee, as though doing up his shoelaces and waited for a gap in the traffic. There were enough of those as the rush hours were ending and when he was satisfied, he calmly took out his handgun with the silencer already fitted on and shot through the furthest large window of the foyer on the ground floor. He was firing at maybe a thirty degree angle to that window and there was no chance of the security guard being hit.

What we were counting on, was that it would sound like someone had thrown half a brick at the window, something that would make him get up and move away from his monitors to check it out and then decide that it wasn't a real threat, just some mindless kids' violence that would have to be reported, but that wasn't an emergency. It would have been better to have actually lobbed a brick, but we'd have to be much closer to do that, probably within camera range and then whoever threw the thing would have to cross back over the road to avoid the CCTV and run like hell back to the side street, before crossing over again. The plan we had was maybe less likely to work as well, but it was safer from our point of view and simpler to execute.

But a lot depended on how the glass smashed.

It didn't.

The bullet passed through and the glass cracked across the whole of the pane, but it didn't smash. I would have heard it, seen some glass falling forwards. But this now could be good or bad. If the pane had smashed, the guard might have been startled into calling the police straight away. As it hadn't, he might notice the round edges of a bullet hole if they were still there and he was good at his job. Hopefully he wasn't. And as nothing else had happened and the place wasn't 'under attack' as far as he could see, with luck he'd make a report about the window and start that process, maybe even call the police, but they wouldn't come out for a bit of vandalism.

But we couldn't worry too much more about it. This would work and we'd buy ourselves some time, or it wouldn't and we'd have to go with whatever happened.

Michel stayed where he was long enough to note the guard standing up to investigate the noise and then crossed over to my side. There were no other pedestrians around and as he reached me, he pulled on his ski mask and I put mine on as well. We walked down the side street rather than ran, which could have been noted from the main road, but when we reached the fire escape stairs thirty yards down the street, we bolted up them and I noticed that I was feeling the climb. I still had the tension in my legs, back and shoulders from the club and the car chase the night before and my body was protesting at having to push myself again. It didn't help that the rain had made the metal slippery as well, but I wasn't going to complain about the building's health and safety at this stage. What amazed me was that Michel could move as quickly as he did on his damaged ankle and I began to wonder what else he might have taken besides the painkilling injections.

At the eighth floor I stopped and waited for Michel.

"They are on the next one up," he said as he reached me and started up the final level and, dammit, he wasn't out of breath.

I stopped him. We hadn't discussed this bit, but we should have done.

"Yes," I said, "I know, but if they have people in the corridor and we blow the fire exit on the same floor, they'll know straight away they're under attack. Go in the floor below and they'll hear something, but they won't know for sure what it is."

"We will lose the chance for surprising them,"

"But we get the chance to see what they have, how they are set up, without stumbling straight into them. They might have no-one outside their offices and we can walk right in."

He hesitated and the truth was I wasn't sure if I was right or not, but I didn't feel good about blowing the door right where they were. Especially as we weren't going to take the whole door out, which would make a huge noise, let everyone know we were here and mean we'd have to be thirty yards away when it happened. We were just trying to blow the basic fire exit bars. So we could be wrestling with a bloody fire door trying to get in, while they shot at us. On the floor below, we'd have a bit more time to get through without armed people directly on the other side.

I hoped.

"We're wasting time," I said to him and I had no real way of gauging how he was reacting behind the ski mask, but then he reached into his bag for the small lumps of plastique and the detonators and I watched him place them at the top and bottom of the doors and frame, approximately where he thought the bars would be. We had talked about this when we'd driven along the front and seen the fire stairs and for once we'd agreed in what we'd thought, that the doors would be push bar fire exits from the inside, the ones with the vertical bars into the frame, top and bottom.

The placement looked about right to me, but I had no way of knowing how good he was at this and if it didn't work, we could be two very embarrassed, would-be assassins, walking down a metal fire escape in thirty seconds from now, on our way home. But I'd seen Michel shoot and I now had faith in what he could do with weapons.

He turned and gestured to me and we went down a floor and he detonated and there was a twin explosion that to me sounded like it must have been heard half a mile away, but in reality was probably lost in most of the general traffic noise from the main road. The door was still on its hinges as I guess Michel had expected it to be, but there were two gaps surrounded by twisted metal at the top and bottom of the door. It took a bit of shifting as one of the bars, the one that went upwards on the inside, had been blown sideways, but was still caught on the door frame and we wasted precious seconds before we forced it down past the edge of the frame and we were inside.

One floor below them and the dumb thought occurred to me that we'd feel really stupid if Lysenkov had simply left the lights on when he'd gone for the day, but then I remembered the moving shadows Michel had seen and I thought that there was no point in worrying, it was too late for that now. Look at Michel. Is he worried about anything? No, he's a heat-seeking missile and he's going to destroy anything in his way. To complete his job. To do his master's bidding. To prove himself.

And I'm with him, I thought, somehow I got myself to a situation where I'm with him. Christl

Then the nerves kicked in fully and I could have turned and walked away that easily, but Michel chose that moment to turn around and, his unrecognisable face behind the ski mask, sneered at me as he said:

"Am I going too quickly for you?"

Nerves and anger mixing as he turned away again and I stopped myself left hooking his bloody mask off his head and instead followed him along the well lit, but deserted corridor to the stairs.

One flight and doors to the Russians. I wasn't sure how we should get from this stairway side of the doors to the other side without presenting a target to anyone there. This wasn't my game anymore. I was a bodyguard, not a commando and the closer I got to this, the less I liked it.

Michel leaned into me and whispered:

"I will go through the door quickly and across the corridor. You will stay in the doorway. Look to the right and shoot anything that moves. You are my cover for this."

I nodded. When he'd told me I was just support, it had wound me up a little, but now I realised that was exactly what I was. Support for the professional in a rite that I didn't fully understand. He held up three fingers and I realised that he was going to count down. Then I noticed my heartbeat was pounding and I checked my hands. They weren't shaking. That, I knew from experience, would come afterwards for me. If I was still alive.

I noticed the gun was in my hand. My Smith and Wesson 686. I hadn't even realised I'd taken it out. My subconscious obviously knew more about staying alive than the rest of me.

I glanced back at Michel who was focussed on the door to the ninth floor and had now only one finger held up.

What the hell was I doing here?

But then the finger disappeared into the fist and there was no time left as he hit the door open and threw himself across the five or six foot width of the corridor to the opposite wall. I filled the gap in the open doorway, looking to my right, with a part of me registering what a target I was making, while the rest focussed on the tall, suited man twenty feet away, the one facing me now and drawing a handgun left-handed from a shoulder holster under his right arm.

I moved automatically into the stance Al had taught me and I had practised that time at Castle's range and more frequently since then in my own flat, left foot slightly forwards, weight and balance spread, left hand forwards supporting the right hand and the gun in it as I squeezed the trigger, absorbing the recoil as the noise exploded in the quiet corridor, my shot missing the tall Russian and as I adjusted the aim, I saw his gun line up for me and I heard a quieter sound from just to the side of me and the man in my sights dropped backwards, blood spreading across his chest as Michel, following his shot, walked to the fallen man and fired again, the silencer still in place and the man lying still.

I turned to check the left side of the corridor and saw a second man, not moving and slumped against the nearside wall, face turned away from me, what was left of it.

I hadn't even seen Michel move or turn in that direction and in the speed of what was happening and the sudden quiet after the noise of the Smith and Wesson, I realised just how far out of my depth I was. And then it came to me as I watched him move back towards the nearest office door, that Michel had me along not really for support at all, but to draw their fire. The man that had aimed at me could have shot Michel if I hadn't been there as a distraction. I didn't even have a silencer on my gun and Michel hadn't worried about that and I hadn't picked up on it. It was the sound of my shot, the one that had missed in the heat of the exchange, which would draw out the Russians. To get Michel to this point, I was integral, not just support. But from here on in, I was fodder.

Michel was walking quickly back up the corridor to me and the office directly opposite me, unslinging the automatic weapon as he came, having already holstered the handgun. The office doors here were wood with a vertical strip of frosted glass running the length of the door, just inside where the handle was. Michel motioned for me to get ready to go through the door once it was opened. It wouldn't be locked unless someone had got to it after they'd heard my shot. More likely they were just waiting for someone to burst in and I didn't think that should be me, so I shook my head.

But I'd misunderstood. He just wanted me to pull down on the handle from the side. He had one of the stun grenades out and that was his plan.

Okay, I could open a door for him.

I moved to the wall next to the office, wondering why no-one had come out yet. I guessed because they had no way of knowing how many people were attacking them and how many guns were trained on the doors, ready to fire the moment they opened.

Hand across to the handle. Michel was against the wall the other side of the door to me and for a second I thought about whether to pull the handle down quickly or slowly, before I realised how stupid that was. There could be a dozen people in that room and all of them would be staring at the door, waiting for any kind of movement, so I yanked down on the handle and pushed inwards and bullets thudded into the wall opposite me as they fired through the opening doorway.

Movement from Michel as he lobbed in the stun grenade and flattened himself back against the wall and more bullets flew before I suddenly thought *stun grenade* and clapped my hands over my ears, not knowing whether that would do any good, or make any difference at all and then there was an explosion that cracked through my head and Michel waited a second and then swung into the room and I could hear the automatic sub-machine gun, or whatever it was, at full blast.

I didn't follow him. This wasn't what I understood and I didn't want any more part in it than I had to be in. I was here. That was bad enough, but then a door opened from further up the corridor, past where the man who had aimed at me was lying dead and someone dived out from that office to lie flat on the floor and fired up the corridor at me and even as I threw myself down as well and aimed my gun at him, a part of my mind was answering the question of why he'd chosen to move at that point and I marvelled at the fact that I could be about to die and yet my brain was working on the facts. That whoever was in the further office had heard the other shots, heard the explosion and realised that the attackers were going for only one office instead of what they should be doing, which would be a multiple, simultaneous attack. So the odds were that there couldn't be that many attackers and they should get out there and help.

All this flashed through my mind as I fired once, then again at the prone figure, but a second man burst out of the office and I felt a sudden vicious burning along the outside of my right arm, the upper

185

part just below the shoulder, almost like someone had hit it with barbed wire and I realised that I'd been shot and I was surprised, because I'd felt no real impact and then the panic set in and I had to move, I *had* to, I'd been *shot* for Christ's sake and I got up from my crouched position without really knowing what I was doing and ran down the corridor towards them, firing all the time, first at one and then the other of them, seeing the second man stagger back and fall and the first just lie there unmoving, his eyes as I got closer, staring at me and then through me as they didn't close.

The gun clicked on empty and I stopped just short of the office, all thought of Michel gone, only one thing registering, the fact that there could be more of them, more of these bastards trying to kill me, heart pounding as I looked at my arm and saw blood on the dark material, but not that much, the burning still there and a slight numbness, but still moving, the arm still moving and I had to forget it, forget the arm, I had no bullets left. No bullets. The brain kicked in and I reached into my left jacket pocket for the speed-loader, again stupidly noting that this was the first time I'd ever used it for real, some kind of dumb pride in that as I went through the process I'd practised many times before and it was smooth despite the adrenalin flowing, Mr Castle would be proud of me, remembering his lesson and now re-loaded, I stepped to the doorway realising that although I wanted to get out, the only way was to take Lysenkov as well.

If Michel hadn't already found him.

I didn't want to go through the open door, but I didn't want to be caught cold as someone came out either, so I took a breath and as I moved forwards, he suddenly appeared, filling the space in the empty doorframe, a gun in his right hand, as I had in mine.

Kirilenko.

Our eyes locked for a split second and then I grabbed for his right wrist as he hit down onto my gun with his gloved left hand.

He was huge, this man and although I'd twisted his arm outwards, I didn't have the strength to hold it there and the force of his blow had knocked my gun to the ground, so I ducked into him, headbutting him full in the centre of the chest and pushing his gun hand outwards, slamming it against the doorframe once, twice and again as he grunted from the impact of the head strike and his gun fell to the floor.

Inside the office now, there was soft carpet under my feet and the impetus was with me as he staggered backwards, then grabbed me with his left arm behind my neck and pulled me down with him and we fell to the floor.

Too strong, he was just too strong for me and although I landed on top of him, I was almost unable to breathe, with my face pulled into his chest, the force of his left arm at the back of my neck almost breaking it, pulling me into him and all of my strength focussed in my left hand, pushing outwards against his right wrist, because if that hand came in and joined his left, the pressure on my neck would be too great and that would be it.

No thought, no time for rational thought and my right fist started striking to his side, but ineffectual, punching with no purchase and having to strike through his jacket and then, again without thinking, the body taking over and trying to save itself, reaching up and striking for his eyes with the fingers of my right hand, missing and missing again, but he had to move his head, had to keep turning his head to keep his eyes away from my clawing hand and the movement shifted the pressure from his left arm slightly and I turned my head sideways and pulled it down and started to slide out of his grip.

Only a few seconds we'd been on the floor, but already I knew about him, knew about the raw power he had, the desire to kill, the fact that dropping the gun hadn't panicked him. He was no pure gunman, Kirilenko, not like Michel. He was an all rounder and all the more dangerous for that.

My head was nearly free now and I was gulping in air again as a part of me recognised that there could be nobody else in this office, otherwise I'd have been hauled off Kirilenko by now.

Unless Lysenkov himself was here.

Shift from him and he'd realised he was losing the grip on my head and rolled and pitched me sideways and there was space suddenly and I struck for his throat with my right again, missing and feeling the pain as his forearm hit into my ribs, the immediacy of it, the wind taken out of me and then the strength again of his right arm taking over, my left hand being forced down as the roll finished and he had me pinned half on my back and left side and I couldn't stop him, he was just too strong and then I remembered I had legs to use and I slammed my right knee into his leg, his upper leg, again and again until he had to move it and I found my right hand free and pounded hook after hook into the left side of his face and head.

I was finally having some kind of effect on him, the leg strikes and repeated punching forcing him to hold and try to block and I got my knee between us and forced him further away.

He had to be tiring now, I'd hit him so many times, but I'd ignored the obvious, with me on the floor and him above me still and his forehead suddenly cracked down, striking me full on the nose and the pain exploded as I felt the bone crunch and I struggled to breathe as the blood started inside the ski mask and my eyes stung and I hated him then, hated him irrationally. Pure, angry hatred for showing me that I could be damaged so easily and irrational because I knew that already and it wasn't the first time that someone had broken my nose, but not like this, not bloody like this and I brought my right hand up inside and smashed the palm up under his chin, striking upwards and snapping his head back.

At last he was forced away and I went after him, scrabbling upwards from the ground, hitting him another right hand as he moved and he fell to the side, landed on his right arm and shoulder and instead of lying still, shook his head clear and began pushing himself upwards again.

But he was down and I was following into him until I saw my gun just inside the open door and lunged for it, my hand closing on the metal as I felt, almost before I saw, a different Russian appear in the doorway. His gun was in his hand by his side and my brain focussed on him as the immediate threat, the unhurt and armed new element in the equation, but even as I expected to fire at him, I found I'd half turned to where Kirilenko had been lying, my mind so taken up with this man, in fact so scared of what he might be capable of, that the instinct had taken over from the brain and made the decision for itself to change the target. And as I turned, I saw him already up on one knee, already reaching for the gun that he had dropped in the struggle, his hand now touching it and again for that heartbeat our eyes locked and then I gently squeezed the trigger, the aim at this distance immaterial and his chest burst as the bullet hit. Still he didn't immediately fall, just swayed for a moment, before the body overbalanced and he went down.

I swung the gun back to the door and fired blindly upwards and maybe he hadn't shot quickly because Kirilenko had been in his view, or maybe he was simply surprised and slow to react, but my shot landed somewhere on him and he screamed, the force of the shot at close range knocking him sideways. Perhaps I didn't hit him cleanly, because he continued to scream as I sat there and tried to breathe. Ripped the mask off my face, there were no cameras here and sucked in air through my mouth, as the blood oozed from my nose and I used my jacket sleeve to try and staunch it.

No-one else in the office, that much was clear and I couldn't do this again, I could *not* go through another door, I'd have to wait for Michel to finish the rest, sat there in my own sweat and blood, the pain in my nose pulsing at me, my right upper arm numb and feeling the intense ache in my left hand and wrist from the effort of keeping Kirilenko's right hand away from me. Then I remembered I didn't have Lysenkov and that he was the key. Michel might have him or might not, but I didn't know yet.

So I pushed myself off the floor with my right hand, the one still holding the gun and looked out into the corridor.

Bodies.

Five bodies. Three outside this office, one halfway up the corridor and one at the far end.

The man I'd just shot had stopped screaming now, had stopped doing anything at all and I walked slowly back up to the first office, too tired to be careful even, the gun held low by my side and pointing at the floor.

When I realised that, I lifted it up again.

The office Michel had entered was a scene of carnage. Brightly lit by neon tubes, the blood from four dead men was pretty much everywhere. Michel must simply have cut down everything that moved, firing so quickly and so many times, that a couple of the bodies were almost cut in two by the bullets. And in the middle of it all, this small, deadly man stood, turning towards me, his mask also removed and with a look that I couldn't describe on his face. A hellish look of triumph and cruelty and I had the same reaction as

189

when I'd seen him kill the Russian in the drinking club, that sickening, gut wrenching nausea. In front of him, lying on his back on the floor, was an older Russian man, pain etched on his face and blood seeping from a gunshot to his left knee.

Michel had switched back to his silenced handgun, the automatic weapon slung tightly once more over his shoulder.

"What are you doing?" I tried to say and my voice didn't work. I'd said the words, but nothing had come out. I coughed and tried again.

"Is that him?"

I think it was almost a physical effort for Michel to tear himself away from his target and answer me. When he did, his voice sounded strange; harsh, but muted and I didn't know if this was because I hadn't adjusted after the noise of the gunshots and the explosion, or if it was, in fact, how he sounded.

"Lysenkov," was all he said, the gun still pointing at the man on the floor.

"What are you doing to him?"

And I sounded calm to myself, calm in the middle of this bloody place, maybe because I knew the answer already and because I couldn't let it happen. I didn't know why I couldn't let him do it, God alone knew what Lysenkov himself had been responsible for, but something inside me knew it was too much, too far. And it had to stop. Not for Lysenkov, but for me.

"A modern crucifixion," he answered me, "Russian style." When I said nothing he carried on: "It is not enough to kill him, a message must be sent. Must be received."

I shook my head.

"I didn't sign up to send messages, or to torture, or whatever you call it."

"It is not your position to tell me what I may do."

We were talking quite normally, could have been in the pub, having a pint, so I raised the gun and pointed it at him.

"You have to kill him, Michel, that's all and that is what you will do. After he answers a question for me."

He laughed, but the gun stayed trained on Lysenkov's right knee.

"You will shoot me? I do not think so. I have seen you shoot and I can aim this gun and fire before you have touched the trigger. And this question of yours, it will be about your friend, yes?"

"No, not about Al," and I surprised myself by adding: "he's gone, history now."

And then Michel surprised me.

"Not him" and it was a sneer, "the other one, Lennox, about how they got to him."

"What do you - "

It was there then, in his eyes and his voice, the laugh, the mocking tone, that cruel superiority.

"You do not see it? Julot leaked Lennox to Lysenkov as being a threat. You had turned him down. No-one turns him down. Julot always gets what he wants and he wanted you to work for him. I did not agree, but he was correct. The Russians hitting your friend brought you back to us and you brought me to here and now." He smiled again. "We have also a person for the police to find here. Someone who will fit in and take at least some of the blame. As Julot has explained to me, even though they will know that someone else was here, they will not put together a man like you, with us."

I was stunned. I had thought of Michel as a threat, but only on a personal level, I hadn't seen any of this. Yes, I was out of my depth in all ways and even though I held the gun on him, I could believe he could kill me, I believed he was that quick, that good.

"You say nothing," Michel again and that bloody smile again, as he started to swing the gun up to me and Lysenkov kicked out at him with his one undamaged leg, catching him a weak strike on his knee, but enough to cause Michel a slight downwards glance, a micro second, even though his gun movement itself didn't alter and I brought my other hand up to support my gun in the firing stance and pulled the trigger.

Michel's shot hit the wall behind me, I swear I felt the air rush past my face as my shot caught him in the middle of the body as I'd been taught, the larger target and he took two steps back and doubled over and raised his gun again and I fired twice more, my aim good as I focussed on him and he fell and a part of me laughed inside at him for his arrogance, for taking the shot to my head instead of the professional one, in this case to my body, which would have landed and effectively finished me. But he'd genuinely thought I wasn't good enough to take him and he'd wanted to prove the point and it had cost him his life.

In the end then, not quite professional enough.

I walked over to check he was dead, I didn't trust him at all, even in death and then I knelt down by Lysenkov, who I realised now had a bullet wound in his right elbow as well as his right knee. 'Russian crucifixion', I thought and let it go.

"One question," I said, thinking that maybe all of it had been a lie. "An English bodyguard, a big man, about three and a half years ago. Did you kill him, have him killed?"

A nod, maybe all he could manage.

I stood up.

For you then, Al. But I didn't really feel that and not even for Mick, since Lysenkov had heard what Michel had said.

So in the end maybe, in truth, to protect myself. To take myself out of this sick world, where life is cheaper than words and the truth is a twisted thing that you make work for yourself.

I looked down at Lysenkov and he closed his eyes.

I aimed at his stationary head and pulled the trigger.

And yes, I felt the sickness again.

*

I was still wearing the thin gloves, but I wiped down the gun anyway and put it in the hands of one of the dead Russians, not just the grip, but got his hands all over it, before dropping the gun near his body. I nearly gagged doing that, but I don't know why, it was no worse than what I'd already seen, what I'd already done, although it seemed more personal. Maybe it was reading the tattoos on a dead man's fingers that did it.

More personal than what, I asked myself. Than taking someone's life?

Time to think later, if I could stomach it. Right now, I had to get out.

I pulled the ski mask back on, ignoring the still wet blood in it and the pain as it pushed in on my nose and ran as fast as I could, on what were fairly shaky legs, down the stairs to the second floor and then slowly opened the fire exit there, expecting to see half of the West London Police armed response teams waiting for me. But there was nothing there and I went down the escape to the ground. I reckoned I had to be on the CCTV for that and the guard might even be watching me, but he wasn't going to come after me on his own and I kept the mask on until I got towards the main street, waited until there were no people walking close by and turned away from the building with my head down walking until I judged I was out of camera range of the one at the front of the office block. Then I rolled the mask up until it looked like a docker's hat. My jacket was torn at the top of the right sleeve, where the bullet had grazed me, but even though I hadn't looked, I knew the bleeding had stopped and against the dark material, it wasn't easily noticeable. Of course, my broken nose would be noted by anyone passing, but it was dark and I kept my head down and my hand up over it and no-one stared as I made it to the car.

In and start the engine, normal actions. Real actions. But after the madness of what had happened, after the insanity of the last twenty minutes, these movements, these common movements that I and others perform unthinkingly day after day, seemed other-worldly. Surreal.

But if they hadn't been commonplace, if they hadn't been routine, I don't think I could have survived them. I was on automatic, the body taking over, the mind on standby, viewing, but not allowing itself to interfere, to think, to remember, to consider. Most of all, not to consider. I was driving and I realised I had no idea where. But it didn't matter. Away from that place. Away from Michel's sneering face, Kirilenko's blank stare and Lysenkov closing his eyes in anticipation, in acceptance, of what was to come.

Five streets away, ten, fifteen and I found a place to pull over and sat there in what must have been shock as the system both shut down and screamed at me alternately.

The shakes came and went and came again and stayed, the images played time and again behind my closed eyes and the adrenalin slowly drained away, leaving me weak and nauseous and scared. Scared of what, I wasn't exactly sure, but the worst fear, the worst, was that I was scared of what I had done. And the old mantra, the old excuse of 'no choice', of 'what else could I have done', just didn't cut it. Not this time. Not now.

How long did I sit there? I don't know. Maybe not as long as it seemed, but I only started to come out of it when the pain in my arm and in my nose cut through. Which meant I was coming down from it, from the pitch I'd been at and, as ever, the ordinary things, the realisation that if I just sat there then I would still be sitting there in five hours time, was what pushed me to move. I checked there was no-one close, more out of habit than worry and got out of the car. I felt weak standing, had to steady myself against the roof, but the rain had stopped and the night air was clear and I breathed deeply and realised I was alive and others weren't.

I felt the speed-loader still in my pocket and walked unsteadily twenty yards to a public bin, wiped it down and pushed it deep into the rubbish. I was still wearing the very thin black gloves and there were patches of darker blood on them, whose I didn't know, so I pulled out of the bin a used Tesco's plastic bag, peeled the gloves off, dropped them in the bag and tied a knot in it. I didn't want to put them in the same bin as the speed-loader, so I went back to the car and drove till I saw another public bin, parked up a little past it, walked back and dumped the gloves. I also had to get rid of the mask which I was still wearing as a hat, so I drove even further and went through the whole thing again with a third bin, stuffing the mask into a KFC box and pushing it well down under the other garbage.

Paranoid? Maybe, but this was evidence for a major crime and the police would be pulling everything they could to piece it together.

My nose hurt like hell, but wasn't still bleeding. I had some tissues in the car and I wet them and cleaned up my face as best I could. I didn't want to walk through the streets with blood showing, it would draw attention. The arm I couldn't look at yet and I wasn't sure I wanted to. I'd never been shot before and I had no idea what to do about it. The pain had settled into a dull ache and I guessed the bullet had only scraped me and not hit properly. Either that or it had gone in, through and out, but then I would've expected to have felt some kind of impact, which I hadn't really. Either way, I would have to look at it when I got home. I certainly wasn't going anywhere near a hospital with a bullet wound tonight.

The jacket would have to go as well, but not until it had helped cover the wounds and got me home. And the phone, I'd ditch the phone. But not until I'd made just a couple more calls on it.

I got the mobile out of the boot and switched it on. One voicemail. This time it was Jenny and not what I wanted to hear.

"I'm back at the flat, but just to collect some of my things. I don't know what's happening to us, but I'm going to stay with one of the girls from the restaurant for a while. I didn't want to leave without telling you, I didn't think that would be fair, but you're not here and I don't know when you'll be back. I need to think about us. I'm sorry."

I called her straight back and she answered.

"Don't go," I said, "where are you? Are you still at the flat?"

Her voice was quiet, but strong when she answered.

"I'm still here, I'm just finishing up."

It sounded so final and I struggled with what to say, with how to stop her, how to keep her.

"Don't go, Jenny, please don't go."

"I can't stay, Garron. This, us, is no longer something I can do. I'm sorry."

"I love you, Jenny, I need you. I need to change myself and I can't do it if you go. I'll have no chance if you go."

I could hear her breathing at the other end of the line, could see her face, could imagine the tears perhaps beginning to form. I was making her cry, I was making her cry again.

"I think I'll always love you, Garron and I know I could never have got from where I was to where I am now, if we hadn't been together, if you hadn't been with me, been there with me." Her voice was cracking now and she paused before carrying on. "But I can't do it. I can't live like this."

"You don't have to," I said and I meant it, found myself meaning every word. "I'm done. I'm finished. Finished with it all. Please just stay there till I get back. Just till then. Let me try."

Silence and I thought she'd gone for a moment, just put the phone down and left, when in a strong voice she said:

"You can't change, you never will."

"Jenny, this stuff, the Russians, Mick, it's all done now and I know I need to get out of it."

There was desperation in my voice, but no theatrics. I couldn't do that and she wouldn't allow it. It was just me speaking with her as we'd spoken together since the beginning. No games. We were too important for that.

"I've ditched the gun, Jenny, I know I need to change. You're the only one that can make that worthwhile. Just let me talk to you. You know I can't lie to you, you know I can't stand there in front of you and tell you something that isn't true. No evasions, no leaving anything out. You'll know it when you see me, when you listen to me. It's the end now."

Silence again and I thought maybe I had a chance. We had a chance.

"I don't know if I can believe you, Garron, I don't know if I can trust what you are now."

That hurt. More than the broken nose and the bullet wound, that hurt. But I realised what she meant. Not that I was lying to her now, but that what might happen in the future would pull at me, take me back into what I was promising I would leave.

"Just wait there for me, Jenny, I'm on the way home. To you. To our home. Just let me come home to you and talk. And then if you want to leave, you'll go knowing that you gave it every last chance, you didn't give up too soon. I'll be under an hour. Can you give us that hour, Jenny? Are we worth that much?"

She was quiet and I found I was sweating again, with a different kind of fear than I'd had earlier in the evening, but one no less real and in many ways more difficult to deal with.

"One hour," she said. "Don't let me down, Garron, please don't let me down, because if you're not here, I won't be waiting."

I started to say I would be there, but she'd already cut the connection.

A chance, I thought, it was a chance.

*

Two calls to make and then I was done.

Mick was the easy one. I told him he was in the clear. Told him his contacts were as well, but I didn't go into the fact that it had been

196

Julot who'd set him up. That could wait. He was worried about what had happened, whether I was okay.

"It was bad," I said, "but it taught me that I don't belong there."

After a moment, he said:

"Well, some good's come of it then" and I thought that he was changing as well, if he was thinking seriously like that.

"You'll need to keep your head down from the police point of view," I told him, "keep out of that Dayton's way, but from the Russians, you're clear."

"You okay though?"

I was quite touched, there was real concern in his voice, but I didn't need a shoulder to cry on, I needed to get home.

"Maybe," was all I said to him. "We'll talk soon, but I'm binning this phone, so check in with Tony in a couple of days and he'll have my new number."

The second call was trickier. Julot.

He answered on the second ring.

"It's over," I said.

There was a pause and then that instantly recognisable deep tone answered.

"And Michel is dead."

He'd assumed it because it was me calling and not Michel.

"Yes, Michel is dead," I confirmed. And then, because I couldn't resist it, I added: "In the end, he wasn't quite good enough."

No response and I waited, knowing that he would have to have confirmation.

"Lysenkov?"

"Dead."

"Michel killed him?"

"No, Julot, Michel did not kill him, I killed him."

I waited again, knowing the question would have to come.

"How did he die?"

Meant Michel of course, not Lysenkov and for a moment the urge to hurt him built in me, or maybe it was ego, maybe after all, Jenny was right and it was ego, because I wanted to tell him that I'd killed Michel, that I'd taken out his golden boy, but as it nearly came out, as I began to speak, I stopped, almost as though someone had touched me on the shoulder, reminded me of how to survive, of the right way to live, of the need to ignore the ego, to look for the best way out, not the most gratifying and I said Kirilenko, Kirilenko had killed Michel, because in the end I didn't know just who Michel was, what he was to Julot and to Julot's empires and I wanted out, I didn't need, I couldn't have, any hangover from this, any reason to be looking over my shoulder. This was it and I was walking away clean.

Another pause as Julot took in this news.

"And Kirilenko?" he asked.

"I shot him. It's all over, Julot."

He started to say something else, but I cut in.

"I know, Julot. I know you set up Mick. Set him up to pull me in. Michel told me."

That would anger him, the fact that Michel had been that unprofessional and had let that information out.

"So this is the end, Julot" and my voice was quiet and even to me, deathly hard. "No more contact from you, ever. And if I get even a hint, a suspicion that you've been anywhere near anyone I know, anyone with access to me, then I'll come for you. I'll track you anywhere, for as long as it takes. I'll find your businesses and burn them down, I'll find your associates and take them down. I'll get to you and I'll finish you and you won't be able to stop me. I'll be one man, untrackable, untraceable. So it ends here, Julot, it ends now."

I didn't wait for him to answer. There was nothing he could say that I was interested in hearing and there could be no debate.

I killed the call and headed for home.

*

Driving slow, everything easy, everything over now. The pain still there and the images lurking, but manageable, manageable if you don't let the mind think about anything. A feeling of release, of relief. London slipping by as I made my way home, the car seeming to know its own way. Jenny would be there. Home.

I couldn't park anywhere near the flat and I circled around for a few minutes until I ended up quite a way off, but it didn't matter. I had told her an hour and I was in good time. I had all the time I needed. And despite the pain and the knowledge of what had happened, of what I'd done, I was feeling as though I'd understood something. As though I knew now where certain lines needed to be drawn and which side of them I was on.

I locked the car and walked back towards the flat, past a church of some kind with posters in the windows, 'Jesus Saves' after which someone had scribbled 'I wish he'd taken over the banks then' and the one that says 'The Wages of Sin is Death'. Probably needed some work on the grammar on that one, but I thought of Michel and Lysenkov and Kirilenko and possibly even of Al and I couldn't believe that it was just as simple as that.

Nearly back and a busker with a saxophone and a backing track as it started to rain again. He carried on, playing a song I knew but couldn't name and I couldn't ask him as he'd have to stop to tell me, so I stood there for a while as he got into it and began to soar, to really take the song and I stayed there as the rain got heavier. I knew he'd stop soon enough, but I was willing him to play on, to keep going, one of those small moments taken out of life, where things come together and you know it will stay with you, a little time out that is somehow worthwhile.

He stopped in mid-phrase as the rain got too much for him and the moment was broken and he hurried to shelter, leaving me with the sound in my head and the song unremembered.

Couple of streets now to the back of the flats and a tiredness beginning to creep over me. I couldn't have that happen though, I still had to talk with Jenny, still had to convince her, but the fact that she was there, the fact that she was waiting, made me think that we were going to be okay. Not easy, but okay.

I needed the flat keys for the back and looked down for a second as I took them out of my pocket and he came out of nowhere, just him on his own, the feral gang leader, out to prove something to himself and right in front of me, standing there, the thousand yard stare two feet from my face and I stopped short, too tired for this and said:

"Not now, son, pick another night, I've had enough tonight."

Not a word and he half turned to go, maybe having proved his point and then he swung back and threw a left hand punch into me.

199

Not much to it and I didn't bother to block properly, or maybe I was just tired, but it was a weak blow to the right hand side of my chest and I thought, 'you little scumbag, got to have the last word, the last punch, now I'll have to show you what a real punch does', but he was gone, fifteen, twenty yards away and jogging, turning every few yards to look back at me and I saw something, something glint in his hand and looked down at my chest as the realisation hit me and I saw the blood pulsing from the wound, not pumping, but pulsing at a steady rate from the bottom of my chest bone on the right of my solar plexus.

Little shit had stabbed me.

No pain at all, but I had to stop the blood and I put my thumb there on the hole and it went in slightly, so I pushed my whole palm against it and realised I was tired and weak.

Reaction, that's all.

- *That's right, it's just the reaction, so don't panic. If you panic your heart rate goes up and the blood will pump faster.*

- Turned up have you? With good advice after I need it.

- *You need a hospital. You can't deal with this on your own.*

- No hospital, not tonight. Not after what happened.

Coughing suddenly and a pull around the wound area and I spat into my hand and looked for blood in my saliva and there was none, but that didn't mean there wouldn't be soon. The voice in my head was right, I needed help. Standing with blood running over my hand now and onto the ground and me doing nothing and if I didn't stop the bleeding, I could go into shock from blood loss and die on this sodding street corner.

- *You're not going to die. Get to the main road, get to help.*

Damn right I'm not going to die, but if I need help, I have to ditch everything, everything that can link me to the Russians. And call Jenny, need to tell her.

- *No time now, you're losing blood, you're getting weak.*

And then not thinking well and staggering, hell, staggering slightly, long way to the main road, thirty yards or so and scared suddenly, scared that I'd run out of time, so get rid of the stuff now, get rid of the jacket with the dried blood on it, just sling it.

Blood now on my hands, all over my hands and I need to get the

SIM out, not just dump the phone, see, Garron, you're still thinking straight, but worrying now because the phone is slippery with the blood and it's taking too much time and I can't get the damn thing open.

Sprung it and picked at the SIM with a fingernail and saw the drain and the SIM went down it and the phone went anywhere.

- Street, get to the main street.

But something else no good, the arm wound with dried blood, old blood, too noticeable, so I used my left hand to rub at it and open it up again, a pin-point of pain, but nothing really, nothing against the fear of what was happening and I smeared some fresh blood from the chest wound on the arm and on my shirt sleeve there, wouldn't fool an expert, but any edge better than none and made it the rest of the way to the main road and face forwards onto the pavement, can't you bloody stand up, you pathetic bastard, now you've just hurt your arm as well, falling over and someone screaming and a man saying, "Call an ambulance," all so silly, just off a weak punch to the chest, no, had a knife in his hand, remember, little bloody knife, at least it was bloody on the way out, gallows humour, only one I've got and someone's arm under my head, breathing a little harder and a bit dark now, or just someone in the way, blocking the street light.

Hearing the voices, but they don't make a lot of sense, someone saying: "Stay with it, mate, don't pass out," stupid thing to say to a guy losing blood and I'm thinking it's okay, just tired now and a little heavy on one side.

'Wages of Sin is Death'. Bloody annoying, can't even get their grammar right, should go and correct it, but not now, not right now.

More voices and a bloody crowd, can't stand crowds and someone in green next to me.

"Okay, mate, I'm a paramedic and there's an ambulance on its way. I'm going to put something on the wound here, try to slow the bleeding, but we'll get you to a hospital very soon. Can you tell me your name, mate?"

Pick a name and I tried Bob, but I'm not sure what came out.

Saying something else, he was saying something and pressure on my chest and a voice saying, "you'll be all right."

Yes, I'll be all right. I have to be all right. I have to get to Jenny in

201

the next ten minutes, 'cos she's waiting for me, she must still be waiting for me, so I can't be too long here.

And I can't die.

Strange thought that. I can die as easily as the next man. But I'm not going to. I'm bloody well not going to. Can't remember the name of that song, though.

Noise, a siren some way off. Might be for me, or might be for some other lucky bastard.

Doesn't matter, I'm not going to die.

- *No, you're not going to die.*

- That's what I said, damn it. I'm not going to die.

- *You're not going to die.*

- I'm *not* going to die.

- *No...you're not going to die...*

About the Author

Joe Stein was born in London in the 1960s. His first job was in a scrap-yard, stripping copper out of electrical cables. He left there before it was raided by Customs and Excise and has been trying to stay out of trouble ever since.

He admits to being an ex-musician and sometime amateur boxer and won't say much else. He has worked in factories, warehouses, markets, spent two days on a building site before he realised it wasn't the place for anyone with even mild vertigo and worked for over ten years in security and as a bodyguard, luckily getting married and being told to get a 'proper' job before the government decided to license the security industry. His training manual for bodyguards is now therefore out of date and a collectors' item.

He always wanted to try to write, and although his first book took many years to complete, he now has three novels and a dozen short stories to his name.

He still lives in North London and has a full time day job to fit around the rest of his life.

His previous novels, soon to be re-released by Ward Wood are:

Cold Fire, Calm Rage (2004)
Another Man's World (2007)

For more about this author online see his pages on www.wardwoodpublishing.co.uk and his own website:

www.joesteinauthor.co.uk